ABOUT THE AUTHO

Gary Engler, who was born and raised in Moose Jaw, Saskatchewan, worked as reporter and editor for 20 years at the Vancouver Sun, before becoming a full-time elected officer for BC's Media Union. In addition, he worked as a cabbie, audio-visual technician, truck driver, postal worker, burner at a steel plant, apprentice millwright, marine engineer and playwright. His play *Sudden Death Overtime* was produced at Factory Theatre Lab and Theatre Calgary in the 1970s.

Engler is also creator of the all-Canadian working class avatar Ernesto (Ernie) Raj Peshkov-Chow, author of *The Great Multicultural North*.

First printing May 2012
Cover by Working Design
Printed and bound in Canada by Transcontinental Printing
A co-publication of
RED Publishing
2736 Cambridge Street, Vancouver, British Columbia V5K 1L7 and
Fernwood Publishing
32 Oceanvista Lane, Black Point, Nova Scotia B0J 1B0
and 748 Broadway Avenue, Winnipeg, Manitoba, R3G 0X3
www.fernwoodpublishing.ca

Fernwood Publishing Company Limited gratefully acknowledges the financial support of the Government of Canada through the Canada Book Fund and the Canada Council for the Arts, the Nova Scotia Department of Communities, Culture and Heritage, the Manitoba Department of Culture, Heritage and Tourism under the Manitoba Publishers Marketing Assistance Program and the Province of Manitoba, through the Book Publishing Tax Credit, for our publishing program.

Library and Archives Canada Cataloguing in Publication
Engler, Gary, 1953-
The year we became us : a novel about the Saskatchewan doctors strike / Gary Engler.
ISBN 978-1-55266-482-7
1. Doctors' Strike, Sask., 1962--Fiction. I. Title.
PS8609.N45Y42 2012   C813'.6   C2011-908418-X

THE YEAR WE BECAME US

A novel about the 1962 Saskatchewan
doctors strike, love, history and politics

By

Gary Engler

RED/Fernwood Publishing

The Assignment

"Welcome to Canada's 1960s — New Approaches to History," said Emma to the five graduate students assembled around a table in the small Academic Quadrangle seminar room. "In this class we are going to take a look at a turbulent decade and in keeping with the subject matter we'll do it through some 'groovy' and rather novel methods."

The three men and two women smiled at her use of the quintessential 1960s' word.

"This will be a hands-on class, focusing as much on alternative sources of studying and presenting history as on the period itself," said Emma. "We will study and report on five topics over the next 15 weeks. They are: The 1962 Saskatchewan Doctors Strike; The Heyday of Canadian Social Democracy; The Rise of Quebec Nationalism; The Election of Pierre Trudeau and Who Created Youth Culture and Why?"

Emma took a calculated, deep breath. You'd think by the third year of being a professor a new class wouldn't make you nervous any more, even if it was the first course you designed.

"We'll be accessing letters from the period, an unpublished novel, pop music, TV news and current affairs shows, newspapers, TV commercials, sitcoms, variety shows and the more common array of books, journals and papers," said Emma. "There will be no papers to write. Instead we will create a single class project, a prototype multimedia e-book about the 1960s. As all of you know, this will be a joint project with the Publishing Program. Our job will be to come up with the history and their job will be to enable us to create the e-book."

Most of the nerves today were a direct result of the shouting match this morning with her mother. How do you prepare with that sort of a distraction? Why couldn't she learn to ignore her mother's provocations? What was the point of fighting about a dead husband and father? What was the point of fighting with her about anything? And then Louise took her side, again, always playing the good daughter to her ungrateful child.

"I hope you are all looking forward to this class as much as I am," said Emma. "It's going to be a lot of work, but I hope rewarding too."

Max says he still gets nervous after 30 years. He also says all good teachers learn from their students. We shouldn't feel like we're exploiting them. We're learning together and so long as we acknowledge their contribution …

A cellphone rang. Everyone stared at Katie as she looked at the screen on her phone.

"I'm very sorry," said Katie. "It's the daycare. Andrew had a fever this morning and I'm sure they're calling to find out when I'm picking him up. Are we going to be much longer?"

"No," said Emma. "Another 20 minutes."

Katie was high maintenance, but a good student.

"I want to give you a short summary about the 1962 Saskatchewan doctors strike," Emma said. "Just a quick overview of the facts and then we'll get into it in depth next week."

Why does my mother keep taking over my thoughts?

"In 1959, Tommy Douglas, socialist premier of Saskatchewan since 1944, announced that, if re-elected for a fifth term, his government would introduce North America's first universal, government-run, tax-funded medical care system. The CCF — Cooperative Commonwealth Federation — government was easily re-elected in 1960 and passed legislation that was to come into effect at the end of 1961. Just after the 1960 election Douglas resigned as premier and became national leader of the New Democratic Party, the successor to the CCF. Woodrow Lloyd became premier and after the doctors of Saskatchewan raised a big fuss, he agreed to postpone implementation of the new Medicare system until July 1, 1962 so that the government had time to listen to the concerns of the doctors. But the doctors weren't really interested in modifying the legislation; they wanted it scrapped. The doctors had mounted a huge propaganda operation going all the way back to the 1960 election — they spent as much money as the CCF and the opposition Liberals' campaigns — characterizing Medicare as a 'government-run compulsory socialist tyranny.' Rather than talk to the government they continued to propagandize and even raised the stakes further by declaring they would withdraw their services if the government went ahead with its plan. Neither side backed down. Medicare came into effect and the doctors struck on July 1, 1962. It was vicious, pitting doctors against patients, neighbor against neighbor; the government brought in replacements, mostly from Great Britain who worked at newly created community clinics. The Saskatchewan news media, which never liked the CCF, went crazy in supporting the doctors. The strike lasted 23 days, ending a few days after what was supposed to be a giant rally supporting the doctors attracted only a few thousand people to the steps of the Legislature in Regina. The government made a few minor changes to its plan, but conceded power to the doctors that made it very difficult for the community clinics to flourish. Within six years Medicare spread to the rest of the country. And today it is the country's most popular social program.

"Anyone have any questions or something to add?"

Katie's daycare problem had put a damper on the possibility of any sort of significant discussion. Perhaps that was why Marc raised his hand.

"Are you saying that the doctors were the bad guys?" said Marc. "It was a simple as that?"

"That's for you to determine yourself," answered Emma. "But the CCF government won an election fought on the issue, then passed legislation and then implemented it. What grounds did the doctors have to defy the democratically elected government? Could you imagine how the media would treat a union that did something similar? And yet the Saskatchewan media supported the doctors all the way."

"So why is there so little written about the strike?" Raj said, as Katie looked at her cellphone screen.

"That's a good question and one we will tackle next week," said Emma, picking up the pile of folders from the table in front of her and passing them to Dorothy beside her. "This is your reading assignment for next week. "It's rather lengthy, but I think you'll find it different and interesting, maybe even fun."

"What is it?" asked Dorothy, as she leafed through the papers.

"An unpublished manuscript," Emma said.

"By whom?" said Katie.

"It's a collection of letters written to President Kennedy during the 1962 Cuban Missile Crisis by two Grade Eight students from Moose Jaw, Saskatchewan, and some diary entries written almost 40 years later by one of the two students after they met in Boston when trying to recover the letters they had sent JFK."

"What's that got to do with the Saskatchewan doctors?" said Marc.

"You'll understand when you read it," Emma said. "On the last page of your package is a short reading list. There was one book — detailed but not particularly insightful — about the strike written not long after the dispute and a variety of articles and books about the origins of Canadian Medicare, but to Raj's point, there's curiously little considering how important socialized medicine is to today's Canadian identity."

Katie began to pick up her things.

"Before you leave I'd also like to give you this," Emma said.

She passed around a single sheet with words on one side.

"Raj, could you please read the first paragraph."

"Sure," he said, picking up the paper. "It's quotes from some famous historians."

"That's obvious," said Marc.

"'History is the witness that testifies to the passing of time; it illuminates reality, vitalizes memory, provides guidance in daily life, and brings us tidings of antiquity.' Cicero."

"I want you all to think very carefully about that and the following quotes while you read next week's assignment," Emma said. "Katie, could you read the next quote."

"'Faithfulness to the truth of history involves far more than a research, however patient and scrupulous, into special facts. Such facts may be detailed with the most minute exactness, and yet the narrative, taken as a whole, may be unmeaning or untrue. The narrator must seek to imbue himself with the life and spirit of the time. He must study events in their bearings near and remote; in the character, habits, and manners of those who took part in them. He must himself be, as it were, a sharer or a spectator of the action he describes.' Francis Parkman."

"Michael."

"'The function of the historian is neither to love the past nor to emancipate himself from the past, but to master and understand it as the key to the understanding of the present.' E. H. Carr."

"Dorothy."

"'What experience and history teach is this — that people and governments never have learned anything from history, or acted on principles deduced from it.' G. W. F. Hegel."

"Marc."

"'History is more or less bunk.' Henry Ford."

Marc smiled. He enjoyed performing.

"Again, think about these quotes as you read the assignment," she said. "That's it. See you next week."

Roy, letter 1

Sept. 5, 1962

Dear President Kennedy,

My name is Roy Schmidt. I'm 12 years old and Catholic, just like you. I live in Moose Jaw, Saskatchewan, Canada and I'm in Grade 8 at St. Michael's Elementary School. Our second day back after summer holidays and already Mr. Rebalski, my new Social Studies and English teacher, is making me write this because he says I talked back, but I didn't mean to. I was just arguing with Katie. I admit I have a big mouth. (My brother Basil is in first year university and he says everyone in our family has one. People probably said the same thing about the Kennedys, but who cares what they think.) Plus I said you were aiming to start a war against Cuba. But I wasn't talking back, I was just telling the truth.

Basil says you are trying to start a war and he's pretty much always right, except when it comes to girls, so unless you tell me something different I'll stick by my brother. (We do that in the Schmidt family, just like Sister Veronica says you do with your brothers.) And if you weren't trying to start a war with Cuba, what about the Bay of Pigs? How do you explain that? I deliver the Moose Jaw Times Herald and it always takes the American side and even it said you were behind that invasion.

I'm not saying Castro is right about everything and maybe he is a Communist, but he played baseball and is a Catholic too, so how bad could he be?

(I'm a pitcher and my team made it almost all the way to the Little League World Series, but got beaten 4-3 in the North Central final by Eau Claire, Wisconsin. It was great even though we lost because I had never been anywhere in the States before except Bismarck, North Dakota, where my grandpa lived before he died, and Grand Forks, Montana where we also played in a tournament. You guys have lots of stuff to buy in stores, like chocolate bars, that we don't have in Canada, but it was kind of funny that the waitress brought me potato chips when I asked for chips and told me down there you call them French fries.)

Anyhow, Cubans got a right to do what they want without another country bossing them around. Basil says Castro is just trying to make things better for poor people and you're siding with the rich guys who want everything for themselves and only leave crumbs for poor people. That's not right. Even Sister Veronica agrees that's not right. She says the Catholic Church is on the side of the poor and the hungry and she's a nun who has given her whole life to Jesus.

Katie and I each have to write you at least 500 words, which I must be getting close to. Mr. Rebalski thinks this is tough, but I like writing. I've kept a journal for almost a whole year. I take notes every day about what happened and then later I turn some of the stuff into stories. I'm going to be a writer and that is good practice.

Mr. Rebalski is going to read this before he sends it to you, so I'll tell you again I never meant to cause any trouble in his class. I just thought the point of social studies is to talk about what's going on in the world. And besides Katie and I were not really talking about Cuba, we were arguing about the doctors strike and it just kind of turned into socialism and then Cuba and you.

What I think is that you should leave Cuba alone. Let the Cubans figure out what's best for them.

It would be really great if you wrote me back. If you do, say hi to Sister Veronica because she thinks you're the best president ever and she's my favourite nun ever.

Yours truly,
Roy Schmidt

P.S. The Moose Jaw Times Herald today says Cuba is receiving hand-me down weapons from Russia and the USA is worried about this. What do you expect Castro to do if you send soldiers to attack him?

Katherine, letter 1

September 5, 1962

Dear President Kennedy,

I hope this letter finds you well. My name is Katherine
Anderson and I currently live in Moose Jaw, Saskatchewan,
Canada, with my mother, Jennifer. But I was born in Cincinnati where my father was attending medical school. He was
born in Kentucky and is an American citizen. Until Febru-
ary, I lived in Regina where my father is the youngest chief
of surgery ever at the biggest hospital in the province. He is
a brilliant man, just like you. He and my mother once loved
each other, but not anymore, so I only spend some weekends
with him now. I miss Regina. People there are so much more
refined than in Moose Jaw. Most people here work in facto-
ries or for the railroad. The only reason my father let me go
to Moose Jaw and attend Catholic school is because he says
Father Athol Murray, from Notre Dame in Wilcox, which
is very close to Moose Jaw, is the only man who has always
stood up to the Saskatchewan socialists. He even called
Woodrow Lloyd a communist, from his pulpit, during the
recent withdrawal of service by physicians. That is a man to
admire, my father says.

Mr. Rebalski, my teacher, asked me to write this letter,
as a class assignment. Or, to be more precise, as a special
assignment for the top two students in his Grade 8 class.
Roy Schmidt and I will certainly both get at least 90s on our
departmental exams at the end of the year. Roy gets at least
90s on every test and has always been the top student at this
school. His older brother Basil is also very smart. Roy and I
were discussing this summer's physicians' withdrawal of services here in Saskatchewan (Have you heard of it?) and Mr.
Rebalski thought it appropriate that we channel our enthusi-
asm for politics into a more quiet activity.

I liked Roy, a lot, when I first met him. He is cute and very
smart, and strong and tall for his age. He's still only 12, but
he acts so much more mature. More like a 14-year old, which

I will be in a few months. He skipped a grade and that's why he's the youngest boy in the class. But he still gets the best marks in every subject. I think that's because the teachers know him and like him better than me, but he did also get better marks than me on all the Grade 7 departmental exams. My Dad says that was only because my school year was disrupted in Grade 7 when I moved. Maybe that's true. I do think I can beat Roy in English, French and certainly in art. Perhaps social studies as well, but he's awfully good at math and science. He doesn't seem to do any homework at all, but still gets a hundred per cent on many of the tests. My father says he will eventually pay a price for things that come too easily. I'm not sure what that means.

I've always gotten the very best marks in most classes, but not at St. Michael's. My father says I just need to listen more carefully and work harder and I guess that's true, but Roy is smart, plus I'm the new girl and I'm not even really Catholic. I was baptized, but I always went to a public school in Regina because my father is a Methodist, which is called United Church here in Canada, but he never really attends. I think my mother sent me to St. Michael's just to make my father angrier than he already was.

A good marriage is one of the most important things in life, don't you agree? Yours is a wonderful marriage and everyone knows how devoted you two are to each other. Your wife is very beautiful, perhaps the most beautiful woman in the world. I love the clothes she wears, especially the hats. She has a sense of style that I very much admire.

My mother dresses very well too, for Moose Jaw. My friends here all think she is gorgeous. She loves shopping. My father says that is the only thing she loves. Sometimes I agree with him. My mother often ignores me. She only pays attention when I make a real fuss or she wants something from me. I think that's because she associates me with my father.

It's sad when a married couple can't get along, don't you think? Especially when children are caught in between. I'm just so glad I don't have a little brother or sister, because this separation would be very difficult for a younger child.

But, I do understand how two people can grow apart and how love can disappear. It was like that with Roy and I. I liked him very much, at first. He is good-looking and intelligent. Most of the girls in our class still think he's terrific. Everyone wanted to hear about it when we held hands at the skating rink. I was the new girl in class and they were so very jealous. And then the next day we went for a walk and we kissed. I told Cindy and I swear five minutes later every girl in class knew. They were all so keen to hear the details.

My opinion about Roy changed when I found out what he is really like. He is the kind of boy who thinks he knows everything, but then shows how stupid he really is, by saying he believes in socialism. My father says Saskatchewan is full of socialist young men who think they know everything. He says the government encourages that and is therefore responsible.

You do know we have a government in Saskatchewan that's every bit as bad as the one in Cuba? The socialist CCF has been running the government since 1944. This summer they started Medicare, which made all the doctors, including my father, withdraw their services. The CCF called it a strike, which reveals its true plans, which is to make all doctors work for the government, like factory workers, the same as in communist Russia.

I say it's a good thing you helped those people trying to overthrow Castro. I just wish they had been successful.

Yours truly,
Katherine Anderson

DIARY ENTRY DEC. 4, 2000

I kissed the Queen of Rightwing Talk Radio today.

The really weird thing? I enjoyed it.

We met at the JFK archives. I was filling out a request form, talking to an archivist, when this woman from the desk beside us interrupted. "Did I hear you say your name is Roy Schmidt? From Moose Jaw?"

It was Katherine from Grade 8 at St. Michael's. Next thing I knew we were in a cab to her hotel room and she was pouring me a drink. We were both nervous and talking a kilometre a second.

"When someone says opposites attract it is usually proof of an inadequate understanding of the whole," he said, sipping the second glass of Madeira she had poured.

"What do you mean?" she said. "That the two of us constitute some sort of long lost complete being?"

"This is very good," he said, rolling the sweet caramelized liquid inside his mouth.

"Malmsey, 1965," she said with a smile that was confident but also hinted at demureness. "I found three bottles today in a wine shop across from the Commons on Tremont."

"Expensive?"

"If you must ask, you can't afford me," she said. "Answer my question."

She seemed flirtatious, but he must be misinterpreting. Her? No way. Perhaps she was one of those women who knew no other way to act in the company of men. Wouldn't that be ironic given her status as "One of the 100 Most Influential Women in America." Or would it? Maybe that's what it takes to be an influential woman in the first year of the twenty-first century. Still it wasn't how he remembered her. Then again, the last time he had seen her she was 13.

"When people say 'opposites attract' they are usually referring to some form of symbiosis, where two supposedly independent entities require the other being in order to survive or thrive," he said. "But, can a symbiotic relationship truly involve independent beings? Or are they, in fact, parts of a whole, with just the illusion of independence?"

He swirled the last bits of amber nectar around the glass and then emptied it. She was staring at him.

"To gain a proper understanding of the complexities of life, one must consider interactions, processes, sub groups, the whole," he said. "Like the Gaia principle."

"This is some sort of ecological explanation for us meeting again after all these years?" she said.

His 'liberal environmental mumbo jumbo' clearly irritated her.

"It's an ecological explanation for relationships and politics and the necessity of what your sort call socialism," he said. The alcohol was definitely having an effect.

"My sort?"

"Libertarians, Ayn Randers, right-wing whackos," he said, hoping his confident smile trumped her smug look. "People who deny the existence of the collective. People who only see trees, but not the forest."

"My sort?" she repeated, shaking her head.

"Every living creature is engaged in some level of symbiosis – Mother Nature's socialism – with every other thing, living or not, on the planet. That's reality. We are all interconnected. Some closer than others, that's all."

She put her right index finger to her mouth, signaling for him to shut up. Her look was that of a magnanimous ruler. She was about to be appointed to an important position in the world's most powerful government. She was important. He was nobody. She was in control, choosing the time and place of her battles, not simply reacting. She was choosing not to argue.

"You remember when we kissed the first time?" she said, putting the glass down and moving towards him, like a cougar stalking its prey.

"I do," he said. "In Elgin Park."

"That was my very first romantic kiss," she said. "I was thirteen and you were twelve."

"A long time ago," he said.

"Could we try it again?" she said, her words sounding planned. "As an experiment? For old times sake?"

He remained completely still. He was 51. That made her 52. Not teenagers, that's for sure. And this was not like him. He'd never cheated on his wife. The situation was weird. She was weird. Beyond weird. This made no sense. Still, it felt good.

She closed the remaining distance between them. Anticipation heightened the sense of touch, smell and taste as she pressed her mouth against his, gently at first then harder. She was the aggressor. The kiss lasted for ten seconds or so, before she pulled back.

"Your taste," she said.

He was conscious of his breathing. A sense memory triggered the smell of lilac and cut grass from that spring day in Elgin Park.

"What?" he said, flustered and flattered, but attempting to recover his poise. "Does it get better or worse with age?"

"It's exactly as I remembered it," she said.

I kissed the Queen of Rightwing Talk Radio and liked it.

"That was nice," she said later, then immediately sounded as if she regretted the banality of her words.

"Nice," he repeated, still a bit winded. "I guess I can live with that. This is the first time I've had sex with somebody new in a long, long time."

Nice was a fair description of how he felt, but it was also like being in a bizarre dream. They were kissing in Elgin Park in Moose Jaw and the next instant the two of them were on this bed in an expensive Boston hotel. He was making out with the Wicked Witch of The Right, rumoured to be in line for a senior position in the new, illegitimate Bush administration, should his stealing of the election from Al Gore be deemed legal, as looked more and more likely.

"That was a first for me too," she said. "Nostalgia sex."

He stared at her. This was all so surreal. She was incredibly irritating. But she did look and feel good. And it was remarkable how at ease he felt with her. Like a childhood best friend, even though the time they had been close was short and long ago.

"I've done it to make up after a fight, to avoid a fight, to end a relationship, to take my mind off something bothering me, because he wanted to even though I didn't really feel like it, to obtain something I've wanted, to make someone angry ..."

"Make up sex, protection sex, last-taste sex, distraction sex, duty sex, barter sex, get-even sex," he said. Why did this feel like a competition?

She smiled. "Are you married?"

Why was she asking? He shrugged. Where was this going? What had he done? She is a predator.

"What does that shrug mean?" she asked.

He shrugged again and tried to keep a poker face as he spoke. "It means I was and still technically am, but functionally not really." After what they had just done it seemed answering her question truthfully was the polite thing to do.

She shook her head. "Men."

"What?" he said, off balance again. Why did she have this effect on him?

"You're all the same," she said. "You think I care? You've already cheated on her. Or not."

"If you don't care, why do you ask?"

"I care in the sense of getting to know you, but not in the sense of not sleeping with you if you are married," she said, enjoying his obvious discomfort. "That's not part of my moral code. And I'm not husband hunting."

"Anymore," he said without thinking and then immediately felt back in the game.

She smiled. "Anymore," she repeated. "I've reached my limit."

"How many has it been?" he said. Information sometimes is power. "Seven? All progressively wealthier than the previous one."

"You've followed my career?" she said.

"It's from a Wall Street Journal story," he said, a little embarrassed. "I looked you up on the Internet a few months ago. I think the kids call it 'Googled'."

"You Googled me?" she said. "So very modern. How sweet! And then we meet after all these years. What a strange coincidence."

"Weird, that's for sure," he said, not liking where this was headed.

"Are you some kind of celebrity stalker?" she said, pressing her advantage.

"You recognized me at the archives, not the other way around."

"But why were you there?"

"To get my letters," he said. "I'm thinking of writing a book based on them."

"Why did you Google me?" she said. "You were lonely?"

"Saw you on TV and thought you looked familiar," he said, deciding he didn't want to play her game anymore. "Then I read about some outrageous comment you made. Something that mentioned you had lived in Canada, so I looked you up and found that you used the last name of your first husband and who you really were."

"And then you found some Wall Street Journal story?" she said, sounding like she had never seen the story even though she probably had a framed copy of the article in her office.

"Yes," he said. "It was full of information. Born in Cincinnati, Ohio. Spent part of your youth in Saskatchewan, Canada. Attended University of

Southern California. A middle distance runner on the track team. Father became president of the American Medical Association. First husband was a medical doctor. Did some acting, mostly TV, daytime soaps. Fourth husband owned a network of radio stations, which was where you got your start as a hotline host. Fifth husband a big player in the Republican Party in California ..."

"You know all this about me, but I know nothing about you," she said.

"One of the advantages of being a nobody," he said, perhaps a little disappointed.

"I've thought about you," she said. "Every first kiss I've ever had, I remembered Elgin Park, Moose Jaw, Saskatchewan. I suppose I judged them all against that one."

"And?" he asked, feeling better. Why? She makes me feel good even though feeling that way gives her power over me.

She smiled.

"How did the rest stack up?" he said. Why is she looking at me like that?

"I know it's a lot to ask of a male your age, but I don't suppose you'd be interested in doing that again?" she said.

"That?" he asked.

She nodded.

"I'm a year younger than you," he said. "Or have you forgotten?"

"As one of my late husbands ruefully said to his very expensive divorce lawyer, 'she never forgets anything'," she said. "But in this case the female gender gets better as we get older, while you boys, I am afraid, peter out."

"Is that a challenge?" he said.

"If a challenge is necessary to boot up your hard drive, consider it a challenge," she said.

"Okay," he said. "I'm game to try anything twice, once."

They both smiled.

Roy, letter 2

Sept. 11, 1962

Dear President Kennedy,

It's Roy Schmidt again. I don't know if you read my letter last week, but I will be writing a lot more and I hope that doesn't bother you. I know you are very busy and have a lot more important things to do than read my letters, but Mr. Rebalski caught Katie and I arguing about politics again in his English class. This time he gave us a special assignment, which is sort of a punishment but also fun because I like writing and can get extra marks to clobber Katie who really wants to beat me. Mr. Rebalski says we have to write a story, based on something that happened to us, which makes a political point. I think I know what he means. We can earn an extra ten per cent on our final marks from him in English and Social Studies. Mr. Rebalski also says he has a friend in the ministry of education who can add ten per cent to our mark on those two Grade 8 departmental exams, but I don't really believe that. Mr. Rebalski says that sometimes he says things not because they are true, but because he wants to produce a reaction, which is probably just a complicated way of saying that lying is okay sometimes. Basil says that's what politicians do all the time, so you should understand.

Anyway, I've been thinking about you a lot because of all the news about Cuba. Today the paper says the "Russians warn U.S. about attacking Cuba" and I'm scared about nuclear war. We saw missile silos when we went to Grand Forks and some of those B52 bombers. They're huge! With the hydrogen bomb and the atom bomb the whole world could be blown to smithereens. That's what Basil says and even the sisters at school agree. They say pray for God to give you guidance, which I could do, but I also want to tell you a story.

I know what you must be thinking: What does a 12-year-old Canadian know about being president of the United States? Not much and maybe it's stupid to write you, because I don't really care much about Mr. Rebalski's extra marks. I always get the top mark in every class anyway so it's no big deal. But, I've been thinking about something that happened to me this summer. It might help you figure out what to do with Russia and Cuba and the Cold War. Sure it's kid stuff, but Basil told me everything in politics is first learned in the classroom or on the playground.

Anyhow, Basil says if I want to be a writer I should write, so I'm going to write you letters like they are chapters in a novel. Each one will have stuff based on my journal earlier this year just before and during the doctors strike. Did you hear about that? Saskatchewan is the first place in North America to have govern-ment health insurance so everybody can see a doctor when they need to. My Dad and Mom are really proud about that, even if we did have to put up with a doctors strike.

But, back to my story. Here goes:

The first time I heard about the problem with Steve McCallum I was collecting for my paper route on Montgomery Street.

"Steve says his cousin is going to beat me up," my baby brother Martin said. "He's thirteen and bigger than you. He's coming to live with Steve cause his Dad and sister got killed by lightning and his Mom has gone cuckoo bird."

I looked up from my collection book. Martin tried to impress me by using words he had heard an adult, or at least a ten-year old, use.

"Cuckoo bird?" I said.

"Crazy," said Martin drawing circles in the air beside his head.

"You're supposed to call it a nervous breakdown when some-thing bad happens and you go a little crazy."

"Steve says she's completely ding dong and the police are go-ing to take her to the funny farm in Weyburn."

Martin didn't mean anything bad. He was just repeating some-thing he heard. Besides, five seconds later he was thinking about something else. The little guy buzzed from thought to thought like a bee in wild roses on the PFRA pasture. In the time it took for me to even think about saying something Martin was three steps ahead singing his favourite verse from a Johnny Horton song — "in 1814 I took a little trip, along with Colonel Jackson down the mighty Mississipp" — looking like he might tip over as the bottom of the paper bag, ten papers left, cleared the cinder sidewalk by barely an inch.

"You want me to carry that?" I said.

Martin shook his head.

"I told Steve you'd beat him up, and his cousin too, if he beats me up," said Martin. "You would, wouldn't ya?"

My eyebrows moved, but I did not deny the possibility as we walked up the steps to Mr. Randall's front door. I knocked and Martin tagged along to sell Little League pull-tab raffle tickets.

"If his cousin is thirteen, he's probably not a lot bigger than you cause you're bigger than any twelve year old in all Moose Jaw," said Martin. "That's what Basil said last week when he told Mom there was no room for him around the couch to say the rosary."

"He just said that cause he's atheist now," I said. "He doesn't believe in the rosary anymore."

"You are," said Martin. "You're the biggest. Even Barry says so."

It must be true if Barry, the dumbest-know-it-all thirteen-year old who sometimes was my best friend, had said it.

"Collect," I said, as Mr. Randall opened the door.

"How much do I owe you?" said the balding man with a white shirt and black suspenders.

"You weren't home last week so two dollars," I said, looking at Mr. Randall's page in the collection book.

"Two dollars! For this Liberal rag?" he said, waving the paper Martin handed him. "I got a good mind to cancel. They're inciting the doctors. Inciting them. Never a good word about the government, why is that?"

"I don't know," I said. "I just deliver the paper."

"I'll tell you why, because the goddamn owners of this rag care more about defending the rich and powerful than they do about reporting the truth," said Mr. Randall. "I don't always see eye to eye with the holy baloney socialists, but Lloyd and the CCF are right. Medicare is a good thing."

"We're CCFers," said Martin. "Holy baloney socialists too."

"You are?" said Mr. Randall.

"We hate the Liberals and that's the truth."

At first I was embarrassed by my little brother.

"You do?" said Mr. Randall, smiling like Ed Sullivan.

"We're socialists, all of us," said Martin. "The whole family. And our big brother Basil is a theist."

"A theist?" said Mr. Randall. "That's good! But no religion?"

"Catholic," said Martin.

"A Catholic theist?

My little brother was too much.

"I'll be one too when I grow up," said Martin.

"Really?" said Mr. Randall, with an even broader smile as he handed me two one-dollar bills.

"You wanna buy a pull tab?" said Martin holding out the half empty book of tickets. "You could win fifty dollars or twenty-five or a tank of gas. It's for a good cause, my brother's Little League baseball team. Roy's gonna be the best pitcher in Saskatchewan. He can throw the ball so hard Kevin the catcher says it feels like one of them Russian rockets flew right into his glove. Isn't that so Roy?"

Little brothers, little bothers. That's what Basil used to call me.

"How much for the raffle ticket?" said Mr. Randall.

"It's a pull tab," said Martin. "Anything from free to fifty cents, depending what you pull."

"Free?" said Mr. Randall.

"There's two in every book," said Martin. "And five cent ones and ten cent ones too. You pick and pull."

Mr. Randall looked over at me and I nodded.

"Well, okay."

Martin handed him the book and Mr. Randall thumbed through it.

"This one."

Martin tore the ticket along the perforation and pulled it out of the book. He looked at it and grimaced at Mr. Randall.

"Not so lucky," he said, handing it to Mr. Randall. "Fifty cents."

"Fifty ..." Mr. Randall stopped himself from swearing and stuck his hand into his right pants pocket. He fished out two quarters as he shook his head.

"Go on, get out of here, before I got no more money and no more heat left in the house," he said, slamming the door.

Martin smiled as we walked to the gate.

"Aren't all the free tickets and five cent ones gone?" I said.

"Two free ones in every book, that's all I said," Martin said, shrugging.

On a sliding scale of one to ten how untrue does an untruth have to be before it becomes a lie? Maybe I should ask Father Phelan.

After we crossed to the other side of the street, Martin dragged the paper bag on a new cement sidewalk poured the previous summer. Funny how the free and five cent tickets all were filled out by our relatives or those of Martin's buddies' parents. The little guy was like the Pied Piper, able to get every kid in the neighborhood to follow him. Came in useful when Martin organized his gang to sell my raffle tickets or candies, stuff I hated. Martin's latest success was a record haul on the cub scout bottle drive when he convinced Old Man Ray to give up his stash of over a hundred milk bottles, which were worth ten cents each. Thing about Martin was he always shared his success fairly, that's why so many kids followed him and why I gave him lots of slack.

I put my arm around his shoulder as we walked the half block to my next customer.

"It's atheist, all one word," I said. "Atheist. And you can't be a Catholic atheist because Catholics got to believe in God and atheist means you don't."

"You sure?" said Martin.

I nodded.

"Then why does Basil go to Mass?"

"Because Mom would kill him if he didn't."

Martin thought about this for a few seconds as we walked.

"Can an alter boy be a atheist?" Martin asked.

"An atheist," I said. "Nope. If the priest found out he'd excommunicate you."

Martin stopped walking. He looked at me carefully.

"With that sharp blade that falls down and cuts your head off and it falls off into a basket?"

"The guillotine," I said.

"Would he excommunicate you with a guillotine?"

"Execute. You mean execute. Excommunicate means something different."

"Oh," said Martin. "What?"

"It means you aren't a Catholic anymore. You can't go to Mass. You can't receive communion, none of the stuff that Catholics do."

"Will you go to Hell?"

"I guess," I said, "except that atheists don't believe in hell either."

Martin stared at me and shrugged. "Doesn't sound so bad. Not like the guillotine."

He had a point.

"Mass is boring," said Martin.

Daily trips to St. Joseph's during Lent had turned Martin off church. The Stations of the Cross every night made atheism look pretty good.

"Why does Steve want to beat you up?" I asked as we walked across the intersection at Tenth Avenue.

Martin shrugged. "He doesn't like me."

"Why?"

"I told him Protestants go straight to Hell."

"You didn't?"

Martin nodded.

"Who said that?"

Martin stopped and looked into my eyes. "You did."

"Me? When?"

"You said I couldn't go to Sunday school with Mikey cause it's a sin to go into a Protestant church. And you said people who comet lots of sins go straight to Hell."

"Commit, not comet, " I said. "A comet is a falling star shooting across the sky."

"You said people who commit lots of sins go straight to Hell, I know you did," said Martin. "And Steve goes to that Protestant church every Sunday."

Martin had a knack of adding two plus two and coming to the answer three plus one, which is correct, but still a surprise.

I collected the dollar for the week's newspapers and Martin sold three pull-tab tickets totaling 60 cents to Mrs. Miller. Hers was the first stop of the best part of my route, which had eight houses on a single block. Twenty minutes later Martin had finished off the last book of tickets and I had successfully collected from all but one of the customers on the ten hundred block of Montgomery and we were headed up Tenth Avenue towards St. Michael's where I was in Grade Seven and Martin in Grade One.

The last two stops on my route were across the street from the school that had been finished the summer between Grades Three and Four. Not long ago the whole area was at the very edge of Moose Jaw, but now houses were being built two blocks farther west.

"What's that word?" said Martin, looking at the front page. "Cos ..."

My little brother preferred asking for help with reading away from Basil and Mom who both gave him a hard time, one more reason to help with my paper delivery.

"Cosmonaut," I said.

"What's that?"

"It's a guy who rides in a rocket to space. Russian for astronaut." I read the story earlier. "He's complaining that there's not much room for him to move."

Martin gave me one of those looks that were inevitably followed by a question.

"But you said the universe is as big as infimity."

"Infinity."

"As big as infinity and that was bigger than anyone could imagine," said Martin. "Bigger than a million cabillion megamillion times how far it is from here to the moon."

"Ya," I said.

"So why is there no room to move?"

"Inside the space capsule," I said. "There's no room to move inside the space capsule."

"What's a capsule?" said Martin.

"Like a car, only instead of an engine it has a rocket and instead of the engine in front, the rocket is behind," I said. "They showed it on TV."

Martin shrugged. He had mostly ignored the television that Dad bought a year ago, preferring to play outside with his many friends, even in January when the temperature hit minus thirty-five.

"A big rocket pushes it up into space and then the capsule circles the earth a few times before a little rocket pushes it out of orbit and back down to earth," I said.

"What's our bit mean?"

"Orbit," I said. "It's the circle that the capsule travels around the earth. It's like a path, only up there in the sky."

Sometimes I wondered if my little brother had a brain big enough to fit the answers to the thousands of questions he asked in a day. Probably, because the little guy hardly ever repeated himself.

Just then Martin stopped and I plowed into him, almost knocking him off the sidewalk that had "1961, City of Moose Jaw" engraved on it.

"Hi Steve," said Martin.

I looked up to see Steve and another guy who must have been six feet tall.

"Hi Martin," said Steve. "This is my cousin Doug. He's thirteen and he's going to live with us."

"Hey," I said. "I'm Roy."

"He's the biggest twelve-year old in Moose Jaw," said Steve to his cousin.

"Hey," said Doug.

"Is it true your Dad and sister were killed by lightning?" said Martin.

"Martin!" Sometimes the little guy said the first thing that popped into his head.

"Ya," said Doug, who then looked at me. "It's okay. Better to tell everybody first time you meet them."

"Both of them, together?" said Martin.

"They were holding hands walking across a schoolyard near our house in Calgary," said Doug.

"Geez, that's terrible," I said.

Doug shrugged. "I'm used to it now."

"And now your mother is having a nervous breakout?" said Martin.

"Who told you that?" said Doug.

Martin realized he had said something wrong.

"Who told you that?" Doug repeated, louder and more aggressive.

As Martin tried to take a step behind me, Doug grabbed his shoulder.

"Who?"

"Roy!"

"Hey!" I said, stepping into the guy, who was two or three inches taller and probably outweighed me by twenty-five pounds.

"Stay out of this," said Doug.

"He's my brother," I said.

We stood so close I could smell the Juicy Fruit on Doug's breath and see his nostrils pulse.

"He's only six and he didn't mean anything by it," I said. "Did you?"

Martin shook his head.

"He's sorry. Aren't you?"

"I'm sorry," said Martin, almost crying.

"He's sorry," I said, backing away, but remaining on guard for a sudden punch. I've had fights on the rink and walking back from the baseball diamond so I know how to back away without backing down.

"He's only six," I said again as a warning. "He just repeats what he hears."

I made sure Doug saw me glance at Steve. The guy had a right to be mad, but at the source of the gossip.

"Come on," I said, grabbing my little brother and pulling him across Mrs. Hayward's lawn to the door of my second last customer.

Ringing the doorbell I snuck a look back towards Doug and Steve. The seven-year old had crossed the street, walking quickly away from his cousin.

"You don't know how lucky you are," I said to Martin.

I didn't know who to feel more sorry for: Doug, because of all the rotten things happening to him? Martin, because he was still shaking in his running shoes? Steve, who was about to get pounded? Or maybe myself, because I knew this was not the last time I'd face that anger.

DIARY ENTRY DEC. 5, 2000

I realized just now that I haven't felt motivated in years. But the Wild Woman on the AM Dial motivates me. She makes me feel good even though she's pushy and obnoxious and her politics are terrible. The past two days I've felt passion. Some of it, maybe a lot, is anger. But there's more to it than just that. She was making fun of my politics and the next thing I know we're making out like teenaged rabbits home alone on a Saturday night. There's something ... chemical. Maybe certain people give off smells that are particularly attractive. It certainly isn't her personality.

Or maybe it's simply fun to be with someone who cares about socialism versus free enterprise and the collective versus the individual. No one wants to argue politics anymore. Her and I share that passion and it leads to others. We fight and that leads to making love because of the passion. Strange.

Who knows where this will lead?

It was fun talking about 1962.

"I tried explaining Saskatchewan politics once to a friend in Palm Beach. 'The Liberals were conservatives and the CCFers were the liberals,' I said. But I couldn't remember what that stood for," she said, emptying the last bottle of Malmsey into her glass.

"Cooperative Commonwealth Federation," he said, holding out his empty glass.

She tipped the bottle upside down to show it was empty and then shrugged, a look that said she paid for it, so why should she feel guilty about finishing it?

"You know, I almost didn't kiss you that first time," she said.

He said nothing. What was her next surprise?

"I hated your name. Where did Roy come from?" she said.

"The name comes from Gaelic meaning red or the French 'roi' meaning king. I'm the red king."

"It's so not German-Canadian socialist, as my 20-year-old new assistant Brooke, would say. So not whatever your parents were supposed to be," she said.

"So-not German was the point," he said. "Because of the war, they stopped speaking the language at home. That's why I never learned it."

"Roy, the singing cowboy, there was one boy who always called you that," she said.

"Doug," he said. "He thought it was funny the thousandth time he said it."

"And the girls all called that other friend of yours 'Trigger'."

"Paul. He could be the hind end of a horse."

"You remember everyone's names?"

"I lived there seventeen years," he said.

"Moose Jaw, 1962," she said. "That was the year I became me. I first read Ayn Rand and learned about politics, my parents separated, I moved away from Regina, my first kiss, and then left for California."

"It was an amazing year," he said. "The doctors strike, the Cuban Missile Crisis, President Kennedy. It had a profound effect on me too."

"Do you remember what you wrote in those letters?" she said.

"More or less," he said. "A story about fighting and the kids of Moose Jaw and the doctors strike that I thought would teach President Kennedy a lesson during the Cuban Missile crisis. Remember Sister Veronica? She convinced me that the role of literature was to improve the world."

"How sweet. You believed her then and I'm sure you still do," she said, smirking.

"I do and I'm sure you agree as well because wasn't that the point of Ayn Rand's novels?" he said, smiling at his cleverness. "To tell people how to improve the world?"

He got her there, so she changed the subject.

"I remember you being a good storyteller but I was a better writer than you," she said. "Your grammar and vocabulary were significantly inferior to mine."

"What's with right-wingers and big words and rules of grammar?" he said. "You worship vocabulary like you venerate money. More is always better and you have some kind of need to flash it around in order to overcome a self-perceived, adolescent inadequacy. And you take pleasure in putting ordinary people down for breaking the rules of grammar. Who cares about conveying meaning? What's important are big words to demonstrate your superior intellect and following the rules."

"You're jealous because I got better marks on every essay in Grade 8," she said. "I remember how happy I was the first time I beat you."

"Trust me, getting better marks on Mr. Rebalski's essays didn't mean you were a better writer," he said.

"He thought you were the smartest kid in his class and he still gave me better marks than you."

"You were a suck-up and he had to reward that. You had a better vocabulary and knowledge of grammar and that's what he was marking. That plus he was to the right of Attila the Hun. But he still liked my stories better than yours."

"How do you know that?" she said.

"He told me. He said I had imagination and creativity, but I needed more discipline. He said I wrote better stories but I could learn from you to pay more attention in class and suck up to the teacher."

"He did not," she said.

He smiled. "You can't help it, you're a conservative. By definition you don't have any imagination."

This comment surprised her.

"Creative people challenge societal norms," he said. "They think outside the box. Conservatives are the box."

"What is that supposed to mean?" Exasperation and contempt dripped off her words.

"Conservatives are the kids back in elementary school who listened to what the teacher said and repeated it back on tests. They never learned to think for themselves. Instead they followed rules. They grew up believing that what exists is the natural order. This is hardly a state of mind conducive to creativity."

"You said conservatives are the box."

"You are the box," he repeated. "The people who grow up believing the existing rules are the natural order. Conservatives defend those rules, because you believe they are the natural order. People who try something different are a threat to that natural order. Conservatives are the defenders of that order, which means they complain when someone tries something new. Conservatives become the box that creative people are told to think outside of."

"You, the socialist believer in state control of thought, are telling me conservatives can't be creative?" she said.

"You don't have a clue what I believe," he said, trying to control the anger he felt. She would use it to her advantage.

"So tell me."

That caught him off guard.

"I'm listening," she said.

"Your sort are never interested in anything beyond clichés," he said.

"I expect them but that's only because the left always speaks in clichés," she said.

"I certainly don't believe in state control of thought or anything else like that," he said.

"That's what you socialists say, but the record shows that when you get in power you attack the free market, which always has the effect of centralizing power in the hands of the state."

"Attack the free market? What does that mean?"

"All socialists believe that the government can allocate resources better than the free market," she said. "That's the point of socialism. "

"I'll admit that historically most socialists thought the opposite of capitalism was government ownership and central planning, but that's not my socialism," he said. "I don't have a problem with a market that is used to allocate resources. That kind of market predates capitalism. What I have a problem with is a so-called 'free market' that is anything but. The capitalist market you defend is simply a system to enforce the unequal distribution of power. It's a set of rules made by the rich and powerful to ensure their complete domination of the economy and government. I believe in the opposite of capitalism, which is democracy."

"Capitalism created democracy," she said, her tone contemptuous.

"Capitalism created representative councils of rich people to take away power from hereditary lords, but I'd hardly call that democracy," he said. "In so far as capitalist countries have a government system approaching democracy it was created by ordinary people through hard fought struggles that got them thrown in jail, deported, fired or killed. And the truth is under capitalism, even with a faintly democratic government, the real power still resides with a small minority of rich and powerful capitalists. Democracy cannot exist until the economy, where most power lies, is run democratically."

He smiled triumphantly.

"I'm talking to a flaming Marxist communist," she said.

"I just kissed a whacko Ayn Rand capitalist," he answered.

They glared at each other.

He smiled first. She joined him.

"Just like back in Moose Jaw," he said.

"Kind of fun," she said. "In a masochistic sort of way."

He smiled again.

"You want to hang out together until Thursday? Sightsee the attractions of Boston," she said. "Then we can share a cab over to the archives. Pick up our letters together and bring them back here to read?"

"Sure, why not," he said.

"We're probably going to talk politics," she asked.

"My guess is it would be hard to avoid," he said.

"You're okay with that?" she said.

"I can defend myself, if that's what you asking," he said. "You're the one who should be worried."

She seemed confident but he wondered what the hell he was doing.

Katherine, letter 2

September 12, 1962

Dear President Kennedy,

Once again, I hope this letter finds you well. My social studies teacher, Mr. Rebalski, has given me another assignment that involves writing you. This time he has set up a competition between Roy Schmidt and I. The one who writes the best story wins ten bonus marks in both English and Social Studies. If I get that, I'm sure to have top marks in both classes.

My father says that the way to beat Roy as top Grade 8 student at St. Michael's is to focus on doing my best in each class, on each assignment and on each test and not to think about how smart he is or anything like that. My mother says I should find Roy's weak spot and take advantage of it. My goal for now is to beat Roy at something in order to gain the confidence that I can do it again.

I've thought for some time about what to write. Our assignment is to explain a political lesson that we learned recently. We can write as many letters as we need to tell the story. Of course, Mr. Rebalski will read each letter first, before he sends them to you, so I've tried to figure out what is important politically to him. I think he is a very smart man who appreciates an intelligent person who is honest and works hard. He says the problem with the world is that smart people are not appreciated. Well, I appreciate him. He's the best social studies and English teacher I've ever had. He really tries to make you understand how important it is to think for yourself. I don't think he likes Communism and the Soviet Union very much because he's Ukrainian and I know that you are one of the people who he looks up to most in the whole world.

Having someone to look up to is so important, don't you agree? My father says this is good both for the person looking up and for the person who is being looked up to. One gets a role model and the other gets an incentive to be a better person. My father also says that the best role model is someone who demonstrates the importance of working hard, rather than of being smart, because most of us can do very little about how smart we are, while everyone can work harder.

I think of Mr. Rebalski as a role model. I like the way he tells a story to make a point or to teach a lesson. I think that's what he wants Roy and I to learn while writing this story. I just hope I can do it half as well as Mr. Rebalski.

My essay will be about events this past summer in Saskatchewan before and during the withdrawal of services by physicians. The importance of fighting communism is certainly one of the most important political lessons I have ever learned.

I know you are a busy man Mr. President, as is Mr. Rebalski. So, I will keep each of my letters short and send you my essay in short pieces that you and Mr. Rebalski can fit into your busy schedules. I will save the beginning of my story until the next letter.

Roy, letter 3

Sept. 14, 1962

Dear President Kennedy,

Well, I got kind of tired Tuesday night and then I had hockey tryouts Wednesday and Thursday so this is the first chance I've had to get back to this story. I like writing, but it's more work than I thought. Today the paper says you have ruled out war on Cuba, which is good, if it's true. Basil says 95 per cent of what's in the paper is true, just not the important stuff. Sister Veronica says she has prayed for you to read these letters. I like Sister Veronica, but I've already told you that.

You got brothers so you know how things can be, right? You got to help out, look after each other. That's what I always try to do. But sometimes it can cause you trouble.

It was in May, a nice day and we were sitting on the back porch after supper.

"What's a 'secret army'?" said Martin, looking at the front page of the paper.

I shrugged.

"A secret army has secret uniforms and secret guns and secret grenades and secret tanks and secret planes," said Basil, who stared out the screen door from inside our house.

Martin's eyes grew wide, but I rolled mine and scrunched up my mouth to show I knew our big brother was fooling.

"Is that true?" Martin had enough experience with Basil's tom-foolery that he checked his stories with me.

"They got secret bombs and they put them in secret places and blow them up with secret detonators," Basil said, stepping out onto the porch, his baseball glove in his throwing hand. "Boom! And then it's not a secret anymore."

"Is that true Roy?" repeated Martin.

I shrugged.

"The Secret Army of Algeria are French colonists fighting against giving the country back to Algerians," said Basil.

"Algeria is in North Africa," I said.

"It's been a French colony for a hundred years and now the

original people want it back," said Basil. "They're the descendents of the people who have lived there for thousands of years."

"Like the Indians?" said Martin.

Basil smiled.

"Ya," I said. "The Algerians are like Indians and the colonists are like cowboys."

"You're pretty smart for a six-year old," said Basil.

Martin beamed at the compliment from his 16-year-old brother, who was the star pitcher for the best Colt League team in Saskatchewan, maybe all of Canada and, with little more than a month to go in the school year, the top student in the graduating Grade 12 class at St. Louis College. He had already been accepted at the University of Saskatchewan and been awarded the Robin Hood Flour scholarship that went to the best student among all the children of those working for Moose Jaw's largest employer. Plus he was a favourite of the priests who saw great potential in him as a candidate for clerical life, which pleased our mother, until she heard some of his recent statements concerning the existence of God. The resulting argument had been the reason Martin and I were on the back porch, instead of in the living room where the family normally said the rosary after supper dishes had been cleaned and put away.

"Steve says the cowboys are the good guys, but I kind of feel sorry for the Indians," said Martin.

He was a smart little brother.

"Me too," said Basil, sitting down beside Martin, whose legs didn't quite reach the ground. "The Indians were just trying to protect themselves and keep their land."

"What did Mom say?" I asked.

"The usual," said Basil. "Father Phelan will straighten me out."

I made a face. Father Phelan was one of my least favourite people, especially since he finked on Maurice Blais to the police. Maurice, one of a family of sixteen children, whose parents were known as the 'Western Producers', lived across the street from St. Michael's and had at least one sibling in each of the school's eight classrooms. One morning he confessed the sin of stealing from the church's collection plate to Father Phelan and later that day, the cops picked him up for questioning. While I told Maurice what he had done was a mortal sin, I didn't think it was right for a priest to rat about something learned in the confessional. That was a mortal sin too.

"Are you crooked?" said Martin.

Basil looked at our baby brother and laughed when he saw the serious look. He stood on the ground behind the porch and bent over, crooked and laughing.

"Mom wants Father Phelan to straighten out Basil's atheism," I said. "Mom thinks his atheism is crooked."

"Is it? Basil?"

Basil looked at the screen door and shook his head. "Look little guy, I promised Mom I wouldn't talk to you or Roy about religion. You'll have to figure it out for yourselves."

Martin looked to me.

"He'll get in trouble if he tells us what he thinks," I said.

"And besides, I'm late," said Basil. "I'm trying out for the Regals tomorrow and Wally promised to work on my slider."

"Hey, I figured out the screw ball," I said. "It goes up and in on a right-handed batter."

"Really?" said Basil.

"I've only tried it in practice cause it's still kind of wild, but I got the grip working the way you showed me. Trick is to release the ball the opposite of a curve."

"That's hard on your elbow and forearm," said Basil. "Season I tried that the chiropractor made me stop."

As far as I knew, Basil was the only kid in Moose Jaw ever to see a chiropractor for his pitching arm. The coach in his first year of Pony League, Mr. Watts, an American pilot stationed at the Air Force base, had paid for the treatment and was rewarded with a provincial championship. Basil gave up a measly three earned runs in six complete games pitched in the league playoffs and provincial tournament.

"You want me to show you?" I asked.

"Maybe tomorrow," said Basil. "Got to get going."

As Basil slipped around the side of the house, I went back to reading my book, but not before I thought about how my older brother seldom had time for me anymore. I suspected a girlfriend. I suspected Wally was really Wendy or Wanda or more likely Isabel, the blonde from Tech who I overhead Basil describing to Dave from across the street as "willing to go all the way."

"Whatcha reading?" said Martin, interrupting my thoughts.

"It's called Fontamara. Basil gave it to me."

The last year or so I'd been reading books that Basil gave me after he read them. It was fun to talk about what they meant.

"Is it good?" said Martin.

"Ya," I nodded. "It's about this poor town in Italy and how everybody takes advantage of the people living there. Especially the fascists."

"What's that?"

"Sort of like Nazis, only not German. They were Italian. Rich people paid to put them in government, to keep the communists and socialists out. Fascists hate democracy and they're really mean to poor people. They make up lots of rules for people to follow and take away their freedom. In the book, the fascists are all squealers. You know, like Charlie Beauchamp, who tells on everyone."

"He gets gold stars even though he's not very smart," said Martin. "He gets half the questions wrong but Mrs. Parker still gives him gold."

"A teacher's pet," I said. "Basil says the teachers who just want you to repeat whatever they tell you are producing good little fascists. Basil says good teachers want you to think for yourself."

My little brother thought about this for a moment. "Is Mrs. Parker a fascist?"

I could see where this conversation might be headed.

"Maybe she is, but you better not call Mrs. Parker that or you'll get in trouble. And don't tell Mom I said she was."

"Basil told Mom the doctors are fascists," said Martin.

This was safer ground since Dad agreed with Basil.

"The ones who don't want Medicare are. They hate socialism. They hate the government. They hate poor people. They think it's okay if you have to pay money to get an operation or if you break a leg or something. All they care about is making money. They say all the doctors will move to the United States or go on strike when the government brings in Medicare."

I could see that Martin was thinking about something.

"Are we poor people?" he asked after a few seconds.

It was a question I'd never considered.

"Steve said his cousin Doug said we're poor and too stupid to know it."

"Us?" I said, thinking about how to answer.

"Steve said Doug said anyone who lives in a tiny house like ours with so many kids has got to be poor."

Was our house tiny? I had to admit it was a lot smaller than the new ones across from the school. And I did share a bed with Martin. Before our sister left home Martin's crib had been in her room while I slept with Basil. Did that make us poor? The bathroom was downstairs and until I was nine we had an outhouse attached to the garage and water pumped from a cistern. There were still a half dozen houses on our block where the honey wagon made regular stops. Did that make ours a poor neighborhood?

"And he said if you had a job filling bags at a flour mill that meant you were working poor at best."

That was certainly true in books. I had read a couple of John Steinbeck novels and factory workers were always poor. But, our family?

"Maybe we are poor," I said.

We looked at each other then Martin jumped down on to the ground. He took a step and then kicked a stone across the yard.

"You want to play catch?" he said.

"Sure," I said. "Get the gloves and put this on my bed."

I handed Martin the book.

"Meet me at the field," I said.

Martin nodded and headed into the house. I walked past the garden our mother was preparing for planting, to the back alley where I turned right.

"Hi Mrs. Erikson," I said to Paul's mother who was digging in her garden.

"Hello Roy," she answered back. "How are you?"

"Pretty good."

"Paul's with his brother at the store," she said, pushing her foot down on a spade.

"I'm going to play catch with Martin."

"Have fun."

Past four yards and across Tenth Avenue I was at the empty field covering half of a block where all the neighborhood kids play catch or kick the can or just hang out to be away from adults. Cindy Shaw was kneeling down, looking at something with a girl I didn't recognize.

"Hey Cindy," I said.

"Hey Roy," she answered. "This is my cousin Mary from Swift Current. She's staying the weekend."

"Hi," I said.

"Hi," said Mary. "How old are you?"

"Twelve in three weeks," I said.

"He's in Grade 7 cause he skipped a grade," said Cindy. "She just turned twelve but she's in Grade 6."

Mary whispered something in Cindy's ear and the two girls laughed.

"What are you doing?" I said.

"Just talking," said Cindy.

"Were you named after Roy Rogers?" Mary said, giggling. "Where's Trigger?"

"So funny I forgot to laugh," I said, having heard this a hundred times before.

Again Mary whispered something to Cindy and they laughed. Girls don't bother me the way they used to, but Cindy was stupid and mean to little kids. And even though Paul heard her say 'I love Roy,' she was always bugging me.

"You want to play spin the bottle?" said Mary, holding up an empty coke bottle, as the two girls laughed harder.

"Maybe later," I said, seeing Martin cross Tenth Avenue. "I'm playing catch with my little brother."

Cindy was always mean to Martin or trying to get him into trouble, so I walked towards him, grabbed my baseball glove and whispered, "Don't let her scare you. That's what bullies want."

Cindy pointed to Martin, said something to Mary, and the two girls laughed again.

"He likes to play catch with his little brother more than he likes to kiss girls," said Mary as loud as she could.

"More than I like to kiss you two," I said. "That's for sure."

I turned back to my little brother who was about ten steps away and lifted up my glove. Martin threw me the baseball and I tossed it back immediately, not too hard. As we lobbed the ball back and forth, I backed up, increasing the distance between us and put a little more heat on each pitch. As a result, Martin, who was pretty good for his age, lost control of the fifth throw, which caused the girls to laugh. Martin glared at Cindy as he walked to where the ball had rolled.

"Butter fingers," said Cindy.

"Butter fingers," repeated Mary.

As the girls giggled, Martin threw the ball back to me and I made sure my return toss was easy and right at my little brother's glove. But, with the laughing and taunting, he dropped the ball again and the girls roared.

"Martin has butter fingers," said Cindy.

"Martin has butter fingers," repeated Mary.

I ran over to pick up the ball. As I reached down I noticed Martin take a step towards the girls and then turn back to me to await another throw.

"You know what Barry told me?" said Martin, in a voice loud enough for the girls to hear over their chanting. "About Cindy?"

Barry was Cindy's seven-year-old brother.

"Barry told me his mom caught Cindy in their garage with her panties around her ankles and Brian Hennessy running away. That's why she was grounded for two weeks."

The chanting stopped as Mary stared at her cousin. I tried not to smile, because people shouldn't say hurtful things, even when someone deserved them.

"I'll kill the little brat," said Cindy, standing.

I stepped between her and Martin.

"Not that one. I'll fix him later," Cindy said. "My little brat."

She stomped off across the field towards her house with her cousin following. "I'll destroy him," were the last words that could be heard as Cindy marched towards revenge.

I threw the ball underhanded to Martin and stared.

"She's always picking on me," said Martin.

"I know."

"She beats up Barry and tells on him and makes up stories to get him in trouble."

I nodded. It was all true, confirmed by numerous sources.

"She tells on kids at school too," said Martin.

This I knew too. About two months earlier she saw me and Geoff Walker smoking behind the barbershop and told Mr. Kalinsky. It was the one and only cigarette I ever smoked — a half dozen drags and I threw up. Fortunately the principal never took anything Cindy said too seriously. For a principal Mr. Kalinsky was pretty nice.

"She's a fink and a bully," said Martin as he threw the ball back underhanded.

"Did it make you feel better when you said that about her?" I asked.

"Ya," said Martin. "I got her back good."

"You did," I said. "She made you feel bad and then you did the same to her."

Martin looked at me with that "I'm-thinking-about-it" look.

"It felt good, but maybe it shouldn't have," said Martin. "Sister Marie-Claire says we should turn the bother cheek."

I had to stop myself from laughing.

"Other cheek," I said, although it was better the way Martin said it.

"Turn the other cheek. You think that's what we should do?"

Was it?

"Most of the time," I said. "It's a good idea, because people get along better. But sometimes it means bullies get away with bad stuff. Or rich guys take everything from the poor."

"Ya," said Martin.

"Turn the bother cheek when you can, but don't let bullies scare you," I said.

Martin threw the ball up in the air as high as he could.

"Hey, that's pretty good," I said, jumping over my little brother to catch the baseball as it descended. "But watch this."

I wound up and pitched the ball straight up.

"Wow," said Martin as the ball soared.

"Catch it," I said. "See if you can catch it."

DIARY ENTRY DEC. 6, 2000

"How many letters did you write?" she said, as they sat in the four-poster with a view of the Boston Commons.

"About two dozen, I think," he said. "You?"

"Maybe half that," she said. "Verbosity is equal to how left wing one is, squared."

"You really do turn the world upside down," he said. "Your country prints a thousand words of what passes for right-wing thought to every left-wing one. And you accuse us of being verbose?"

"Our words makes sense," she said.

"To the owners of newspapers and the advertisers who pay the bills," he said.

"To the people that count," she said.

"So you admit it?"

"That some people count more than others?" She smiled at his foolishness. "You call me an 'Ayn Rander' and then it surprises you that I believe a small minority of people are absolutely more important than the majority? That's the point of all her novels."

"The point of all her novels is to appeal to adolescent angst. 'No one appreciates me. Everyone else is stupid. I am the centre of my very own universe. They'll miss me when I'm gone.'" He hated Ayn Rand.

"The novels are propaganda and what bothers you Marxists is that they work," she said. "You've got nothing even remotely close to their effectiveness. They've wiped you guys off the map."

She had a point there. But there was an easy answer.

"Her books blame individual failure on government and collectivism," he said. "They offer an easy excuse to people who wish to avoid personal responsibility for their lack of success. They work because they offer an idealized explanation of how capitalism works that appeals to a simple mind who cannot see the big picture, cannot grasp the possibility of another kind of economic system. The irony is these books promote a loser ideology by making people think they are smarter than the rest of us."

"A loser ideology?" Her tone turned to anger. "What the hell are you talking about?"

"You convince people, who by your own elitist ideology, cannot possibly be great people, to believe the world should be run by greedy, great people," he said, feeling good that she was agitated. "You have a supposed democracy in which people vote for an oligarchy. How much more of a loser philosophy can you get?"

She glared at him as he continued.

"It's the same thing as making people believe that everyone can be rich, when they obviously can't, because if everyone were rich, no one would be rich. You use the language of populism and democracy. In public you pretend to be populists when in private you admit to being elitists."

"Come to one of my talks," she said. "I speak very publicly about the importance of creating a society that enables the few great people, the doers."

"Do you tell the assembled masses that most of them can never be one of the 'few great people'?" He had her on the ropes. "You're really going to deny that you pretend to be a populist? All your sort perform the same trick. You claim to speak on behalf of the people, even though you really believe you're part of the elite. And then you attack the so-called liberal elites that pretty much don't exist. It's a complete scam that only works because so many people are kept in ignorance by a useless education system and a media that's even worse."

She was about to say something, but he cut her off.

"A media your sort claim is liberal or even socialistic, despite it being owned by some of the biggest corporations in the world," he said. "But don't get me wrong. I hope you continue to thrive and prosper. If you Ayn Randers actually ran the world most people would be so miserable capitalism would collapse quicker than you can say 'Who is John Galt?'"

"What planet are you from?" she said.

"That's your best shot?" he replied.

"You really are an unrepentant socialist," she said.

"I believe in democracy, one person one vote in every area where people come together, including the economy," he said. "If that makes me a socialist in your books, I wear the label proudly."

"Perhaps we should change the subject," she said.

This was a rule they had agreed to. At any time either party could request a time out or a change in subject.

"How about Al Gore and election stealing?" he said, smiling.

She shook her head.

"You choose the topic then," he said.

"Do you have any children?" she said, almost certainly buying time to regroup.

"Three girls, each a year apart," he said. "Two still in university, getting their PhDs, Emma in history and Sylvia in English literature. The oldest, Louise, is an elementary school teacher. No grandchildren yet. How about you?"

She turned away then looked back at him as if deciding whether or not to say something. "A son by my fourth husband," she said.

"How old is he?"

Silence. She actually had to think about it.

"He's fourteen," she said. "I had him when I was 38. He was a Down's baby."

"Oh geez," he said. "How was that?"

"Not the best time of my life," she said. "But we found him a good home. Down's babies are a lot of work. My husband and I certainly did not have the time."

"That must have been tough," he said.

"It all worked out for the best," she said. "I would have been a terrible parent. My mother was not a good role model."

She smiled weakly.

It was not fair to judge her. Time to change the subject again, but what else did they have to talk about if politics was a forbidden subject? They stared at each other for a few seconds.

She walked toward the window. She didn't know what to say either.

He thought of the letters.

"I'll let you read mine if you let me read yours," he said. "The letters."

She turned to look at him. She was having a hard time deciding how to answer.

"Why not?" he said.

"Maybe," she said.

"You're embarrassed?" he said.

"I'll think about it," she said.

"You who claim to have been the better writer," he said. "What did you say? 'The more prodigious child prodigy.' And now you're scared?"

"No," she said.

"You are."

"That's not it," she said.

"What then?"

"I have concerns regarding my new position," she said. "Discretion is required."

"You can't remember what you wrote and you're worried something in the letters could be embarrassing?" he said. "You're worried the press might get hold of the letters. That's why you're here?"

He could tell from her look that he was right.

"You can let me read them," he said. "I won't tell."

"I'd like to read them, before I decide, that's all," she said.

"You're afraid of what you wrote."

"No," she said.

"Chicken," he said, tickling her foot.

"I am not," she said.

"Chicken," he said then began clucking.

"Don't tickle," she said, with anger in her voice.

He pulled his hand away.

"If you're going to touch me, touch me hard," she said. She grabbed his hand and put it on her shoulder.

He stared, unable to figure out what she wanted.

"Massage me," she said. "Hard. All over. Every square inch."

Once again she surprised him.

"Come on," she said. "You do know how?"

She was brazen. Asked for what she wants. Different, but it was kind of nice.

"In certain circles, back in the late sixties, I was known as 'Magic Fingers Bliss'," he said.

"I can hardly wait to meet him," she said.

Roy, letter 4

Sept. 27, 1962

Dear President Kennedy,

Sorry it's taken so long to get back to you, but Mr. Rebalski has been giving us a lot of homework. And I sort of got in trouble with the principal because all the boys in my class voted for me to stop this new kid who was a really bad tattletale.

Grade 8 is the last year of elementary and we write departmental exams to decide if we take academic or technical courses in high school, so you got to do well. Not that I'm worried, all of my marks have been in the 90s, but Basil says sometimes your marks from Grade 8 are tiebreakers to decide who gets a university scholarship. I really want to go to university.

Hockey season has also started and I made the midget team, which is mostly for 14 and 15 year olds even though I'm only 12. We play at the Civic Centre instead of outside, which is pretty good. I haven't forgotten about baseball either. I guess you heard Maury Wills got his 100th stolen base. Wish I could run that fast. The paper today says the Cuban government discovered a plot to kill Castro and they executed 75 people involved in the planning. You weren't behind any plan to kill him, were you? Basil is up in Saskatoon at university, but he came home last weekend and said your government has hundreds of agents trying to kill Castro. Do you know about that? Sister Veronica says it's probably just bad guys running the army and the CIA. I sure hope that's true. Anyhow, back to the story.

"The doctors will all leave Saskatchewan and then what will happen when you get sick?" said Paul, as he pumped higher on one of the old Elgin Park wooden flat board swings.

"They won't leave," I said, sitting on one of the newer rubber-strap bottom swings. "They're just saying that to scare the government."

"My Mom says they will," said Paul.

Mrs. Erikson was a nurse at the training school for retarded people.

"And even if some do leave my Dad says the government has

plans to get new ones from England," I said. "That's what his union president said."

"Socialist doctors," said Paul, as he jumped off the swing and flew about ten feet before crash landing into the dirt, showing off like always.

"What's wrong with being a socialist?" I said, following Paul away from the swings. "I'm a socialist. Basil is a Marxist. The mayor is a socialist. Half the province voted socialist."

"Ya and my Mom says now they're going to get what they deserve."

"Your Mom voted CCF," I said. "She told me."

"She voted for them when Tommy Douglas was premier. He's a Baptist, like us, but Woodrow Lloyd is a communist, that's what she says," said Paul.

This was pointless. Arguing political theory with Paul was like playing canasta with him, he was so easy to beat I felt guilty instead of good. Paul had always lived two houses west of ours and even though he was a year older, he was a year behind in school since flunking Grade 4 and me skipping Grade 2. As long as I can remember Paul would knock on our door and ask, "can Roy come out to play," or follow me around, more like a little brother than an older neighbor.

Of course sometimes it was fun to hang around with him, like when we went shooting down on the flats by Thunder Creek. Paul had a .22, a B.B. gun and a pellet rifle, the only presents Jiggs ever gave him in the decade he had been his stepfather. We shot frogs and tin cans and gophers, experimenting with each weapon. The B.B. gun is pretty much useless against frogs or gophers but is fun for tin cans, which clang and sometimes even jump a little if the target is not too far away. The best thing about it is you can fire a dozen shots real fast, only having to pump the lever before pulling the trigger. The single-shot pellet gun is a little more powerful and, if you're close enough, you can explode a frog, which is pretty cool. The .22 goes right through both sides of a can at a hundred feet, blows up frogs and once I downed a duck flying a hundred feet above us. (Paul claims it isn't true but I swear it is.) Problem is the .22 bullets are expensive, but sometimes Paul sneaks a few from Jiggs.

I guess we're good friends, a lot of time best friends. Except for when Paul gets mad, when he's dangerous, not because of his guns, but because of his arm. He is the best rock thrower in Moose Jaw, maybe in the whole world, especially when he's peed off. Doesn't matter who makes him angry, Jiggs, his big brother, me, or a baseball coach, Paul chucks rocks hard and straight when he's mad. In May he cut me for seven stitches. Of course I never told my parents what happened. I said the rock flew up from the wheel of a passing truck, but every kid in the neighborhood knows the true story. I teased Paul about Frida Folkstone while we played catch at the field.

"You're always hanging around with her. What are you doing, playing dolls?" I said, joking, but that's not how he took it. Paul turned wild and started firing rocks. His aim is always good with small, round ones and the back alley had lots of his favourite ammunition.

I ran and thought I was beyond his range but my "nah, nah, nah, nah, nah, nah" made him madder and his arm stronger. He fired and hit me right above the left eye. The blood came pouring out, the most ever, even counting the time two winters ago when Max Miner's skate clipped my wrist and Doc Baxter said a quarter of an inch over and I could have bled to death. There was so much blood it made me shut my eyes and it ran down my face into my mouth, making it hard for me to breathe. Scared the crap out of Paul, but it didn't hurt that much. Not like Max's skate.

"The cut is pretty much healed?" said Paul, staring at my face as we sat on the merry-go-round.

"Pretty much," I answered.

"Does it still hurt?"

I shook my head.

"So it's okay if I slug you?" said Paul snapping his fist at me, stopping an inch from my face.

"I'm so scared," I said.

"I know you are," said Paul.

I made a show of putting up my dukes and jabbing five or six times before almost landing a right on Paul's nose. We boxed a lot after he got gloves two Christmases ago and I always beat him cause his nose spurts blood with just a little tap.

Instead of snapping his head back like he always did when I pretended to punch him, Paul looked at something behind me.

"Look who's here," he whispered, pointing with a scrunch of his face.

I turned around. It was Doug with Cindy and Katie from Regina, the new girl at school.

"He **is** big," said Paul, staring at Doug.

But I was more interested in Katie Anderson, the new girl in my class who seemed pretty smart, especially in English and French. A few times she even came close to me in math and science tests. Plus she was pretty good in Phys. Ed., played softball and belonged to the figure skating club. A few days earlier, the last time I went public skating at the Civic Centre before they shut it down for the summer, we held hands, until Martin showed up. Katie was nice, but maybe a little stuck up. Her Dad was a doctor and a Protestant, but her Mom was Catholic. People say mixed marriages are hard on kids.

"Hi Roy," she said.

"Hi," I answered.

"Where's your little brother?" said Cindy.

I shrugged.

"Ya, where's that little jerk brother of yours?" said Doug, who followed up these aggressive words with an even more hostile stance.

Cindy giggled. Paul glanced at me to gauge my reaction. Katie smiled nervously and took a step away from Doug.

"My little bother?" I said.

Cindy giggled again and Katie laughed.

"He's probably organizing his gang to knock off the milk truck again," I said. "You heard they struck it rich yesterday with a roll of pennies?"

My attempt at being funny caused Doug to glare, but the two girls liked it.

"Really?" said Cindy. "Was my little bother with him?"

She valued any information that could be used against Barry.

"Dunno," I said. "A swarm of them distracted Mr. Pratt and one snuck into the van."

"That's all they got?" said Cindy. "A roll of pennies?"

"That's what I heard," I said. I had mixed feelings about the theft. On one hand stealing was wrong, on the other Mr. Pratt was the umpire who blew a call at home that allowed the Reds to beat me in the bottom of the sixth inning the season before. Kelly missed the plate by at least six inches. I knew this to be true because I was backing up home on the throw and had a much better view of the play than the ump or anyone else.

"Did you know all Mr. Pratt's kids have six fingers?" said Paul. "It's true, my Mom said so."

"A roll of pennies?" repeated Cindy. "You sure?"

I shrugged.

"Wouldn't have got anything if they still used horses to deliver milk," said Paul.

He was trying to help me avoid the fight that Doug was trying to start.

"They used horses until I was in Grade 3," Paul said. "You remember?"

Cindy and I nodded.

"Grade 3," repeated Paul. "George, that was Mr. Pratt's horse. Remember his feedbag? Remember when Marty Manson fed George five packages of Exlax mixed with cayenne pepper over on Montgomery Street? Shit everywhere."

"Oooh," said Cindy. "We don't want to hear about it."

"You're disgusting," said Katie.

It was Paul's all-time favourite story. Jiggs claimed to have been a witness to what happened and asking about that day was one of the few ways Paul could get his stepfather to talk.

"You're the one full of shit," said Doug, poking Paul hard on the shoulder.

What was this guy's problem?

"It's a true story," said Paul, trying his best to sound friendly and not scared. "My step dad saw it happen."

"Then he's full of shit too," said Doug, poking Paul again.

"We're all full of it," I said. "Him, you, me, them."

Paul was scared and relieved that I was trying to divert the big guy's attention, instead of confronting him. Paul had always been a coward so everyone picked on him. As Doug took a step towards him, Paul began to spin.

"Trick is who can keep it in," said Paul as he turned.

Doug and the girls looked at him like he was mental. He stopped and stared back.

"What's the matter? You chicken?"

"Of you?" said Doug.

"Of spinning," I said. "It proves who is most full of shit."

Paul smiled slyly. He and I were champion spinners.

"Spin fast for one minute and the one who is most full of shit, will puke it all out," I said. "That's how we do it here in Elgin Park."

The girls laughed. Doug was trapped and he knew it.

"What's wrong? You can't do it? One minute, that's all," I said.

"I can do it," said Doug.

"Katie counts and the rest of us spin," I said. "Come on, over here on the grass."

I ran the 20 feet or so to the middle of the biggest patch of green in the half-square-block park. The others followed.

"You got to try keep it tight and fast," I said demonstrating. "And you count, one one hundred, two one hundred, up to 60."

We took our positions as Katie stood back about 10 feet.

"Okay, go."

"One one hundred, two one hundred, three one hundred ..."

Paul and I kept our spins in tight circumference at a steady pace, but not too fast. We had experienced what happened if you showed off.

Doug, however, spun twice as fast and Cindy did as well.

"Twenty one hundred, 21 one hundred, 22 one hundred ..."

Katie was ... what? She looked nice and she was smart.

"Thirty one hundred, 31 one hundred, 32 one hundred ..."

Cindy fell to the ground, giggling.

Doug's circles were growing large and out of control.

"It's cheating if you make the circle too big," I said. "Keep em tight."

"Forty-five one hundred, 46 one hundred, 47 one hundred ..."

Katie, Doug, doctors strike, Martin milkman, Basil girlfriend, baseball season, 99 on math test, sore arm, Bertrand Russell, second base ... My head was spinning.

"Fifty-six one hundred, 57 one hundred, 58 one hundred ..."

President Kennedy, atom bomb, Fidel Castro, sugarcane, George Diefenbaker, funny cheeks, Woodrow Lloyd ...

The moment your blackout ended felt good, but almost immediately a headache started. I tried to focus and that made the pain sharper than usual, but I knew it would go away quickly, just like the times before.

Doug was doubled over what was left of his supper. Paul giggled like a happy drunk as he weaved in a circle almost as wide as the patch of open grass. Katie and Cindy stared at Doug.

"I guess he was the one full of shit," said Cindy, laughing.

"Full of shit," said Paul, quietly smiling.

I said nothing. I smiled at Katie and felt good, except for the headache. I noticed Doug stand up, but lost in the stare between me and Katie, missed him moving toward me, the twist of his shoulder and the roundhouse motion of his arm. All I saw was the last few inches of the fist as it traveled fast at me. Then ...

Katie was kneeling over me, her hand touching my forehead.

"Are you okay?" she said.

Okay?

"You're bleeding,"

Bleeding?

"He hit you right where you got the stitches," said Paul, standing above me.

He?

Both Paul and Katie looked to their right at Doug, who stood, hands in his back pockets, eyes to the ground, about ten feet away.

"He sucker punched you," said Paul.

"When you weren't looking," said Katie.

That's what sucker punch means, I thought. What's the word to describe that? Redundant.

"Right on your stitches," said Katie, glaring at Doug.

"Dirty fighting," said Paul.

Katie's face leaned towards mine, so close I could smell her sweet breath.

"Are you okay?"

Was I? Better than okay. This was nice. I thought of kissing Katie. It must have been the sucker punch or the spinning.

"I'm fine," I said, sitting up.

"Careful," said Katie, touching my arm.

"The blood is oozing," said Paul.

I touched the wound and felt stickiness.

"He's probably gonna have to go back to the hospital and get new stitches," said Paul, glaring at Doug.

"Do you pick on five year olds too?" said Katie, also glaring.

"Cindy?" said Doug. "Come on, let's go."

Cindy looked at Katie and then at Doug. She took a few steps in his direction.

"Let's get out of here," said Doug. "Leave these losers to their stupid games."

Cindy glanced at Katie then back at Doug. I knew she'd choose to go with whoever she thought was more powerful because Cindy was always like that.

"A fair fight would be a different story," said Katie as Doug and Cindy left.

"That's for sure," said Paul. "A different story."

Doug glanced back, but said nothing. He had the humiliated look of a batter, just struck out by a roundhouse curve he missed by half a foot. I felt good, like the pitcher after that strikeout, but I knew it was dangerous to humiliate some batters. It was still early innings.

Katherine, letter 3

October 2, 1962,

Dear President Kennedy,

This is Katherine Anderson again. I hope you remember me. I promised to send you my essay and here it is:

The socialist government of Saskatchewan was first elected in 1944. My father says the date is important because it was during the Second World War when the Reds were our allies in the fight against Hitler. Because of that not many people noticed or cared that the communists took over in Regina.

Like communists everywhere the CCF did not reveal its true intentions for some time. Instead they tried to gain the support of the common people by buying their votes through taking money from the few and giving it to the many. This is called taxation. My father says taxes are especially bad when they are what the communists call progressive. That means the government takes more and more money from the people who work the hardest, such as doctors and lawyers and businessmen. Poor people become slaves to the government and start to believe that the wealthy are their enemies.

The CCF also took over private business and set up new companies, but just like government-run companies everywhere they were mostly failures and today only a few of them, like the Saskatchewan Transit Company, remain. They require subsidies from the government that make them unfair competitors with free enterprise companies.

But the worst thing the CCF ever did was to start a compulsory socialist medical system called Medicare. They passed a law last year that made all physicians work for the government, taking away their freedom to practice medicine in the way they were trained. Instead, the government is now telling physicians what to do, where to do it and how much to charge for it.

The brave doctors of Saskatchewan and their supporters tried their best to stop the socialists from creating Medicare. They vowed not to practice medicine under the new law. All around the province Keep Our Doctors committees were formed to fight the government. We sent letters and we marched, telling the CCF to withdraw the law, but the government would not listen to us. When the new law came into effect, on July 1ˢᵗ, almost all of the physicians in the province withdrew their services and the good people of the province got very angry at the government. All of us in the KOD committees sent more letters, many businessmen shut their doors to support the doctors and attend rallies, but still the government would not change the law.

Instead of listening to the physicians and their supporters, the CCF started bringing in socialist doctors from Great Britain and other places where communists had already taken over. They opened medical clinics with these foreign doctors to take over the business of those physicians, like my father, who were taking a stand against government control of medicine and our lives. The CCF used all the strength of the government to crush the physicians of Saskatchewan and force them back to work under the socialist Medicare system.

The doctors kept up their brave fight for over three weeks, although a few returned to work before that. They did force the government to make a few changes to Medicare so it is not quite so bad, but most of the doctors are so angry that they will probably leave the province. My father is certainly looking for a position in the United States, possibly in California, and I might soon leave Moose Jaw to go live with him. My father says he is disgusted with Saskatchewan and all of Canada because there is already talk about how the socialists in the New Democratic Party will force the federal government to create Medicare all across the country.

But the worst part of Medicare is not what it has done to the physicians of this province, but rather what it has done to the people who live here. Many of them, perhaps most, seem to like Medicare. They want the government to run the medical system. In the eighteen years since the CCF first won an election it has made the people socialists.

How has it done that? By taking the wealth created by the few and giving it to the many. By making the many jealous of the few. By lying and manipulating the ignorance of the masses. Lying and manipulating are what the socialists are good at because they have lots of practice. Only a brave few, like my father, have the courage to stand up to the socialists who have all the power of government.

Quite honestly, most people are ignorant and not even capable of understanding what is really going on. They are easily manipulated by the socialists, who promise them everything. But wait and see what happens next. All the government has really done is drive away the smartest and the best. They won't stand for Medicare. They won't stand for socialism. The people who are really important, the people who are brilliant, the people who create new things and who everyone relies on, they will not keep working for a society that does not value them. If society takes away the wealth and independence of the brilliant visionaries, people like my father, they will go on strike, just like the Saskatchewan physicians. They will leave the province and then what will happen? The medical system will collapse. Soon the entire economic system will collapse. That's where socialism leads.

If you really want to understand this better the book to read is Atlas Shrugged by Ayn Rand, my favourite author. My father told me I should wait until I was sixteen before reading that book and Fountainhead, but I went ahead and read them anyway and now I understand the world much better. I understand people like Roy Schmidt much better too.

To sum up, the most important political lesson I have learned is that socialism is dangerous because it hurts those few people that society needs the most. Saskatchewan Medicare and the recent withdrawal of services by physicians was a good example of how this happens.

Roy, letter 5

Oct. 2, 1962

Dear President Kennedy,

What is going on at the University of Mississippi? What's the big deal that James Meredith wants to go to school? Just cause he's Negro all those mean-looking white people are screaming at him and soldiers have to protect him. Sometimes I don't understand your country. Sister Veronica says you are trying to stop prejudice against the Negroes and that's a good thing. Last weekend Basil brought home a friend who is from Ethiopia. I never saw black skin up close before. Ben's a nice guy and real good buddies with Basil. Who cares about your colour? Like Sister Veronica says, it is just skin deep.

This story is taking longer than I planned, but I keep thinking of more parts and Basil says it's important to give the whole picture. He's a pretty good writer so I listen to what he says. Here goes again.

"You gotta fight Doug," said Martin, in bed beside me. "You're the only one who has a chance of beating him."

My little brother had lost his marbles.

"You're tougher than him, I know you are," said Martin.

I shook my head.

"You afraid?" said Martin, eyes wide and honest in that alter boy look he was so good at. "Cause of your cut?"

I reached up to touch the scar tissue on my forehead. The bruise on top of the original cut had almost disappeared, but there was still a slight swelling and the scab had not yet fallen off the freshest part of the wound.

"We can wait till it's all healed up," said Martin.

"Why should I fight Doug?" I said.

"Cause he's mean and picks on little kids and he hit you when you weren't looking and you got three more stitches on top of the ones you already had and Dad got so mad I thought he was going to blow his top like the time Barry's steam engine exploded when you stuffed rubber bands in the smoke snack to see what would happen."

I sat up and reached over to flip the bedroom light switch.

"Stack," I said, lying down again. "Smoke stack."

"Smoke stack," repeated Martin.

There was always some logic to what Martin said, which was why he could persuade over a dozen kids living on the 900 and 1000 blocks of Albert and Brown streets to fight their counterparts from Carleton and Hall.

"What's a stack?" said Martin. "Like a stack of cards?"

"Pack of cards," I said.

"Mom says stack of cards when she's playing solitaire," said Martin.

"Ya, there's a pack of cards, which is the whole deck, but then you can put them into a stack, which means like a pile," I said.

"Barry calls their big porch out back a deck," said Martin.

"It's just a different word for the same thing," I said. "His Dad is from Ontario. Different places use different words, even though it's all English. Like we say chesterfield but Grandpa Dietrich said couch."

"And Grandpa Schmidt says it in German or Russian or Ukrainian."

"He used to speak more English," I said. "But he forgets as he gets older."

"Is there a porch of cards?" said Martin.

"No," I said.

"Why not?" asked Martin.

"Just because two words can mean the same about one thing doesn't mean they mean the same about everything," I said. "So 'table' can mean the place where we sit and eat, or it can mean a chart on a piece of paper, but you'd never call any piece of furniture a chart."

Silence. Maybe the little guy had fallen asleep.

"Why don't you want to fight Doug?" said Martin, just as I thought it might be safe to think about other things.

"Why do you want me to?"

"Because I got to have somebody to fight everybody Steve gets to be on his side," said Martin. "First it was gonna be him and me and then he said he'd win because Larry Tait would be on his side too and so I said Barry would fight Larry and then he said Mark Mainman and I said Billy Borg and pretty soon we had everybody I could think of on Brown and Albert and he had everybody he knew on Carleton and Hall."

"Like the Cold War," I said. "But instead of missiles, you guys got friends."

"What's the Gold War?"

"Cold War," I said. "Between Russia and the United States."

"They're fighting over cold?" said Martin.

A gold war did make more sense.

"They're fighting over communism versus capitalism," I said.

"Which side are we on?" said Martin.

"I'm not a capitalist or a communist," I said. "I'm a socialist."

"Me too," said Martin.

"Americans got more freedom, like for books and stuff like that, so we're on their side for that," I said. "And President Kennedy is a Catholic, like us."

"I like President Kennedy," said Martin.

"Mom says we have to be with the Americans because communism is against religion, but Dad hates the Americans because they won't let Robin Hood sell flour to Red China and the mill might close down if they can't get the business and then we'd have to move, maybe to Alberta or Ontario."

"Why is China red?" said Martin.

"Red means communist," I said.

"I hate the Mericans too," said Martin.

"Americans," I said.

"Americans," repeated Martin.

"Basil says both sides hate socialists," I said. "He says the Americans are real capitalists and the Russians call themselves communists but are really state capitalists."

"What's a capitalist?" said Martin.

"Rich people," I said. "Rich people who boss you around and try to run everything."

"Like a bully?"

"Ya," I said. "Like a bully."

"Like a principal?"

"That's more like a state capitalist," I said.

"I hate state capitalists," said Martin.

"Me too," I said. "If we had socialism everyone would be equal and we'd get to vote on everything."

"Like how long was recess?"

I smiled. Why not?

"I'd vote for half an hour and no more stupid art class."

"Sounds good," I said.

"Just cause I can't draw doesn't mean girls should laugh at me."

"They shouldn't laugh at anybody, just cause you're not good at something," I said. "You don't laugh at other kids, do you when you get best marks in arithmetic or science or spelling? Because they're not as good at something as you?"

"Never," said Martin.

"Good. You try your best at school, to learn everything really well so you can go to university, right? You know that every Schmidt, every one of us, gets the best marks in their class?"

"Ya," said Martin. "That's what Mom tells me all the time."

"We always do our best and we help each other, right? We help everybody, not just our family."

"'Do into others as you would have them do into you,' that's what Sister Marie-Claire says."

"Unto," I said. "Do unto others."

"Unto others," said Martin.

"If you know how to do something that somebody else doesn't, you should help them, show them how," I said. "That's what socialism is. Working together, helping each other. If all the ordinary people did that then the rich people wouldn't win all the time. Sticking together and helping each other, that's what Dad says a union is all about."

"Sticking together and fighting for what you believe," said Martin. "That's what Uncle Gregor says."

Basil told me that Uncle Gregor had been blacklisted after the Swift's meatpacking plant strike and that's why he now worked as a school janitor. The school board was all CCFers and they helped out the guys who lost their jobs. But I didn't think it was a good time to share this information with Martin. Better to let him think that sticking together meant you would win.

"So why won't you fight Doug?" said Martin, interrupting the thought. "Sticking together to fight for what you believe."

"What I believe?"

"You said it was important never to back down from bullies," said Martin, "and he's a bully. So is Steve. He tried to make me trade baseball gloves because he liked mine more than his."

"Did you give it to him?"

"No."

"Then you didn't back down. You don't have to fight him."

"He's going to keep picking on me until I fight him," said Martin.

"How do you know he won't keep picking on you even if you do fight him?"

"If he does, then I'll fight him again."

"And again and again?"

"Maybe," said Martin.

"For how long?" I said.

"As long as it takes," said Martin.

"Forever?"

"Maybe."

"And all your friends? And me? We should just keep on fighting forever and ever, as long as it takes?"

"Don't you want to get even with Doug?" said Martin. "Stick together and fight for what you believe."

"I want a million dollars too and I want Mom to make a whole Saskatoon berry pie just for me every day, but that doesn't mean it's going to happen."

Maybe I should have told Martin about Uncle Gregor being blacklisted. Maybe it was important to understand that you don't always win.

Silence. Maybe this time he had fallen asleep.

"You said a chart was like a map when you read me Treasure Island, but now you say it's like a table."

"Martin," I said. "Go to sleep."

I lay perfectly still for a few minutes.

Martin is pretty good, for a little brother. He is fun sometimes and you can trust him not to squeal. In fact, Martin would take any punishment rather than tell on friends or brothers.

Martin's breathing was more regular.

Imagine if you had nobody you could trust? The evening after Doug sucker punched me, Katie and I went for a walk back in Elgin Park. She told me about how her parents were always fighting and so she couldn't talk to either of them anymore without taking sides and so she just stopped saying anything. Even her grandma wanted her to takes sides, so she couldn't trust anyone any more. Then she said she felt like she could trust me and only me and we kissed.

Katie isn't like most girls. She has a good arm and throws like a boy. She is better than all the other girls, and lots of the boys, at everything from running, to jumping, to throwing, even the three-legged race where during Phys. Ed. she had to carry Marianne Laflamme the whole way. She is smart, but not a complete teacher's pet like some of the girls. She tells funny jokes and sometimes even uses swear words. Best of all I can talk to her about books and ideas and she has opinions. She likes to argue almost as much as me.

In fact, she always argues with me. Her Dad is a doctor and rich and she says he deserves all the money he makes and Medicare is going to destroy the province and turn the place into a soviet republic and I say, good, I hope so. She gets really mad.

Katie is almost as tall as me. Sure she is nine months older, but all the other girls in my class are older and only a few of them are as developed as Katie.

Sometimes it's hard not to think about the kinds of things you aren't supposed to. Maybe Paul over on Albert Street is right that adults just want to save all the good stuff for themselves.

Katie.

The newspaper had a story about Marilyn Munroe singing Happy Birthday to the first Catholic president of the United States. Paul showed me pictures of Marilyn Munroe. They were from a magazine called Playboy that Paul found in a box of Jiggs' stuff in the basement and she was completely naked.

I can see why you'd like her to sing happy birthday, Mr. President. I can see why they say you like the girls. Sometimes I like girls too.

It's hard not to think about the sort of stuff that you aren't supposed to. Hard.

DIARY ENTRY DEC. 7, 2000

"You sent President Kennedy an entire novel?" she said, staring at the pile of papers the clerk had just delivered to the desk.

"Three hundred and eighty-one pages it says here," he said, looking at the handwritten figure on the cover page that was attached to the bundle of photocopies by an elastic band.

"You wrote all this when you were twelve?" she said, either impressed or annoyed.

"I guess I must have," he said. "I started telling him about my family, my friends and then the story of what happened during the doctors strike and it just kept on getting longer and longer."

"Wow, you peaked as a writer when you were twelve." She knew exactly how to humiliate him.

"And here's yours," said the clerk, delivering a much smaller pile to Betty Bitch, a moniker she had no doubt earned, maybe even invented to tease giggles from her politically incorrect followers.

"Thank you," the "bitch" replied, perhaps a little embarrassed at the meager size of her pile.

"Could I have your autograph?" the clerk said, after taking a step away and then turning back.

"Of course," said the Big Bad Blonde, another of the nicknames that her legions of knuckle dragging fans called her, but only on air when ratings were falling. "On?"

The clerk did not understand at first.

"What would you like me to write the autograph on? And to whom?"

"Oh, yes, sorry," the clerk said, reaching for a blank piece of paper. "Here."

"To whom?" Lady Loudmouth repeated, somewhat sternly.

"Could you make it out to John. That's my boyfriend's father. He's a fan of yours."

"John?"

"Dear John," said the clerk. "If you would. Thank you."

"Dear John," the Wailing Witch said in a slightly sarcastic tone, pen in hand, looking up at the clerk. "This is not the first time I've written that."

"Thank you," said the clerk.

"Anything for my fans," said the Queen Bee of the Ayn Rand Hive.

"I don't really care for your views," said the clerk. "Too right wing. But John thinks you're clever and funny. He's always taunting me with some comment of yours. I don't know how you live with yourself, empowering women-hating men like that."

He could not help the smile that infuriated Lady Libertarian.

That was the highlight of the day.

Roy, letter 6

Oct. 10, 1962

Dear President Kennedy,

I hate the American League and the rotten Yankees are leading the Giants in the World Series. I guess you're probably an American League fan cause you're from Boston, but the Red Sox are okay. I don't need to worry about them beating the Dodgers or the Giants or the Cardinals. They are my favourite teams, especially Los Angeles. I'm a pitcher (probably already told you that) and I love Sandy Koufax, Juan Marichal and Bob Gibson. Whitey Ford is pretty good too, even though he plays for the Yankees. Before I continue my story, I just want to say I think you're doing the right thing in sending those federal troops to protect that Negro student at the university. Did you know we had the KKK in Saskatchewan, back in the 1930s and they attacked Catholics? French people too. That's what Basil told me. He's taking history at university. He says it's important to remember what happened years ago and to know what's going on today. That's why I read the newspaper. Which reminds me about my story.

"'May 26, 1962. High today 70. Manitoba doctors try to find jobs for Sask. docs on strike,'" read Martin as we walked up Montgomery Street. "What does that mean?"

"You know that Manitoba is another province, right?" I said, wearing my Giants uniform as I delivered newspapers. We were doing the route backwards in order to finish nearest the baseball diamonds on the flats.

"Ten provinces in Canada," said Martin. "I know that."

"Name them." I ordered. "Quick."

"British Columbia, Alberta, Saskatchewan, Manitoba, Ontario, Quebec, New Brunswick, Nova Scotia, Prince Edward Island and Newfloundlund."

"New found land," I said. "Newfoundland."

"They just found it?" said Martin.

"No, but it was the last province to join," I said. "Year before I was born."

"Join? Like cubs or the Y?"

"Sort of," I said. "Newfoundland was a British colony and then they voted to join Canada."

"Did we vote to join?"

"No," I said. "Saskatchewan was given to Canada and the federal government decided it could be a province in 1905."

"Who gave us?"

"The Hudson's Bay Company," I said.

"The store in Regina? They owned Saskatchewan?" said Martin.

"Claimed they did," I said.

"I thought it belonged to the Indians," said Martin.

"It did, but an English king gave it to the Hudson's Bay Company," I said.

"Was the king of the English the king of the Indians too?"

"No," I said. "But he claimed to be."

"Then how could he give it away?" said Martin.

"It's called imperialism, Basil says. One country takes over another."

Martin did not look satisfied by my answer.

"Wait here," I said. "The dog is probably loose in the yard."

Martin is scared of dogs and on a nice Saturday afternoon it was safest to assume pets were in the backyard. I opened the gate, walked quickly to the steps and dropped a folded paper.

"Why are the Manitoba doctors finding jobs for Saskatchewan doctors?" said Martin, who was staring at the front page of the paper when I returned.

"You know the doctors here say they are going to strike when the government starts Medicare?" I said.

"Ya," said Martin. "That's all Mom and Dad talk about."

"So the Manitoba doctors are going to help them by finding jobs during the strike. It's all political, the people voted for Medicare but the doctors don't like it."

"Why?" said Martin.

"Cause they think Medicare is socialist and they're brainwashed to hate socialism," I said. "The capitalists and businessmen and all the other doctors across Canada and the United States are giving the doctors here money so they can stop working and still get paid. They think if we get Medicare here in Saskatchewan and it works then it will spread everywhere else."

"They're fighting it?"

"That's right," I said.

"So we're fighting them," said Martin. "Us socialists?"

"Exactly," I said.

As we came to the next house, I handed my little brother a paper. Martin ran up to the mailbox beside the front door and stuck it inside.

"Doctor Henderson was nice to me when I got my tonsils out," said Martin, as he came back down the sidewalk. "He told the nurse to get me ice cream."

"I remember," I said.

"But we have to fight him because he's a doctor and he doesn't like Medicare. Right? We have to because we're socialists."

I figured out where my little brother was headed with these questions. When the little guy wanted something bad enough he had a way of getting to you.

"This is all about me fighting Doug?" I said.

Martin said nothing, but I could see the look in his eyes as he stared at the front page of the paper. We walked silently for a few feet.

"What's 'L, A, O, S?'"

"A country," I said.

"'Communists close to L, A, O, S capital,'" read Martin.

"Laos," I said.

"Communists close to Laos capital," repeated Martin. "We don't like communists? They're straight capitalists, right?"

"State capitalists," I said.

"Ya, and we don't like them," said Martin.

"Depends. We're not communists, but sometimes we like them better than the other guys."

"The guys they're fighting?"

"Ya," I said. "Like when the Russian communists and the American capitalists fought on the same side against the Nazis in World War II."

"The communists are good when they're fighting the Nazis?"

"Exactly," I said.

"Are they fighting Nazis in Laos?" asked Martin.

"I don't know," I said. "I think they're fighting the Americans."

"We don't like Americans," said Martin.

"It's not so simple as liking or not liking Americans. Sometimes we do," I said. "Depends on who they're fighting and it depends on which Americans you're talking about. Our grandpa was an American."

"I don't remember him," said Martin.

"You were only two when he died. You rolled off the bunk bed and hurt your shoulder when we went to Bismarck for his funeral. Do you remember that?"

Martin shook his head and placed his right hand on his left shoulder. "Is that why my shoulder feels funny?"

"Maybe," I said, handing him the last paper. "Sometimes figuring out good guys and bad guys is kind of complicated."

Martin stared at me for a few seconds, as if he were thinking what to say, then he walked slowly up the sidewalk towards the day's last stop on the paper route. I knew the little guy would have something interesting to say when he returned.

"I think the good guys are the ones on my side," said Martin carefully. "But sometimes my side can change. When Steve's on my team in kickball, he's a good guy, but when he's mean and wants to take my glove, he's a bad guy."

"Exactly," I said. "And if one person can sometimes be a good guy and sometimes a bad guy, think how complicated it is when you're talking about 200 million Americans."

Martin thought about this as we headed down Tenth Avenue across Caribou Street and I sang, "Duke, Duke, Duke of Earl."

"If you're an American do you have to be on the side of the Americans all the time or can you sometimes cheer for another team," said Martin, interrupting the song, which was just as well since I only knew those five words. "Did Grandpa have to be on the side of the Americans about everything?"

"What do you think?" I said.

Martin shrugged, but then thought of something. "At field day I cheered for St. Agnes in the high jump because Steve got picked to jump for St. Michael's even though Barry can go a lot higher."

My little brother was right.

"You're never just on one team," I said. "You're on St. Michael's team and you're on Barry's team and you're on the Schmidt team and you're on the socialist team and the Canadian team and the Saskatchewan team and the Catholic team and the Brown Street team and the boys team and the Moose Jaw team — all at the same time — and every day you gotta choose who to cheer for."

"You're on the Giants team and you're pitching today," said Martin, suddenly thinking about baseball. "And I'm going to cheer for you."

But I wasn't listening. This idea of all those teams seemed important. Why hadn't I thought about it before?

"I play for the Giants and I hate everybody on the Pirates," I said.

"You'll mow em down," said Martin, doing his version of a wind-up. "Steee-rike one, steee-rike two, steee-rike three!"

"But then I get picked for the all star team and so do a few of the Pirates and then we like each other," I said. "We're never just on one team and we're always choosing which one we're going to cheer for."

"Steeeeeeeeee-rike three," shouted Martin, mimicking Mr. Pratt, who was the loudest, most colourful umpire in the city.

"If Mr. Pratt is umping you better not let him see you, or I won't get any calls today," I said, reminding my little brother of the great milk van robbery.

"You think he might be there?" said Martin.

"Maybe."

Martin slowed down as we walked west along the train tracks, but all I could think about was the idea of belonging to different teams at the same time. I kept up the fast pace, but my little brother dawdled.

"If the Liberals won the next election, we'd still be socialists, even if Ross Thatcher said Saskatchewan this and Saskatchewan that. We'd have to decide which one of our teams, Saskatchewan or socialists was more important to us and I know which one I'd choose. The capitalists never side with a socialist government no matter how many people vote for it, that's for sure. Why should we be any different?"

When I glanced over to see my brother's reaction I noticed Martin was about 20 feet behind, walking "tightrope" on the metal rail.

"Hey, hurry up."

Martin looked up, but didn't go any faster.

"Come on," I said. "I'm gonna be late."

As I turned back there were two kids on bikes coming fast down the Eleventh Avenue hill. It was Tim McMahon, our catcher and his little brother Jimmy.

"Hey Martin," I shouted as I turned back to my little brother. "It's Jimmy."

I pointed up the hill and Martin began to run, but still "tight-rope" on the tracks.

"Hey Tim," I shouted, waving. Then I noticed something was wrong. Jimmy was out in front of his older brother and going very, very fast. He was screaming and Tim was trying to catch up, but couldn't because the little guy's bike was speeding out of control.

"Oh man," I said as Martin caught up to me. We stared up the hill at an unfolding disaster.

"Tim, I can't stop, I can't stop," screamed Jimmy.

"Jump," screamed Tim. "You gotta jump."

"If he hits these tracks he's gonna go flying," I said, pulling my little brother out of the bike's projected path.

"Jump!"

Jimmy was on the last stretch of the hill and going faster than I had ever seen a six-year-old travel, except in a car.

"Jump," I screamed when Jimmy hit the gravel where the road flattened out.

"Jump," screamed his older brother from behind.

But we needn't have bothered because, at the moment Jimmy's front wheel hit the loose gravel, the bike went into a skid, on a slight angle at first, then sideways, then suddenly Jimmy was flying and the bike was doing summersaults like the gymnasts on Ed Sullivan.

From the corner of my eye I also saw Tim hit the gravel. At the centre of my vision was the perfect three-point landing performed by Jimmy. Chin, belly and knees all hit the loose gravel at the same instant and he slid to a stop like one of those big U.S. Air Force transport planes with the parachute behind them I saw at last year's air show. Jimmy was smiling!

His older brother was not so lucky.

While Jimmy's ancient, brakeless two-wheeler twisted through the air after bouncing once, twice, three times, Tim's right shoulder, then left knee and right elbow hit the ground hard. But, while the bike, which had been abused by at least a dozen kids over three decades, survived, to be ridden another day, Tim was not so lucky.

Because of trying to rescue a little brother who had been warned dozens of times about riding down the hill, Tim's shoulder was looking broken or maybe dislocated, his knee swelled up to twice its normal size and he was scraped so bad you could actually see three inches of bone from his elbow to part way down the forearm. Plus his baseball uniform was shredded.

As I stood over my teammate, trying to determine if he was dead or alive, Tim's first words were: "I don't think I can catch today." When I told this story that night to Paul's older brother John, he said, "well no shit, Sherlock" a few words I liked so much I used them over and over for months afterward.

Tim stood up and his next words were aimed at his little brother. "I'm going to kill you," a phrase Jimmy must have heard a million times, but never with so much emotion. Jimmy stared at his big brother, ragged and bleeding, and burst into tears. Then, just to make everything more serious, Tim collapsed, falling to the ground, unconscious. Jimmy, Martin and me just stood there amazed for maybe 10, 20 seconds before we even moved and then Jimmy goes running and screaming up the hill towards his house. So I tell Martin to hurry to the nearest house and get somebody to call an ambulance.

I knelt beside Tim who lay face down in the gravel. I thought about turning him on his back but remembered you're not supposed to move anyone who may have a back injury.

"Tim? Tim? Can you hear me?" I thought my teammate might be dead.

Then all heck broke loose. Adults from nearby houses came running. A siren could be heard getting closer and pretty soon Martin and I were no longer needed. As soon as the fire truck and the ambulance arrived and I told the woman who made the emergency call what happened, there was really no point in staying. Adults always ignore you or tell you to get out of the way, so I grabbed my little brother's hand. We could still make the start of the game at the diamond a few hundred yards away.

As we hurried towards the baseball field, I noticed Tim's catcher's mitt on the ground, a few feet from the tracks. It must have flown out of the rattrap above his back wheel where he always kept it when the bike smashed into the ground. I picked it up and was about to take it back to the accident scene, when I noticed the crowd was even larger and the ambulance guys were lifting Tim onto a stretcher. Someone yelled to another person on the other side of the crowd, "Looks like he's got broken bones and they're taking him to the hospital."

The Giants would have to forfeit the game if we didn't have anyone to catch. Or maybe Coach Miller would make me catch — he'd done it a few times when I was ten — and put Maurice on the mound. That would be a drag.

I put Tim's mitt into my paper bag. I'd return it tonight or tomorrow. That was the best thing to do.

DIARY ENTRY TWO DEC. 7, 2000

Fresh snow covered the Commons as they lay beside each other reading, heads propped up on pillows, both wearing plush white, crested hotel bathrobes. He turned over to take pressure off a sore shoulder and once again crossed the invisible line separating the two sides of the king-sized bed. She pushed him back onto his own side.

"My side," she said.

"Why so territorial?" he said. The first time he thought she was playing, but now realized she was serious.

"I'm paying for the room so the least you can do is stay on your own side of the bed," she said.

"Did I bump into you?" he said, more than a little annoyed. What was her problem? "Were you using those particular six inches of the bed?"

"That's not the point," she said.

"What is the point?" he said. She made everything political. "That this half of the bed belongs to you whether you are using it or not? Your private property?"

"As a matter of fact, yes," she said. "It is my private property. What do you think it is? Public property?"

"How about a commons?" he said, smiling at his cleverness. "Available for use by anyone inhabiting the room who has a need for it. Based on the customary right of those guests staying at this hotel."

He thought she didn't know what he was talking about.

"I have enclosed this particular commons," she said, smiling back. "Clearly defined property rights are the foundation of capitalism and the central basis for progress over the last three centuries. Just look at countries where property rights are not clear. They're a mess."

She was well read and certainly not ignorant, he had to give her that. So why did she talk like a fool?

"Might makes right and it also makes private property," he said. Arguing with her definitely felt almost as good as making love. "That's the real basis of capitalism. The mafia, feudal lords, capitalists, you all share the same origin."

"That's why we need to maintain a strong military," she said, trumping his argument by agreeing with it. "America understands this and that's why the rest of the world loves us."

"I can't believe you American right-wingers," he said, grabbing his pile of papers and walking to the desk. "You really don't get how much the rest of the world thinks the USA is a crazy, evil, militaristic imperial power."

He sat on the chair in front of the desk.

"There's a difference between don't get it and don't care," she said, wearing a smug smile. "Liberals have a need to be liked. We can live quite comfortably with being feared."

He stared at her for a few seconds. He was about to throw another jab, but then decided to change the subject. "Have you decided yet if you'll let me read your letters?" he said.

She nodded.

"Yes I can read it or yes you've decided?"

"You can read them if you tell me what you've done with your life since 1962," she said. "I need to know more about you before I decide."

"You know who I am."

"I know who you were in Grade 8, in Moose Jaw, Saskatchewan," she said. "A much-too-smart-for-his-own-good, but cute, socialist."

"I haven't changed much," he said.

"You are still cute, in that older man sort of way" she said. "But what have you done in all those years since? Aside from writing a film script called 'The Wobbly Cowboy' which I'm told got you a hundred grand from a Hollywood studio in 1972 and then getting a Master's degree in history from Simon Fraser University and being accepted into the PhD program at York University in Toronto."

What was she after? She couldn't possibly care.

"You gave back $95,000 rather than agree to the changes a certain important producer wanted and then dropped out of the film scene entirely. A few years later you are a rising star in the Canadian social history world but don't even finish your thesis. You join some Maoist group called the Red Star Collective."

"How do you know all this?"

"A few phone calls to friends of mine with connections in the intelligence community."

He looked away, angry and embarrassed.

Why was he embarrassed? Anger makes sense. She had been spying on him. Why should anything he'd done embarrass him? The past few days, being with her, that's what should embarrass him.

"You've taught history at Langara Community College for over 20 years and you are currently head of the faculty union. You are very popular with your students, but you completely abandoned any serious academic work. No publications could be found except for one paper, published in an obscure journal, that I had faxed to me this morning."

She walked to the desk near the window and opened a large envelope.

"The title is: 'The 1962 Saskatchewan Doctors – A Classic Right Wing Disinformation Campaign.' Should be scintillating reading."

She flopped back on the bed with the paperback journal in her hands and then opened it.

"Maybe you will learn something," he said.

"I'll read it right now," she said. "But then I want you to justify your life to me."

"Justify?"

"Explain in the light of contemporary history."

He stared at her for a moment. Why did he understand her?

"Justify wasting my life as an advocate of working class power and socialism in light of the complete and utter triumph of capitalism around the world?" he said.

"That would do," she said, her smugness growing. "You catch on fast."

"You really are too much," he said. Once again she had gotten under his skin.

"Are you embarrassed?" He was beet red and she enjoyed his discomfort.

"What's embarrassing is that I may be forced to explain spending five days with the most right wing radio host in America," he said. "If my friends find out, they'll turn me in to the leftwing thought police."

"After all the intimacies we've shared this week, it seems strange that you'd draw the line at telling me what you've done since we last met," she said. "What are you hiding?"

"I'm not interested in being fodder for one of your attack columns," he said. She was planning to write something, that's why she was interested.

"You're afraid I will judge you?" she said.

"I'm afraid you will twist and distort and lie to fit your pre-conceived neo-conservative agenda," he said. "How do you know when a neo-conservative is lying? When she says it in public."

"Very funny. I promise I won't write or talk about you," she said.

"What's the other way to know a neo-conservative is lying? When she makes a promise," he said.

"Even if I were to write or talk on air about you, why would you care?" she said. "I'd have more to explain than you."

She had a point.

"Tell me," she said. "I won't judge. I'll read this paper of yours and you can think about what you want to say. Then you tell me. Explain your life to me. I won't even comment if you don't want me to. And then I'll let you read my letters to President Kennedy. I'll read yours while you read mine."

"My life would make no sense to you," he said. Sometimes it didn't make any sense to him.

"Now I am even more intrigued," she said.

He walked to the other side of the bed, before facing her. Maybe she is right. After sleeping with her, maybe I owe her a little bit about who I am. I'm not embarrassed by my life. I am proud of it. Perhaps, in hindsight, I would have done some things differently, but so what?

"Okay," he said. "Why not?"

Roy, letter 7

Oct. 13, 1962

Dear President Kennedy,

I agree with Castro that your government ought to pay for all the damage you caused when you invaded the Bay of Pigs. The story in the paper says Cuba wants $62 million to release the prisoners they captured. I think that's fair. It's just like when Paul and I were fooling around in the back alley and I hit the baseball through Mrs. Shaw's kitchen window. It was fair that I had to pay to get it fixed. I know you can't tell me the truth because the CIA would probably do something bad to you, but I think deep down you're a socialist just like me. I think you're on the side of poor people. I mean why else would you help the Negroes down south? They're the poorest of the poor. Also, I think it's a good thing the World Series game was cancelled because of rain. It gives the Giants more time to rest Juan Marichal and maybe his finger will heal. Baseball, that's where I left off the story last time.

It took me three pitches to figure out Brian Epstein was a better catcher than Tim.

"He's crowding the plate, so throw it on the inside corner," Brian said as we met half way between home plate and the mound. "Throw it as hard as you can and none of these guys can hit you."

"I'm fast, but my control isn't always so good," I said.

"You're a right-handed Sandy Koufax, compared to these guys," said Brian, who had moved from Winnipeg to Moose Jaw a few months earlier. "Don't worry, if you bean somebody, so what? We're looking for a no-hitter, not a perfect game."

A no-hitter, I thought, that would be neat. Mow the batters down like Sandy Koufax and Don Drysdale. Or the big kicking Juan Marichal. Or Bob Gibson, the way he stares from the top of the mound.

Brian gave me a target, waist high, on the inside edge of the plate, so if I hit the catcher's mitt, the ball would graze the batter. I stared at the glove, made eye contact with the batter, cold, intense, like Basil showed me, and then focused back on the target.

Winding up, right hand hidden inside my glove I gripped the ball with index and middle finger across the narrowest part of the seams, leaned back with my weight on my left foot, then shifted to my right leg, as I kicked up my left and twisted slightly. I threw myself towards home plate and released the ball just as my left foot hit the ground. I knew the pitch would be fast. But where it would go was the question. "Strike two," came the answer from the ump. The batter jumped backwards, frightened by the speed and location.

Brian nodded as he returned the ball to the mound and set up the target for the next pitch on the outside corner.

"Streeee rike three," roared Mr. Pratt.

The next two batters went down swinging on three pitches each.

When I had speed and control nothing was more fun than pitching. It was as good as, or maybe better than, scoring the winning goal while winning the peewee hockey championship the previous season.

We went up 2-0 in the bottom of the first, then 5-0 in the bottom of the third. Going into the top of the fifth inning I still had a no-hitter and had only walked one batter, so I had to try out my screwball. I had successfully thrown the pitch a few times playing catch but never in a game. Mike Mackie was going to be the second batter and he always swung for the fence. He'd be perfect.

In the dugout, while we were batting, I told Brian what to expect.

"Why do you want to try out something new when the game is going so well?" he answered. "You want to blow the no hitter?"

"The way I'm throwing today, it will work," I said. "Mackie will swing but the ball will jump over his bat."

"You don't need another pitch," said Brian. "They can't hit your fastball."

"It's too easy," I said.

"Getting a no-hitter is too easy?"

"My brother says try to pitch a little better every inning," I said.

Brian raised his eyebrows like he thought I was crazy.

"You got the signs?" I said.

"Ya, one finger for a fastball, two a curve, three a screwball, four a change-up."

"One a fastball, two a curve, three a screwball, four a change-up," I repeated.

"Thought you said your curve didn't curve," said Brian.

"Maybe it will today," I said.

Brian shook his head, but didn't argue.

After the first batter in the top of fifth went down swinging on three straight fastballs, I shook off the sign for another when Mackie came to bat. He was the Pirates best hitter and a pretty good hockey player who I fought twice in the playoffs a few months earlier. I nodded when Brian flashed four fingers. Mackie always swung for a homer on the first pitch and a change-up would fool him completely.

With the same intense glare I had used all game, I wound up, kicked and delivered the ball at about half my usual my fastball speed. Mackie swung so hard the bat was behind him before the ball even crossed the plate. Hal, our third baseman snorted. Gary, the second baseman laughed at Hal's snort and Maurice, the shortstop kept up the continuous banter that opponents hated at the best of times. "Good pitch, good pitch. Hey batter, batter, you could have swung twice and the ball still wouldn't have crossed the plate. Good pitch, good pitch. Hey batter, batter."

Mackie was angry. As a buzz ran through the crowd of sixty or so people and the Giants infield laughed, he stared at me. I glared back and took up my position, right foot on the rubber at the top of the mound. Down came a single finger from Brian and I nodded. The target was low on the outside corner. Perfect place, if I could hit it and I did. This time the ball slapped leather before Mackie got his bat half way around.

Hal snorted louder and Gary found it even funnier. "That's it big guy, what a pitch, what a pitch. You got him off balance. Way to go big guy."

As Mackie quickly stepped back into the batter's box, I imagined steam rising out of his nose and ears, like a cartoon bull on Bugs Bunny. Down came the single finger again, but this time I shook it off. The only pitch that could top the two previous ones would be a screwball so I had to try.

My windup was smooth and my grip on the ball was firm. As I brought my arm down, I twisted my hand inwards and down, the ball spinning off my fingers towards the plate. It looked headed for the inside corner, letters high, a spot that Mackie liked to pull the ball deep into leftfield. Because of the last little awkward twist of my hand, its speed was slightly less than a fastball and I worried Mackie might slam it out of the park, but a few feet in front of the plate it popped up and in.

As Mackie swung, the ball climbed over his bat and headed for the back of his neck. The sound when it hit unprotected flesh was a slightly lower pitch than leather smacking leather.

At first he looked startled more than anything, then Mackie dropped into the dirt as if someone had swung an axe, chopping off both legs at the knees. The screwball worked, I thought, then 'oh shit' followed by 'is he okay'?

An hour later, as Brian and I walked up Tenth Avenue, followed ten feet behind by Martin and two friends, events of the day had already been repeated a dozen times.

"I swear the ball jumped a foot up and in," said Brian. "Mackie swung at it like it was right over the centre of the plate. Then it beans him and he just stands there, thinking what hit him, maybe it was a mosquito that bit him on the back of the neck. Then boom, he crashes to the ground like a skydiver whose parachute didn't open. Splat!"

We laughed as we walked up the hill. Behind us Martin was telling his own tall tales to his pals.

"Tim is chasing his little brother down the hill when Jimmy's brakes stop working and he's going a megamillion miles an hour. Me and Roy are standing at the bottom of the hill and Jimmy's flying down straight at us, screaming, 'help me, help me' but what can we do? Tim is going almost as fast, right behind his little brother hollering 'I'm going to get you, I'm going to get you' like a wild guy. Jimmy must have swiped his marbles or something. Tim was mad. Then, when Jimmy hits the pile a stones at the bottom, he jumps off his bike, which goes bouncing like maybe a hundred feet and he goes up in the air, floating like a kite, and lands, hands out like this, flat on his belly in a big pile of rocks."

"Was he hurt?" said one of the little guys I did not recognize.

"A couple cuts and scratches, that's all," said Martin. "But Tim, you shoulda seen what happened to him."

"What?" said the other little guy.

"When he hit the rocks, he slams on his brakes, you know like the 'leven-year-olds do to show off, and the bike it skids and Tim goes bouncing, bouncing across the road like that indi rubber ball Mikey was playing with over at the diamond. Bouncy, bouncy, bouncy. He smacks his shoulder, he smacks his elbow, he smacks his knee, he smacks his head. I hadda call the amblance and he must have had like a gazillion broken bones, or maybe he even died, we don't know cause we had to go to the baseball game so Roy could pitch his no-hitter."

"Wow," said both of Martin's friends at the same time.

"You saw it?"

"I hadda run and get the neighbor lady to call the amblance," said Martin. "Fire truck showed up too and maybe a cop car, but I couldn't really tell cause we were almost at the baseball place when I turned around to see."

Martin's two friends had wide eyes.

"Roy went to see if he was dead or what, right after he landed, but Tim was talking crazy."

I was thinking it had been one of the most eventful days of my life. How often do you see an accident like that, pitch a no-hitter and see one of your worst enemies carried off the baseball diamond on a stretcher?

"You think he was really hurt?" said Brian.

"No," I shrugged.

"Must have stung like heck, but nothing serious," said Brian. "He's really, really tough."

Brian had been in the same class as Mackie for the first two months he spent in Moose Jaw.

"I heard you fought him a couple of times in hockey," said Brian.

"Two playoff games in a row," I said. "He's hacking and chopping and butt-ending the smallest guy on the team, The Beetle, Fran Hawkins, you know him?"

Brian nodded. "He's about six inches smaller than me."

"Exactly," I said. "Mackie runs Fran into the boards, hard, cuts him with the blade of his stick, which he claimed accidentally went up in his face, so I drop my gloves, didn't even think about it I was so mad. I must have hit him thirty times and he's really bleeding, but he just stands there taking it. Acts like it didn't hurt him a single bit. I wouldn't worry about him being hurt."

"He's a bully too and an anti-Semite," said Brian. "Called me a dirty Jew."

I said nothing. I hadn't known Brian was Jewish. I'd never met a Jew before.

"You're Jewish?" I said after a few seconds.

"Ya," said Brian. "Well sort of."

"Sort of?"

"My Dad's Jewish, but my Mom's an atheist. Well so is my Dad, but he's Jewish as well."

I stared.

"Technically, your mother is supposed to be Jewish for you to be one, but my grandparents say my Mom is Jewish cause her grandmother was, so they've arranged for my bar mitzvah when I go back to Winnipeg."

"That's like confirmation?"

"What's confirmation?"

"A Catholic thing when you turn twelve."

Brian shrugged. "I don't know too much about religion."

"Are you an atheist?" I said. "My brother Basil is."

"Probably," said Brian. "Maybe an agnostic, because I don't know if you can be so sure about anything."

"You're going back to Winnipeg?"

"In August, or maybe December," said Brian. "My Dad is teaching accounting at STI. My Mom and him split up and he took the job to get away for awhile."

"You live with your Dad?"

Brian nodded.

I had never met any kid before who lived just with a father.

"You got any brothers or sisters?"

"No," said Brian. "Don't have any friends either here in Moose Jaw."

I had never known anybody before who said he had no friends. I liked Brian; he was smart and talked about interesting things. Maybe he could be my friend.

"You've only been here since January, so it's not really a long time."

"Ya," said Brian. "And I'm a Jew and an atheist and a communist and I can't skate."

I laughed.

"I'm serious," said Brian.

"You can't skate?" I said. "That is pretty weird."

Brian smiled.

"But you're a good catcher," I said. "That counts for something."

"Will coach keep me behind the plate? I hate right field."

"Even if you weren't so good, you're the only catcher we got cause Tim ain't playing sports anytime soon."

"He was hurt pretty bad?" said Brian.

"You should have seen it. Almost as bad as the time we were coming back from Lancer, where my uncle and grandpa live, and we were the first to come across a head-on collision. There was a woman with her head right through the windshield."

"You saw it?"

"No further away than you and me," I said. "Tim was bleeding almost as bad. You want to go to the hospital with me, to see him? I got his glove."

"Sure," said Brian.

"I'll phone his house and find out when we can go," I said. "Are you really a communist? I'm a socialist."

"My Mom and Dad left the Party when I was nine. Or, like my Mom says, the Party left us."

I had never met a real capital "C" Communist before, either.

"Did you belong to the Young Pioneers?"

"That's only in the Soviet Union," said Brian. "I went to camp, that was about it."

"Communist camp?"

Brian shrugged.

"Was it fun?" I said. "I've never been to any kind of camp."

"Not really," said Brian. "I hate the outdoors, mosquitoes, campfires, singalongs, all the camp stuff. I like cities. I'm a musician. I play the piano."

I had never met a boy piano player before.

"You mean, like seriously?" I said. "What kind of music?"

"Classical," said Brian. "Chopin is my favourite. You know, the Polish revolutionary?"

I didn't. In fact, while I had read or heard the name "Chopin" somewhere before, I knew nothing about the guy.

"Only thing I know about music is what I hear on the radio, and in music class, which is not very much," I said.

"You like it?" said Brian.

"Sure, I guess. Never thought about it much. My older brother Basil takes accordion lessons, but it's expensive. My Dad used to play the fiddle and the accordion and the piano. He loves Louis Armstrong."

"I spend four or five hours a day practicing."

"Four or five hours? A day?"

"That's what you have to do if you want to be a concert pianist."

"Geez, I never do anything four or five hours a day, except sometimes read," I said. "You don't get bored?"

Brian shrugged.

"How do you find time for anything else?" I said.

"Mostly I don't, except for baseball, which I love almost as much as the piano."

No wonder he doesn't have any friends, I thought.

"It's probably why I don't have any friends," said Brian.

"That's just what I was thinking," I said, smiling.

We walked silently for a few seconds.

"You want to come to my place for dinner?" said Brian. "I could show you my piano and then my Dad would probably take us for hamburgers or something. You like A&W?"

"Love it," I said.

"We go there a lot because my Dad doesn't like to cook," said Brian. "That or Chinese — Moose Jaw has a couple of pretty good Chinese restaurants."

While I had been to the Exchange Café and the National, I had never actually eaten Chinese food. Truth was, we hardly ever eat out. Kentucky Fried Chicken on Mother's Day, Teenburger and root beer a couple of times, when Basil had had a really good Pony League or Colt League game, a couple of times at the Husky truck stop in Swift Current, on the way to Uncle George's farm, that was about it.

"You want to come? My Dad won't mind. He's been bugging me about making friends."

"Sure, so long as it's okay with my Mom," I said. "We'll stop at my house."

Brian smiled, but the moment I mentioned my house, I had a bad feeling. Brian probably lived in one of those new houses, up by his school. I had been embarrassed a few months earlier when Joey Krosch, whose father was a dentist and lived in a new split level, came over and went on and on about how small our house was and how could I sleep with my little brother and why was our bathroom in the basement and 'geez some of the houses on your block still have outhouses.'

But it was too late to back out since we were already near Albert Street. Besides, Brian said he was a communist. He shouldn't care about how big my stupid house was.

As I thought about this, I was surprised by Martin's voice.

"Roy, Roy, watch out," Martin shouted.

I turned to see my little brother with a dozen or so other kids, ranging in age from six to eleven.

"Steve and Doug are going to ambush us," shouted Martin, who was about twenty yards down the street, almost back at Montgomery, surrounded by his gang, waving at me to come over to him. I looked at Brian and shrugged. We headed back down Tenth.

"It's a trap," said Martin as I approached. "Paulie saw them. They're hiding behind Mr. Gunn's fence. They're gonna jump us and fight us all. Steve told Paulie. Said they got fourteen guys."

What had my little brother gotten us into?

"They're going to jump us?" I said to Paulie. "And fight us?"

Paulie nodded. I had known the kid his whole life. All six years of it. He mostly told the truth.

"Why?"

"Stevie said Doug hates you," said Paulie.

"I don't hate him," I said. "I don't hate anybody, except maybe the damn doctors who are going to go on strike cause they hate socialism."

I said the last bit mostly to impress Brian.

"I'm not in the mood for a fight," I said.

"You're the toughest 'leven year-old in all of Moose Jaw," said Paulie. His friends all nodded their agreement.

"I just turned twelve," I said.

"You're the toughest twelve year-old in all of Moose Jaw," said Paulie.

"This is stupid," I said.

"Steve said he's gonna fight us and now he is," said Martin.

"You need help?" said Brian. "I'm not very good, but I have been beaten up a few times."

"This is really stupid," I said.

DIARY ENTRY THREE DEC. 7, 2000

She threw the journal on the desk then glared at him as he entered the room. Her face was contorted in disgust.

"You liked my exposé of the conspiracy between the doctors, the right-wing and the media?" he said, a big smile calculated to irritate her.

"You're just pissed off that us cynical right-wingers are better at propaganda that you earnest liberal-lefties," she said. "The so-called facts you cite, what makes them any more true than what the Moose Jaw Times-Herald reported?"

"What makes them true is evidence," he said, handing her a coffee and then taking off his coat. "No one disputes the facts. Even the Times-Herald, usually, reported the facts. The problem is it also reported lies. And more important it obfuscated the facts. It created its own truth based on distortions, narrow self-interest, rhetoric, fear and only looking at one side of the story."

"And it did a pretty good job of it," she said, sipping the coffee, then reading from the pamphlet. "'The people of Saskatchewan are now awakening and find that their province has been slowly, and in recent months much more rapidly transformed from a free democracy into a totalitarian state, ruled by men drunk with power. They not only say the citizens must do this and thus, but they make the threat of what will be done to them, otherwise. Truly it was a sorry day Sunday, July 1, 1962. A day that will be marked with a black blotch on the calendar, the day when freedom died.' The Moose Jaw Times Herald, Tuesday July 3, 1962. 'When the nuts on the bolts that lock the tire frame and a tire securely in place, and all but one nut are removed from a wheel on a medical doctor's car; when tires are slashed on the cars that bear license plates indicating that the vehicle is owned by a doctor; when threats of injury are made to the members of a doctor's family; then the people of Saskatchewan know that there are people wandering the streets of the cities of this province who are seeking to intimidate those who rebel against regimentation.' Times Herald, Tuesday July 24, 1962. I'm surprised how modern this is. It could have been written yesterday."

"That's a point my article makes," he said. "It argues the right-wing has done the same con job over and over. Creating fear, creating a crisis. McCarthyism, destabilizing governments in Iran, Guatemala, Chile, Nicaragua ..."

"I know," she said, looking down at the pamphlet to read from its pages. "'What was the goal of the 1962 doctors strike and media campaign against Medicare? To stop the government from implementing its socialized medicine plan? To make the plan more palatable to the doctors? To send a message to other governments that might be thinking of similar legislation? To overthrow the government? I would argue all four were goals, but that the primary purpose, like all such covert psychological warfare operations, was to create a crisis, which could then be exploited to achieve any or all of those goals.'"

She looked up at him and made another sour face.

He smiled. He liked that this bothered her.

"You really believe this nonsense?" she said and continued reading. "'The central objective of the strike and its support operations, which included the media campaign, was to manufacture a crisis. While on a much smaller scale, the Saskatchewan doctors strike was no different than the CIA's destabilization campaigns in Iran in 1953, Guatemala in 1954, Chile in 1973, Nicaragua in the 1980s, and other lesser-known psychological warfare operations. Each of these campaigns manufactured a crisis that was then exploited to overthrow an elected government. Each used a small group of dedicated "fighters" to create the crisis. Each used the media to help create and sustain the crisis. Each used the crisis to justify overthrowing the government.'"

Again she looked up at him, but this time said nothing. Instead she simply shook her head then continued reading.

"'The point of this short article is to help ordinary people understand what the forces of reaction might do when they feel threatened by a government's attempts to upset the status quo. The rich and powerful and their allies will lie, distort, blackmail and even use force to create a crisis that they can then use to overthrow a government they don't like. Given what the doctors did in the face of the introduction of Medicare, imagine what might happen if a truly progressive government was ever elected in Ottawa.'"

She put the pamphlet down and again shook her head.

"What?" he said. "You disagree that the newspaper distorted the truth of what was happening? They lied and exaggerated because they were at war with the government."

"What you call the truth is really just your interpretation," she said. "How do you know only four thousand people showed up at the rally in

Regina? I was there and that's not what I remember. There were at least 10,000."

"I've seen pictures, including one that was in the Leader-Post the following day. I counted the people. Four thousand is a generous assessment. I'd say more like 3,500 and if you deduct all the doctors and their families, at best a couple thousand. Say 2,500, to be more than fair. After all the promotion the doctors received from the media only 2,500 supporters show up? I'd say that was a spectacular failure. And the College of Physicians and Surgeons must have interpreted the turnout as a failure as well, because a few days later they started talking to the government and a few days after that, gave in."

"That's your interpretation," she said. "Your truth."

"Which part of what I said are you disputing?" he said.

"It doesn't matter how many people showed up at a demonstration," she said. "Numbers are not what's important. The majority can be wrong and the minority right. In fact the majority is often wrong. And my father, who was very involved with College at the time, was not discouraged by the turnout. Unlike you, he understood that truth is related to perception and understanding rather than to some absolute, definable reality. Truth is not simply there, waiting to be discovered. We create it."

"The truth is most Canadians like socialized medicine."

"And your point is?" she said. "You're the one who believes 'in one person, one vote everywhere people come together', not me. I believe in 'one dollar, one vote' was the way you described it. I'm an elitist, remember? I understand the majority is often wrong."

"My point isn't about being right or wrong," he said. "My point is that your so-called truth, which you claim to be able to construct regardless of any objective reality, doesn't apply in the case of Canadian Medicare. Reality and truth are the same. People like Medicare. They liked it in 1962 and they like it today. Most people disagreed with the doctors strike. Your father was the bad guy. This was not clear in 1962 only because the media lied, obfuscated and exaggerated to create a crisis, exactly what the right wing has always been good at."

"We created a truth to suit our purposes," she said. "We were successful."

"For a time, a few months at best," he replied.

"That's because we were just learning," she said, making sure to look smug. "We are much better at it today. Look at the past forty years. Even you must admit that we won and you lost. We run the world."

"For now," he said. "History is full of examples of winners who quickly became losers."

"History is over," she said.

"Another right wing lie," he said.

"History is over because there are no challenges to the existing system. Socialism has been discredited and capitalism proved right. History existed to explain how the world changed, but if there are no more changes ...

"Lying to yourself is even crazier than lying to others," he said.

"You're just jealous that we won."

"What's with right wingers and the denial of reality?" he said. "Do you really believe you can base an economy, a political system, any sort of science on lies?"

"We don't deny reality. We just don't think it's as important as truth."

"Are you a creationist as well?"

"Science has its theories and other people have theirs," she said. "I don't take sides in that dispute."

"That's it," he said. "I can't do this anymore."

"Can't do what?"

"Be here, with you," he said. "Sleeping with the enemy. I'm leaving."

"Before we read each other's letters?"

"I can't do this," he said. "I could never explain this. It makes no sense."

"Don't worry," she said, a calculated smile adding to the effect of her words. "Your leftwing friends will love it when you tell them you screwed Betty Bitch. And, if it comes up, which it most likely won't, my friends will be equally amused."

She did have a point. About his male friends anyway.

"So, if you find my company interesting and the sex pleasurable, what's the harm?" she said, turning on a little girl smile. "Unless you're scared that I will shake your fundamental beliefs with the power of my arguments?"

A challenge. She was a salesman and knew how to clinch a sale. But he wasn't buying her bullshit. He could see through her. She was using her predatory sexuality to get what she wanted. But that was the part of it he did not understand. What was it she wanted? He had to stick it out to discover the answer. And if there was a little more sex to come, he would enjoy it. Two could play the 'I'll use you if it feels good game.'

Roy, letter 8

Oct. 16, 1962

Dear President Kennedy,

Hey, too bad the Yankees had to win the World Series. I was really cheering for the Giants. I like all the Alou brothers and Orlando Cepada and Juan Marichal. I guess now that New York has a team in the National League again, maybe I can cheer for them. But the Mets sure were bad. I mean, the most losses since 1899. Basil says he's good enough to pitch for them.

I kind of left you hanging with my last letter, so I'm writing this now, even though it's a school night, plus I had a hockey practice. This is a good part of the story, especially when I read in today's paper about your army firing rockets at the Reds in Vietnam. Sister Veronica says war is terrible and we should always look for alternatives. She's right, don't you think? I've been lucky with the nuns I had for teachers. They've all been pretty nice. Did you have nuns in grade school? Back to the story.

"We hafta fight em now or they'll think we're scared and next time they come, there'll be more of them," said Martin.

"Ya," said Paulie. "More and bigger too. Pretty soon Doug is gonna be fourteen."

"Steve's telling everyone you have to be in his gang if you wanta play anywhere this side of Ninth Avenue. Only reason his gang isn't bigger is cause kids are scared you're on our side," Martin said to me. "Everybody knows you're the toughest twelve year old in all Moose Jaw."

"Ya, he can beat up all the toughest 13-year-olds and even sixteeners," said Paulie. "You'll pound Doug real good."

"That's some reputation," said Brian. "How did you get it?"

"A little brother who exaggerates," I said, evil eying Martin.

"He beat up the toughest 12-year-old on the east side, Mike Fisher in a fair fight, everyone knows that," said Paulie. "And he'll beat that Doug from Calgary just the same."

The crowd of kids around them nodded and said "ya" and told each other to "pound" their opponent or "make 'em give" in the upcoming fight.

"Who is this Mike Fisher?" said Brian.

"East end kid, good pitcher and hitter, challenged me to a fight a couple of months ago when Paul and I were walking back from the Natatorium. He went to slug me and I took the punch but grabbed his head. Great hammer lock. He had to give," I said.

"Tell him 'bout the time you kicked that 16-year-old right in the nuts," said Martin. "He never bothered you again."

This Brian had to hear.

"A couple of weeks after the fight I was at Sunday public skate at the Civic Centre when Mike's older brother comes up to me and says 'I'm going to teach you not to pick on my little brother.' He's almost six feet and 180 pounds. And he had four other guys the same size with him."

"They fought you in the rink?" said Brian.

"No, the older brother says, 'I'm going to be waiting for you outside. And don't even think about trying to sneak out, cause we'll have all the doors covered.'"

"What did you do?" said Brian.

"Worried, mostly. Hard to have fun skating," I said.

"I'd have phoned my Dad and got him to pick me up," said Brian. "Or told one of the adults there what was going on. Or called the cops."

I gave my new friend a look.

"What?" said Brian.

"That's not the way it works around here," I said. "Unless you plan on having an adult everywhere you go, cause the next time they find you alone it'll be one beating and then another for squealing."

"So what did you do?" said Brian.

"I acted like everything was normal. Skated and then when it was time to go, me and Paul walked out the front door, just like we always do and the big guy was there waiting. As Mike goes around the building to get the guys who had been covering the side doors, his big brother grabs my arm and pulls me down towards the far end of the building where I guess he's planning on pounding me in private. I pull free and the big guy says, 'Okay you want to do it right here and be embarrassed in front of your friends?' But I just glare at him."

"And?" said Brian.

"Well, it occurred to me that I was pretty much up shit creek and I might as well hit him first. So, I kicked him in the balls as hard as I could. Thump, dead on and hard. He went down in serious pain."

"You didn't?" said Brian.

"I did."

"And?"

"And then he pounded the crap out of me," I said. "Except I hurt him worse than he hurt me, cause Mr. Poulsen, the mailman, sees what's going on and breaks it up after only about four or five punches. A nosebleed and a couple of bruises, that's all I got. That big guy was hurting a lot worse, let me tell you and he's never bothered me since. Mike mostly walks on the other side of the street when he sees me coming."

"Everybody knows Roy is the toughest twelve-year-old in all Skatchgewan," said Paulie.

"Saskatchewan," said Martin.

"Saskatchewan," said Paulie.

"Never let them see fear," I said.

"That's why I stay indoors," said Brian.

He was funny.

"But I never start a fight," I said, mostly to Martin. "Cause I don't like them. Fighting means big, tough guys get to run the world."

"We don't like it neither," said Martin. 'We're just trying to stop Steve from being a bully."

Paulie and the rest of the gang said "ya" and "we gotta stop him" and nodded.

"Steve is trying to imitate us," said Martin and his little friends nodded again.

"Intimidate," I said.

"Intimidate," repeated Martin.

"You've tried everything you could to avoid fighting?" I asked.

"Ya," said Martin. "I told him Basil said fighting was barberic."

"It's pronounced barbaric," said Brian.

"Barbaric," repeated Martin as I smiled at Brian for being nice to my little brother. "And we could settle our fight by playing cards or seeing who could throw stones the farthest or who could run around the block the fastest, just like Basil said, but Steve knows I always beat him at that stuff."

"Everyone knows Martin always wins at Go Fish and cribbage and marbles and throwing and runs the fastest to get away from big kids," said Paulie. "Everyone knows."

And now everyone was supposed to learn that he can also get together the toughest gang.

"So, what are we supposed to do in this fight?" said Brian. "Pick somebody our size and go at it? Are kicking, scratching and punching allowed or just wrestling? You keep at it until your opponent gives or until everyone on the other side is beaten to a pulp? How do you decide who wins?"

I looked to Martin for an answer.

"Do we all have to win or is it like best of thirteen?" said Brian. "Cause if we all have to win maybe you should drop some of the weaker fighters."

I stared at my little brother, who shrugged his shoulders.

"I dunno," said Martin. "Maybe they'll be scaredy cats and run away when they see us coming."

"Ya, scaredy cats," said Paulie. "When they see you, Roy, they'll run."

The tough talk motivated a few of the nine and ten-year olds to move up the street towards Steve's gang. "Come on, let's go fight 'em," said Darryl, a particularly obnoxious Albert Street nine-year-old, who bragged he could piss further than any kid in the neighborhood and claimed to be an expert on absolutely every-thing there was to know about garter snakes, gophers and sex.

Martin looked at me like he was pleading for help and then followed the crowd, to lead it. Brian and I walked behind them.

"You're not really going to fight this Doug, are you?" said Brian.

"He sucker punched me in the park. That's where I got this," I said, touching the not quite healed cut on my forehead.

"So? The guy's a loser who fights because some seven-year-old tells him to," said Brian. "Why should you sink to his level?"

He had a point.

"I'll watch and see what happens," I said. "My little brother is up there. I've got responsibilities."

"One benefit of being an only child," said Brian.

"You coming?" I said, picking up my pace.

"To think I could be home, working on an étude," said Brian, who nonetheless followed.

Martin made it to the front of the group of kids just as Steve's gang appeared from the back alley between Brown and Albert streets.

"Where's your brother?" said Doug, who was standing beside his cousin, like a mean guard dog. "He chicken out?"

Some of the guys in Steve's pack began to "cluck" like chickens.

"You wish," said Martin.

"You wish," repeated Paulie.

"Shut-up," said Steve as he shoved Paulie's shoulder.

"Pick on someone you own size," said Martin, jabbing at Steve.

"Hey," said Doug, grabbing Martin's hand and twisting it.

"Hey Dougie, you beating up seven year olds now?" I said, from about twenty feet away. The crowd of kids opened up to let Brian and I pass. "I mean, I don't mind. The little brat really pissed me off today. But it doesn't look too good for you. You might get a reputation and our older brother Basil and his friends might have to do to you what you do to Martin."

Doug freed Martin's hand.

"You're going to get your big brother to do your fighting for you?" said Doug. "Figures, after what I hear about you."

"I'm not the one grabbing six-year-olds," I said. "What did you hear about me?"

We stood about two feet apart, staring at each other. Brian stepped up from behind me to stand beside Martin.

"So how is this going to work? Do we just start wrestling, right here on the road? How are we going to pick partners? Can I have first pick? I want that one." Brian pointed to the smallest kid in Steve's gang,

I had to keep myself from smiling. Brian was very funny.

"Who is this?" said Doug.

"Brian," said Brian holding out his hand as if to shake. "Brian Epstein. I'm from Winnipeg and we don't do this sort of thing there, at least not where I live, so I'm not familiar with all the rules."

Doug stared. Brian put his hand down.

"I'm Roy's new catcher," he said. "Did you hear he threw a no-hitter today? Fifteen strike outs in six innings. And he threw a screwball that jumped up and in over a foot and hit Mike Mackie, right in the back of the neck. Knocked him out cold. Had to be carried off the field on a stretcher."

The stare continued as Brian made a show of looking at Doug carefully.

"Haven't I seen you somewhere before?" said Brian. "I have. I know it. Were you at the Kiwanis Festival?"

"Let's go into the field," Doug said to me. "Talk about how we're going to do this."

"Fine by me," I said.

The swarm of kids crossed the street into the vacant half block, a more suitable location for fighting than the street. Except for the occasional piece of broken glass, the ground was more forgiving than the gravel-covered, hard-packed road surface that had been oiled only the week before.

"I saw him at the Kiwanis Music Festival, I know I did," Brian whispered to me as we headed to the field. "Just trying to remember where and when."

Steve's gang formed a line with Doug and their leader in the centre. Martin's guys took spots opposite them.

"What's the deal?" said Doug to his younger cousin.

Steve looked at Martin.

"Everybody get a guy his own size," said Martin.

Doug and I stood opposite each other.

"What did you hear about me?" I asked again. "From who?"

"That you've been telling stories about my mother," said Doug, tears almost coming to his eyes.

"That's not true," I said. "I'd never do that. In fact I'd punch out anybody I heard doing that."

Doug stared at me. Brian searched in vain for a partner, every few seconds looking back at Doug, trying to figure out exactly where he had seen him before.

"You really knock out Mike Mackie?" said Doug, quietly to me.

"I hit him hard in the back of the neck, but who knows, he could have been faking it," I said.

"Know what you mean," said Doug. "He's a little prick and his brother is a big prick."

"You know Kevin?"

Doug nodded.

"He jump you?"

Doug nodded again.

Kevin Mackie was fifteen and the west side's most notorious bully. He lived two blocks on the other side of Elgin Park but terrorized kids almost all the way to Main Street. He never went after me, but that was only because of Basil. Kevin never picked on anyone with a tough older brother or anyone he thought stood a remote chance of beating him in a fight. Having an older brother like Kevin explained why Mike was the way he was.

Everyone but Brian and another kid had picked partners. It was Sam Wong, a short ten-year-old who had the misfortune to be both Chinese and the fattest kid in the neighborhood. His parents owned Elgin Park Grocery and Confectionary, which meant he could eat all the penny candy he wanted.

"I can't fight him," said Brian. "He's too little and too big."

"Don't worry," I said. 'He's on our side. He lives on Brown Street."

"Oh, too bad," said Brian. "Sorry, I thought you were from over there, but I wouldn't have fought you, not really."

"No one ever fights me," said Sam. "They just call me names."

"Oh. Perhaps you and I share that in common," said Brian, who then suddenly turned back to face Doug.

"You were in the Bach choir from Calgary," said Brian, raising his hand and pointing. "You sang a solo and have a wonderful voice, absolutely beautiful."

Every kid on the field stared at Doug.

"You look different, without the white shirt and bow tie," said Brian. "I was in the piano competition."

Doug glared.

"Do you take private lessons? Do you do conservatory voice? Do you sing with anybody here in Moose Jaw? Are you looking for a pianist?"

Doug was enraged. He took a step towards Brian, eyes filled with anger. Brian immediately took a step backwards.

"What did I say?"

I stepped beside Brian and whispered in his ear. "Let him hit you once, in the stomach." Then I stepped in front of Doug.

"Get out of my way," said Doug.

I stood my ground.

"Get out of my way," repeated Doug.

I leaned forward and whispered to Doug. "Push me out of the way and slug Brian once in the belly."

Our eyes met for a moment as Doug pushed my shoulder and then did it again. I stumbled out of the way and Brian look terrified as Doug took a step towards him, then kneed him in the gut and pushed him down to the ground. All the kids gathered round to watch, expecting more fighting, but Brian lay completely still, hugging the earth like he was in love with it. Doug stood over him, waiting.

"You know what I heard," I said to Steve. "Before the baseball game today. Before I beaned Mike Mackie?"

"What?" said Steve who remained focused on his cousin.

"Mike and Kevin are getting together a gang from the other side of Ninth Avenue and they plan to keep everyone else out of Elgin Park," I said. "They're going to beat the crap out of anyone from this side of Ninth Avenue who tries to get in."

I had the attention of the entire crowd of kids. Even Doug was interested.

"Who told you that?" said Steve.

"Mike," I said. "That's why I hit him."

"They can't do that," said Martin.

"It's not fair," said Paulie.

"They'll try," said Steve, sharing a look with his cousin. "That's just the way the Mackies are."

"We won't let 'em get away with it," said Martin.

"We hafta stop them," said Sam, who would be especially affected since he lived right across the street from the park.

"The only chance we have of stopping them is for all of us here to join together," I said. "Not fight each other. That's what the Mackies want."

There were nods of agreement from throughout the crowd. "That's right. Stick together. All of us. We'll show them."

"There's a lot of tough kids from the other side of the park," I said.

"That Mike and Kevin are awfully mean," said Sam.

"Can you and Steve call a truce?" I said to Martin. "And then start cooperating on getting together a new gang to protect us in the park? That might work, but only if all of us from the west side of Ninth Avenue stick together."

Martin looked at Steve, who looked at Doug, who looked at me. I looked down at Brian, who looked back. Then the looks moved in the opposite direction and finally Martin said, "Ya, we can do that."

"Okay," I said. "Shake hands."

They did and so did some of the other kids who moments before were about to fight each other. I offered my hand to Doug. Our eyes met as we shook hands.

"If you really want to make this thing work you could cut your wrists and then press them against each other to become blood brothers," said Brian as he got up from the ground. "I read about that in a book."

I smiled. My new friend was hilarious.

DIARY ENTRY ONE DEC. 8, 2000

"Did you see the paper?" he said. "The Florida Supreme Court has ordered the hand recount of about 45,000 votes."

She smiled.

"What?" he said.

"We won the election and the U.S. Supreme Court will sooner or later agree," she said.

"Why are you so sure? What do you know?"

"I have my sources," she said, smiling mysteriously.

He had no doubt that she had authoritative sources.

"You promised to explain yourself before I give you these to read," she said, changing the subject. She held her small pile of papers picked up the day before at the archives.

"Nothing in there that's too embarrassing?" he said.

"I was definitely a child prodigy," she said. "Some of it was a bit naïve, but what else would you expect from a 13-year-old?"

She held out the papers for him to take, but pulled them away as he reached out.

"You promised," she said. "You've accused me of ignoring reality, of basing my entire political philosophy on lies, but here you are in the new millennium, an unrepentant Marxist who has devoted his life to a 'working class' that doesn't exist and to ideas that were ridiculous at best a hundred years ago. You were smart. You could have been a great screenwriter and made a fortune or at least became a hot-shot academic, writing books to explain the past. What happened to you? Why did you drop out of screenwriting and then graduate school? Explain the life you've led. Justify yourself."

"Justify myself to you?"

"Yes."

"Okay," he said, having thought carefully about his answer. "I believe capitalism is a rotten system that causes war and is destroying the environment, as well as severely limiting the creativity and intelligence of most human beings who are trapped within it. For some reason this is a message that the system prefers not to hear, so rather than being a rich and famous writer I got stuck with the not so bad job of being a college instructor."

"Tell me at least you dropped out to become some kind of Red Brigades terrorist," she said. "At least that would be romantic."

"No, not even close," he said.

"A South American guerrilla?"

He shook his head. He walked to the far side of the room to be as far away from her as possible.

"The suspense is killing me," she said. "Why did you stop screenwriting and drop out of the PhD program to become a college instructor? You had to be doing something on the side."

He turned around the chair in front of the desk and sat on it.

"You wrote pornography for a living?" she said, smiling.

He raised his eyebrows.

"What?" she said, having fun.

"Nothing romantic whatsoever," he said. "The studio wanted to change my script to take out all the politics. It was the story of an anarchist cowboy. How can you take the politics out? I refused. Gave most of the money back. I thought some other studio would pick it up but it didn't happen. Why would I want to work in that kind of world? Then I met my wife and wanted a steady income to look after my family."

He could see she understood.

"You made her pregnant? Your girlfriend?"

He tried for a look of nonchalance as he nodded.

"What a cliché," she said. "Right down to growing up Catholic."

"Sorry to disappoint you," he said. "I thought teaching would be an easy job, giving me time to write. I wanted to be an authentic voice of the working class. And then I never really did write much, except for editing a few newspapers and political journals. I wrote hundreds of leaflets."

He shrugged as she stared at him.

"Call me an enemy of the system or call me a failure, I really don't care," he said. "Maybe I am just lazy, but I still write. I'm thinking of turning these letters into a novel. I have a couple of other novels in storage. A few plays, some poetry. Sent them out a few times but there was no interest. I think they were too political, but maybe they were just lousy. And then I learned to like teaching. Got involved with the faculty union. Elected president and I've been doing that for a decade."

She said nothing.

"That's the one paragraph summary," he said.

"Weren't you also a pretty good ball player? A pitcher?"

He nodded. He had not thought about baseball for a long time.

"What happened with that?" she asked.

"Tried out for the Moose Jaw Regals when I was 17," he said. "If I had been willing to stay in Moose Jaw, they would have kept me on the roster and maybe I would have been noticed by a scout. But I wanted to go to university. One of the Regal coaches said he'd talk to a friend about a baseball scholarship in Texas, but nothing ever came of it. No one was looking for Canadians in those days."

"So you quit that too?"

"You talk like my life's been a failure because I never became famous," he said. "That's your definition of success, not mine."

"What's yours?" she said.

"Being happy, which mostly comes from believing in something and working hard to make it happen," he said. "Doing your best to make the world a better place."

"You've been happy?" she asked.

"Pretty much," he said.

"No disappointments?"

"I never said that," he replied quickly. "I'm disappointed that I never saw my film script up on the silver screen. I'm disappointed I never got a chance to wander the world, doing all sorts of jobs and writing about the experience of the contemporary working class. Be a literary Woody Guthrie. But would I trade all the years of fun I had raising my three girls for any of that? No."

"Funny how you never bring up your wife," she said.

"My relationship with her has been another disappointment."

He could feel her looking into his eyes. What was she looking for? It felt like she was reading his thoughts.

"She had lots of affairs?"

"Why do you ask that?"

"She's good looking isn't she?"

He nodded.

"She came from a middle class or even upper class background?"

He nodded again.

"And she was disappointed in you, wasn't she?" she said. "You promised her the romance of Hollywood or a revolution and all you delivered was the life of a junior college professor. She bought into your bullshit, she thought you were going to be a great writer, and what happened?"

"Did you get this from your spy friend too?" he said, trying to scramble away from the edge of a big black hole.

"I knew it," she said. "You really are a walking cliché. You could have been a great writer, but your politics held you back. You stuck with Marxism even when the world was abandoning it. Your loser philosophy made you a loser. Even your wife understood that."

He stared at the deep blue woolen rug.

"You wasted your life trying to become an 'authentic voice' for the working class," she said, sarcastically. "You fell for that 'write about what you know' bullshit. That's what losers tell you. No one, except creative writing professors, cares about authentic voices. People want to be entertained, distracted from their dreary lives. They want imagination, not authenticity. They get enough of the real world every day."

"You're right," he said, pulling out of a momentary funk. "How could I have been so stupid? I should have written Harlequin romances."

"I said books with imagination," she said. "You had a great imagination. You were full of ideas. I saw that when you were twelve, even if I didn't agree with most of them. But you gave up writing to do things any monkey can be trained to do."

"I never gave up writing," he said. "I've always written. And don't insult the people who do jobs a lot more socially useful than yours."

"You could have been a brilliant writer, but instead you teach history to kids who don't have good enough marks to get into university," she said.

"I told you I've written a few novels," he said.

"None of which have ever been published," she said. "Because no one is interested. Your novels are all about changing the world, right? But no one cares."

"I don't regret anything," he said.

"That's even worse," she said.

"I still have the same dream," he said. "To write the great working class novel that changes the world. Which means I can never 'make it' as part of the system. That's the life I chose and I'd do it all over again. The absolute best the system allows is for mainstream literature to describe some small part of reality. As Marx said, the point of philosophy should be to change the world, not to simply describe it."

She shook her head. "Sad," she said. "This is what socialism does to true believers."

"What?" he said. "You don't believe me?"

"I believe that's what you believe," she said. "But you're fooling your-self. You have constructed an elaborate excuse for avoiding success. You're smart, funny and probably a great writer. Why waste your life?"

"I could say the same about you," he said. "You're smart, funny and a talented actor. Why waste your life supporting an unfair, rotten-to-the-core system that benefits the few at the expense of the many?"

"It's the only system we have," she said. "You claim to be an environ-mentalist, but you deny the natural order."

"That's what our economic and political system is?" he said. "The natu-ral order?"

"That's what reality demonstrates," she said.

He stared at her for a few seconds and then smiled.

"That really is the fundamental divide, isn't it?" he said. "On one side are those who see the system as the natural order and on the other those who believe human beings created it and therefore can change it."

"Whatever you say, big red," she said. "Whatever you say."

"Can I read your letters now?" he said.

She handed them to him and then walked across the room to pick up his pile of papers from the desk.

"Wait. Before we begin we need some more wine," she said.

Katherine, letter 4

October 8, 1962

Dear President Kennedy,

This is Katherine Anderson once again. Whilst Mr. Rebalski gave me a mark of 93 on my previous essay and said it was excellent, in terms of grammar, spelling and clarity, he also said I misinterpreted his instructions regarding what the assignment was about. I certainly don't mind writing more for my favourite teacher.

What Mr. Rebalski would like me to write is a story that is based on something that has actually happened to me. It should suggest a political message, like Ayn Rand's Atlas Shrugged, which I have read, or Charles Dickens' Oliver Twist, which I have not. I can send the story in one or many parts, it is up to me.

Since my conversation with Mr. Rebalski, I have been thinking very carefully about what to write and must confess to not making up my mind yet. I have one good idea, but am not certain, so will consider the matter for a few more days.

Mr. Rebalski also told me that Roy Schmidt has already sent you many chapters of his story. What I would like to say about that is please don't judge his story better than mine simply because he understood the assignment first. I'm sure my story will be at least as interesting as his.

I promise to begin sending you my story within the week.

Roy, letter 9

Oct. 19, 1962

Dear President Kennedy,

I'm starting to get nervous again because the paper says you want to talk to Mr. Khrushchev. Why? What's going on? Paul says his Mom says there's going to be a war. I think it's a good thing if you talk. I mean, if you're talking and not fighting.

We won our first regular-season game tonight, beating South Hill 3-2. I didn't play much for the first two periods, but then I got regular shifts in the third and I got an assist on the winning goal. Most of the guys on my team have been treating me like I'm a little kid and making fun of me, but they were pretty nice after that pass. People are prejudiced about lots of things, not just the colour of your skin or your religion. Most 14 or 15 year olds act like everybody who is 12 is a little kid and doesn't know anything about being a teenager or about how to play hockey with older guys. But maybe I do and maybe I can. That's what I like about my brother Basil. He always treated me like I have a brain. And that's what I try to do with Martin. I hate prejudice, just like everybody says you do too.

To get back to the story, it was early June.

"Are you gonna throw another no-batter?" said Martin, as he walked beside me to help deliver the Saturday paper.

"No-hitter," I said, in my freshly washed Giants uniform.

"You said a batter and a hitter were the same thing," said Martin.

"They mean the same when you're talking about the person with a bat in his hands, standing at the plate," I said. "But a no-batter would mean you didn't face any batters, while a no-hitter means you didn't allow any hits."

I grabbed a Moose Jaw Times Herald from the paper bag slung over Martin's shoulder and walked up a narrow sidewalk to put it into the mailbox beside the light blue bungalow's front door. Martin had a point. A hitter was the same thing as a batter, therefore a no-hitter should mean the same things as a no-batter. Sometimes English was a strange language.

"Are you gonna throw another no-hitter?" said Martin, when I returned.

"I'll try," I said. "Brian's gonna catch again and my arm's feeling pretty good."

"Is Brian your best friend now?"

"He's a friend," I said. "He's smart and he's funny."

"I never knew boys could play piano," said Martin.

"Dad can play piano," I said. "You never saw him?"

Martin shook his head.

"Well he can," I said. "I remember him playing at Grandpa's house in Bismarck."

"I never saw it," said Martin.

"He used to do lots of things when he was younger that he doesn't do anymore," I said. "Basil says Michael told him that Dad used to ride horses."

"Horses?" said Martin. "Like a cowboy?"

"Ya, they had horses when Mom and Dad first got married and lived on the farm. Dad was like Roy Rogers."

Martin had a hard time believing this.

"People change as they get older, even moms and dads," I said. "You've changed a lot since you were five, right?"

"Before Grade 1? Ya, I changed a whole lot."

"And that's only a year," I said. "Imagine how much Mom and Dad have changed since Michael was born."

"How old is Michael?" asked Martin.

"He's nineteen years older than you," I said. "So, how old does that make him?"

"Twenty-five?" said Martin.

I nodded.

"I don't remember," said Martin. "Does he look like me and you?"

I shrugged. "I sort of remember him from before I went to school and then when he came to Grandpa's funeral. He joined the Air Force when he was nineteen."

"I'd like to join the Air Force and fly those big planes," said Martin.

"Ya," I said. "It'd be fun."

I dreamed about being a pilot. A pilot and a writer, that would be perfect.

"I'm thinking about joining air cadets next year," I said. "They'll help you get a pilot's license if you stay in long enough and do all the tests and have good eyes."

Martin spread his arms, as if he were the airplane. I picked up the bag from my little brother's shoulders and handed him a paper. Martin flew it to Mrs. Fox, who waved from her front stairs.

"You're gonna throw another no-hitter, I know it," said Martin as he landed back on the sidewalk in front of me. "I think every Saturday you'll throw them out, one, two, three. Saturday is the day you can do anything you want."

"Last Saturday was fun, that's for sure," I said. "See Tim break his arm, dislocate his knee and his shoulder, get a no-hitter, throw a screwball right into Mackie's neck so he gets carried off the field on a stretcher, make a new friend, create a new gang — all in one day."

"Jimmy says Tim doesn't have to go back to school," said Martin. "Says he's probably gonna hafta get a peration for his knee."

"Operation," I said.

"Operation," said Martin. "Cut into him with a satchel and a saw and pointy long things that look like pliers."

It took me a few seconds to figure out what my little brother meant.

"Scalpel, not satchel," I said. "A satchel is a like a bag that hangs over Roy Roger's horse."

"Trigger," said Martin.

"Ya," I said. "A scalpel is what a surgeon uses to cut into your body."

"Steve loves Roy Rogers," said Martin.

I lifted the paper bag to my other shoulder.

"How's it going with you and Steve?"

"I told him he could be leader of the gang, like you said and now we're best friends," said Martin.

"Sometimes the guy who calls himself leader and the real leader is not the same person," I said. "You understand?"

"Like when the teacher leaves the room and says everyone listen to Cathy Conacher, but no one does?"

"Exactly," I said. "Real leaders aren't appointed by the teacher or the boss or the adults. The real leader is the person who people look to cause they make the most sense."

Martin took two newspapers as he went to a house on the north side of the street while I delivered to one on the south side. When we met back on the sidewalk Martin was staring at the front page of the Times Herald.

"'Castro fears new attack might be launched by U.S.'," Martin said. "What does that mean?"

"It means the Americans are going to invade again," I said.

"With an army, like in the Longest Day?" said Martin, about his favourite movie, which he had seen a few months earlier at the Capitol. "With boats and planes and guys jumping out of parachutes?"

"Sure, last time they used ships and planes and guys in parachutes, but not near as big as D-Day, like in the movie," I said. "That was the biggest invasion in history. Cuba is a tiny island, not even as big as Saskatchewan."

"What's Cuba?"

"Cuba is the country where the guy in the story lives," I said. "Castro led a revolution against a bad government run by gangsters. They were killing everybody who tried to make things better for poor Cubans."

"So why do the Americans want to attack him?" said Martin.

"Cause the old bad government did pretty much what American companies wanted, so they made lots of money. Now they don't. Plus Castro says he's a communist."

"The 'Mericans never like communists, do they?" said Martin.

"That's just what they call anybody they don't like," I said. "Doesn't matter if you really are. You can be a socialist or a nationalist or just not like Americans and they call you a communist."

"What's a nashalist?"

"Nationalist," I repeated, slowly.

"Nationalist," said Martin.

"A nationalist is someone who loves their country and thinks it's the best place in the world," I said.

"Are we nationalists?" said Martin.

"Basil says he's an internationalist," I said.

"What's that?"

"It's someone who thinks all the people in the whole world and all the countries are equal and you have to treat everybody the same," I said.

"Kind of like the Golden Rule?" said Martin.

"Ya, kind of like that," I said.

"So nationalists are bad guys and inter ... the other ones, are good guys?" said Martin.

"No, the nationalists are the good guys lots of the time because they're fighting for their country's freedom against the imperialists," I said.

Martin stared.

"I told you, imperialists are big countries that make little countries do what they tell them," I said.

"Is Canada a perialist?" said Martin.

"Imperialist," I said.

"Is Canada imperialist?" said Martin. "You said Canada is the second biggest country in the world."

"That's big in terms of land," I said. "Canada covers the second most land of any country, but it doesn't have a big army. That's what counts for imperialism."

I could see Martin didn't understand.

"Are imperialists like bullies?" said Martin.

"Exactly," I said. "Not all big kids are bullies, right? Only mean, tough ones who push you around to get what they want. They force you to do what they want, even if it's not what you want."

"Does Canada do that to smaller countries?" asked Martin.

"I don't think so," I said. "Maybe sometimes, like when we stole the Indian land. But if Canada is an imperialist it's mostly when we go along with the United States."

"The United States is imperialist?"

"Ya," I said. "And Britain and France. They make countries in Africa and Asia and South America do what they tell them. Last year the Americans invaded Cuba at the Bay of Pigs. That's why that story says Castro is worried they'll do it again."

"What's a Bay of Pigs?"

"It's just the name of a place, like Hudson's Bay or Bay of Fundy," I said.

"Funny name," said Martin.

"It's where the anti-communists landed and tried to take over the island," I said.

"Aunt Communists?" said Martin. "Whose that?"

"Anti-communists," I said. "That means people who are against communists."

"The 'Mericans don't like Castro cause he's a communist?"

"That's what they say, but the real reason is they don't like him cause he won't do what they tell him," I said. "He cares more about ordinary Cubans than he does about American companies. He's a real communist, that's what Basil says."

"A real communist is a good guy?" said Martin. "But not the communists who are state capitalists?"

The little guy remembered every word. "Exactly," I said.

"What's a true communist?" said Martin.

"Someone who tries to build a system where everyone is equal and people live from each according to their abilities to each according to their needs," I said. "That's in the Communist Manifesto. Remember I showed you it outside St. Joseph's when you got bored and said you had to go to the bathroom during Good Friday High Mass? I told you we have to keep it secret from Mom, even though Basil says real communism is what Jesus preached."

"That was the longest mass ever," said Martin.

"You told Mom you were old enough to go," I said.

"I remember you showed me a book called Looking Backward," said Martin.

"That's about socialism too," I said.

"I remember that name cause I thought about it when Steve told me Mackie's gang is following us."

"When did he tell you that?"

"Monday, after school," said Martin. "Some of the kids in the Mackie gang told Steve they were keeping a spy on us."

"You mean 'keeping an eye on us?'" I said.

"They send little kids across Ninth Avenue to keep a spy on us."

"To keep an eye on us."

Martin shrugged. "That's why I have to be looking backward."

The little guy was like a sponge soaking up everything and if you squeezed him, you never knew what might squirt you in the eye.

"Steve said he talked to some members of Mackie's gang?" I asked.

"They're in his class at Queen Elizabeth," said Martin. "Kids who live on the other side of the park. They told him all about the plan to keep us out."

"Steve asked and they told him?" I said.

"Doug helped," said Martin.

"Doug helped Steve ask about the Mackie gang?"

"He wasn't really gonna do anything," said Martin. "But the little kids are scared of him, so they told Steve everything."

"Steve told the little kids that Doug would beat them up if they didn't tell him about the gang?"

He nodded.

"Martin!" I said, annoyed. "You didn't understand I made all that stuff up about the park and the Mackie gang to prevent your crazy fight?"

Martin looked skeptical.

"It was all a story," I said.

Martin shook his head.

"I made it up because I didn't want to fight Doug," I said. "Why should I? It's sad about his Dad and sister and mother. And then he has to move here to Moose Jaw to live with cousins. How'd you feel if that happened to you? Would you like it if someone beat you up on top of everything else?"

"He sucker punched you," said Martin. "You told me."

"He did, but only because he was trying to impress stupid Cindy and make himself seem tough so no one else would pick on him," I said. "Sometimes people do mean things, but it's better to understand why they do it, rather than just beat them up."

"But you said you have to fight back if a bully is mean to you," said Martin.

"But that's the point, Doug's not a bully. That's not why he sucker punched me," I said. "Think things through. Just because someone slugs you and gives you a black eye doesn't mean you have to give him one back."

"The bible says 'an eye for an eye and a tooth for a tooth,' that's what Paul told me," said Martin.

"It also says 'turn the other cheek'," I said. "And what's the golden rule? 'Do unto others as you would have them do unto you,' right?"

Martin stared.

"If you do something stupid and have a big fight with Mom and she slaps your bottom, then you come to the bedroom and hit me, cause you're mad at Mom, would it be better for me just to hit you back or to try and understand why you hit me?"

Still Martin said nothing.

"Look, the point is, I made up that story about the Mackies and Elgin Park so you guys would see that cooperation makes more sense than fighting," I said. "There's no Mackie gang and no plan to stop kids from this side of Ninth Avenue playing in Elgin Park."

"Then why would six kids say there was?" said Martin, defiantly.

"Because they'd say anything to avoid a beating from Doug," I said.

"Why would Mike Mackie shove Sam and tell him if he ever stepped a foot in the park again there'd be twenty kids pounding the crap out of him and he'd hafta give every single one of them two jawbreakers, two leaves and two jujubes every day or they'd pound him again?" said Martin, with growing certainty in his voice.

"How do you know he said that?"

"Sam told me," said Martin.

"When?"

"It happened yesterday and Sam told me this morning when I went to the store to buy baseball cards."

"Baseball cards? Where did you get the money?"

"None of your business," said Martin.

"Have you been stealing again?"

Martin shook his head and he looked like he was telling the truth, but he was a pretty good liar, so who knew?

Mackies and the park? Something was not right. Could I have accidentally dreamed up something that was about to come true?

GARY ENGLER

DIARY ENTRY TWO, DEC. 8, 2000

How can one person have two different personalities? Nice, charming, fun to be with one minute, and then the last person on earth you'd choose to spend any time with, the next. It finally made sense after he returned from the liquor store with the most expensive wine he'd ever bought.

"Your first three chapters are pretty good," she said, as he entered the room with the two bottles of Cote de Beaune Grand Cru she had asked for. "You should stick to fiction. This is a lot better than that crap you wrote in the pamphlet."

"One hundred and seventy-four dollars for two bottles of wine?" he said. "This had better be good."

"Trust me, it is," she said, then kissed him.

Was she feeling guilty about what she said? He pulled away and stared at her.

"What?" she asked.

"I was thinking I should get to know you better," he said. "As a human being."

"What?" she repeated.

"Like you said about me. Some questions. Have you been happy? Have you always done what you believe in? Do you believe everything you write and say?" he said, blurting out what was on his mind. "I answered your questions, now you answer mine."

She stared at him.

"Okay, she finally said. "One, not always. Two, not always, but that's the price of success. And three, not always, but that's definitely the price of success."

"Are you happy now?" he said.

"That's four questions."

"Add it to my bill," he answered.

"Yes," she said.

"Really?" he said. He knew something was not right.

"Right now I feel quite happy," she said.

He could see something bothered her.

"Why are you happy?" he asked.

She said nothing.

"Because I'm here with you?" he said.

She scrunched up her face at the ridiculousness of his question. "Because I'm in a hypomanic phase of my bipolar disorder." She said it matter-of-factly, as if it were something revealed to new acquaintances at a party.

Bipolar disorder?

"You're bipolar?" he asked. "For how long?"

"I was diagnosed eight years ago," she said. "But I'm told I probably had it all my life."

He wasn't surprised.

"Sometimes I'm manic and sometimes I'm depressed. I take lithium, which I'm sure you saw in the bathroom."

"Wow," was the only response he could think of. She must have planned to tell him. Why?

She stood six feet away and for the first time looked vulnerable.

"Does George W. know about this?" he said, before considering how the question could be interpreted.

"I suffer from a disease that has nothing to do with what I write or say," she answered defensively. "If anyone asks I tell them the truth."

Did she regret telling him? She was reacting to his look of sympathy. She couldn't stand that he felt sorry for her. Too bad. There was nothing he could do about his sympathy. He felt sorry for the most obnoxious person on the world's airways.

"My advisers tell me I should be honest and matter-of-fact about my condition," she said, perhaps noticing his look of concern. "You're the first person I told. It takes a little getting used to."

His level of concern dropped quickly. She had not revealed some deep dark secret because she felt close to him. She had been instructed by her advisers that blabbing loudly to the whole world would be the safest course of action and it would probably get her some sympathetic stories in the media. He felt used, again.

"You have more questions for me?" he said, trying to end the conversation after the silence between them became too long.

"You found me attractive when I was thirteen," she seemed to say the first thing that popped into her head.

"If that's a question, yes," he said.

"How attractive?" she asked.

"You were my first sexual fantasy," he said.

"How about now?"

It was a pathetic question. Maybe she was vulnerable.

"Do you still find me attractive?"

"Very," he answered.

"Even now that you know about my disease?"

Her defiance of the vulnerability she clearly felt was kind of sexy. She saw his pity.

"I'm not asking for sympathy," she said. "Some of the greatest people in the world were bipolar."

"What do you want from me?" he said.

"Nothing," she said. "I take what I want."

She opened the front of her robe and turned to face him.

He stared. Her body looked good, but he wondered if plastic surgery was part of the reason. She could be the type. Shallow.

"A pair of breasts can get a man to do anything," she said, then closed her robe. "It's not a criticism. That's the way men are built. The No. 1 goal is to spread your little seeds all around the garden. Women have to consider other things so we learn how to manipulate men for our own ends. We get good at it."

"Your sexism would drive most of the women I know crazy," he said, the moments of sympathy past.

"Trust me, I know all about confronting women's lib," she said, back in control of her emotions. "The Femi-nazis hate me."

"Because, like the economic system, you understand the natural order that divides the sexes and you defend it, while the feminists attack it," he said. She was a piece of work.

"Very good," she said, countering sarcasm with sarcasm.

"At least you're consistent," he said.

"All the way back to Grade 8," she said.

"Me too," he said.

"Which proves very little changes in the natural order," she said. "Form but not substance. Liberals are seduced by the appearance of change, but the reality is, whatever the system, the many are followers and a few are leaders. Women are mothers and men are fathers. The family is the foundation of happiness, both personal and social. These are eternal truths."

"You forgot another one," he said. "That the role of intellectuals is to suck up to those in power. Tell them what they want to hear."

"If you want to have power you must reside where power lives," she said. "I'm not ashamed of choosing to be an important person. I am not a coward like people who are afraid of power and success."

"I'm a coward, afraid of power and success, because I choose to oppose the existing system?" he said. "The teachers' pets, the camp followers, the whores to the system, they are the brave ones, while the people who challenge power are cowards. Wow, you really do have the world turned upside down."

"Did you live up to your potential?" she asked.

"My potential for what?" he said. "To become a rich and famous writer by selling out everything I believe in?"

"So you admit you couldn't make a living writing about what you believe?" she said, triumphant. "Because no one is interested."

"No one who owns a film studio or publishing company," he said, weakly because he knew where this was headed.

"No one who has paid any attention to what's happened in the world the last few decades," she answered quickly. "No one believes in communism or socialism anymore because it was proved it can't compete with capitalism. We won, you lost. You're like a fan who stands outside the arena weeks after the big game saying to passersby: 'The game's not really over. Give us another chance. If you give us another chance, we'll beat them for sure this time.' Get on with your life."

"Capitalism is the perfect system?" he said, moving the argument to where he had a better chance of success. "One that will last forever?"

"There's no perfection in human affairs," she answered.

"Exactly. Capitalism will exist until people no longer find it useful. The proper sports analogy is we've moved on to a new season and the big game is coming up once again, and maybe this time capitalism won't look quite so good," he said. "You may be the reigning champion, but they don't hand out the Cup until the final game of the playoffs is over. And then there's next year and the year after that. Nobody wins every season and all it's going to take for capitalism to go down is one really bad season. "

"The only way your team ever wins is by changing the game," she said. She was one of those women who specialized in sports analogies.

"The only way you guys will win the Stanley Cup is if they take body checking out of the game and replace the goons with figure skaters who get points for the best Quadruple Salchow."

She smiled, once again exuding smugness.

And he was once again irritated with her, the few moments of sympathy all but forgotten. He stared at nothing in particular. He wished he was anywhere but where he was.

This time she changed the subject.

"What happened to your brothers? Martin and Basil? What do they do now? Are they still socialists too?"

"Basil is the president of the longshoremen's union local in Vancouver."

"Figures," she said. "A communist and a gangster."

"You want me to answer your question or not?""

"Sorry," she responded. "And Martin?"

"You'd never ever guess, but you'd probably approve," he said.

"Now you've piqued my curiosity," she said, then held out her pile of letters. "Answer it and you can read these."

"Martin became a linguist, moved to the States and taught at Berkeley," he said.

She shrugged. "Why would I approve of that?"

"Ten years ago he was recruited by a voice recognition software company," he said. "A couple of years back he became the CEO and when it went public just over a year ago at the height of the market, he made over $20 million."

"Little Martin?" she said. "He was kind of cute, even when he was seven."

He shook his head.

She smiled. They understood each other well enough now that she did not have to say she was joking.

"May I read your letters now?" he said.

"After you open the Montrachet and pour us each a great big glass."

"No talking until we're both done," he said.

"Suits me," she said, handing him the stack of papers.

Katherine, letter 5

October 14, 1962

Dear President Kennedy,

This is a true story. Mr. Rebalski told us we can be completely honest without any worry that our parents, the principal or anyone else will find out. We know he will keep his word because Roy and I know a secret about him too. Roy's brother Basil has a friend in Saskatoon who knew Mr. Rebalski in university. He was very surprised to learn that Rick got a job at a Catholic school. Of course, we promise to keep Rick's secret as long as he keeps ours.

My story is called The Girl Who Could Make Anything Happen.

Once upon a time there was a 13-year-old girl named Katherine who moved to a new city with her mother, who was very beautiful, but also very mean. That meanness caused her marriage to break up and was also the reason why she moved to Moose Jaw. Sometimes Katherine thought that the move to Moose Jaw was because her mother was being mean to her. Other times she thought it was because her mother was being mean to her father. Probably she was being mean to both of them.

But Katherine was determined to make the best of her situation regardless of how much she preferred Regina and living with her father who was good looking and smart and never ever was mean to his daughter. So, Katherine made friends. She knew that her mother was hoping to make her life miserable, and the way that her mother would judge just how miserable she was, was by the number of friends she made. So, Katherine joined every club she could, Guides, figure skating, track, chess, choir, home economics, swimming, marching band and gymnastics, where she found girls from every corner of the city. She made so many friends so quickly that within six months of moving to Moose Jaw Katherine knew at least two girls in every Grade 8 class in all 14 elementary schools in the city. She also knew at least one girl in every Grade 9 class at Tech, Central, Riverview and Sion high schools.

Most school days and every weekend Katherine would invite at least one of her new friends over to her house so that her mother would know just how well she was doing. All the girls loved her mother because she was the most fashionable woman in all of Moose Jaw and a very gracious host.

Katherine was pleased with herself, but one day, Cindy, her very first friend in Moose Jaw, said to her as they were walking home from school: "You spend so much time making new friends that you don't have anytime for me anymore. It's been weeks since you invited me to your house. Is it because you don't like me anymore?"

Katherine assured her that wasn't true.

Still, Cindy was upset. "I don't understand why you need that many friends. How can you possibly get to know so many people? What's the point?"

Katherine didn't want to tell her the truth, about how mean her mother could be and all that, so she made up another story. It wasn't a lie. In fact, as it turned out, it was the best reason of all to make many friends.

I'll tell you why in the next letter.

Roy, letter 10

Oct. 21, 1962

Dear President Kennedy,

My Dad says something bad is going to happen between the USA and the Soviet Union. He says you are going to talk on TV tomorrow night and everyone thinks you will declare war. I sure hope not. I'm going to try to finish this story as quick as I can so I'll try to write every day. Maybe you don't read these and it's a waste of my time, but I don't have anything better to do, especially if there's going to be a war and the world is about to end. I told the principal Mr. Kalinsky last week that I was writing these letters and he laughed, but Sister Veronica says I should continue. She says she is sure my story is a good one and important and something that could help you. Sister Veronica says: "Listen to the children for they are innocent and wise." Her and I talk a lot about God and religion and stuff. She's not like my Mom who gets mad if I tell her that I don't know if God really exists. Sister Veronica thinks about stuff and she really cares about making the world better. She made a vow of poverty and spends all her time helping the poor and educating people. She doesn't say one thing and do another. I trust her. So here goes again.

"Two no-hitters in a row. How can that be bad pitching?" asked Brian, as he sat on the back steps of my house.

"I walked nine batters and gave up four runs," I said.

"We won and no one got a hit," said Brian.

"I didn't pitch well," I said. "I got distracted before the game."

"By what?"

"A bunch of things, but that first inning when I walked in two runs I was thinking about the doctors and Medicare and that story in the Times Herald today about 44 Regina doctors offered jobs in the U.S.," I said.

"You were thinking about that while you were pitching?" said Brian. "Even Young Communists are allowed to stop thinking about politics when playing baseball."

"It wasn't the politics I was thinking about, it was Mark Collins," I said.

"The Reds shortstop?"

"Ya," I said. "Before the game him and Paul and I got into this big argument over what the doctors are doing to stop Medicare."

"Paul from down your street?"

"Ya, Paul who I've known my whole life and his mother is a nurse at the training school," I said. "I can't go over to her house anymore. She's gone completely nuts over Medicare. Says Woodrow Lloyd is worse than Stalin. Says if the CCF can control doctors the next step will be state control over motherhood."

"She said that?" said Brian.

"Wish I was kidding," I said. "And Mark Collins, whose Dad is a doctor at the Training School, before the game says 'he wouldn't be surprised if someone shot the commie bastard premier.'"

"Seriously?"

"He's screaming and I'm screaming and Paul's screaming and Martin is staring like we're all nuts," I said. "The doctors and the right wingers have gone completely stark raving nuts. Over something they've had in England for 20 years."

"Good point," said Brian. "They make us memorize every king and queen since 1066, but we better not copy English socialized medicine."

"I was so mad, I was shaking by the time Collins bat leadoff in the first inning," I said.

"That explains the two balls in the dirt and two over his head."

"If I had any control, he'd have been on the same stretcher that carried Mackie off last week," I said.

"You were trying to hit him?" Brian laughed. "You missed by a mile."

"I can't pitch when I don't focus," I said. "Whole game all I could think about was those damn doctors."

"You were still good enough they couldn't hit you."

"If Tim was catching, there would have been a half dozen wild pitches," I said. "And they would have beat us."

"You were pretty wild," said Brian. "The pitch that landed a yard behind the batter, that was a lucky block. I dove blind and somehow it hit my glove."

"Yogi Berra would have been proud of that one," I said.

"At least you didn't hit anybody," said Brian.

"Everyone heard what happened to Mackie last week and they were jumping out of the batter's box before the ball left my fingers," I said, smiling.

"A reputation for killing batters isn't so bad," said Brian. "Fear is a pitcher's best friend."

"The Reds are scared of everybody," I said. "They haven't won a game. They're the worst team in the league."

"And we're the best, thanks to your fourth straight win."

"You're the best catcher in the league, that's why we won," I said.

Brian kind of smiled and kind of blushed.

"You going out for the all-star team?" I said.

"You think I have a chance?" said Brian.

"You're the best catcher in the league," I repeated.

"My hitting is not great," said Brian.

"A double, a bunt single, two RBI and two runs scored?" I said. "That's pretty good. You're the best base-runner on the team, except for me."

"I'm the best," said Brian, smiling again. "Trust me."

"I stole a base once," I said. "But the groundskeeper caught me and I had to give it back."

"Old joke," said Brian.

"You are pretty fast," I said.

"You have to be when you're as scared as me," said Brian. "I go fast to avoid getting beat up."

"You could stay and fight."

"Not when you got delicate, piano playing fingers like these."

As we talked, about ten kids of Martin's age assembled in a circle in the backyard.

"What are they doing?" asked Brian.

"Spinning the broom to see who is it first," I said.

The kids screamed as the broom pointed at Steve.

"What's it like playing piano in front of hundreds of people?" I asked.

"It's scary sometimes, especially just before going onstage," said Brian. "But it's also fun. Probably a lot like pitching. It feels great when you have a good performance."

"You sounded good to me," I said. "That piano is amazing."

"Steinway baby grand," said Brian. "Belongs to the family we are renting the house from. Friend of my Dad's cousin. Capitalist pigs. They own a fur store."

"Only other one I ever saw like that is in the Tech auditorium," I said.

"A Heintzman," said Brian. "I like it. Rich, full sound. Made in Ontario. As good as anything I played in Winnipeg."

"I know nothing about music," I said. "Chopin, Liszt, Beethoven, Bach — just names I read. I don't have a clue what their music sounds like."

"Like me with Doug Harvey, Tim Horton, Stan Makita, Eric something enko."

"Eric Nestorenko, Chicago Blackhawks, my favourite team."

"Or football. What's the name of the guy who throws the ball for the Blue Bombers? Everybody loves him."

"Kenny Pleon, my favourite quarterback," I said. "Wish the Riders had him."

"If you want to learn about music, I'll help," said Brian.

"Count on me about hockey or football or the entire Catholic mass in Latin."

"Seriously? You know it all in Latin?"

"I'm an alter boy, I got the whole thing memorized," I said. "Which may be useless cause Sister Veronica says the church is talking about changing to English."

"Together we have the entire sum of human knowledge covered," said Brian.

We smiled at each and watched the little kids running around the yard.

"What did you think of my father?" said Brian.

"He's great," I said. "Funny. I liked those Khrushchev jokes. I thought accountants were supposed to be all serious."

"They're also supposed to be capitalists," said Brian. "He wanted to be a composer, but he got married and had me."

"You made him give up music?" I said.

Brian shrugged.

"And the food was great," I said.

"Can't believe you never had sweet and sour before."

"Never ate Chinese food," I said.

"Not even chop suey?" said Brian. "Moo goo gui pan?"

I shook my head.

"Incredible," said Brian.

He said nothing more. I liked that he had not made a comment about how small our house was or anything like that.

"This is a very strange game," said Brian, as the kids scrambled in all directions, screaming as Steve chased them with a broom.

"Why?" I said.

"Old Lady Witch? Running around your house smacking each other with a broom?"

"Tag, that's all, with a twist," I said. "Instead of "it" you become "old lady witch" and little kids like it."

"It has to be played here, at your house?" asked Brian.

"It only works here because we have that narrow path there between the house and the fence, which makes it impossible to swing the broom, and then there's the caragana bushes out front where little kids can squeeze through but bigger kids can't and good hiding places in the back here," I said. "It's a neighborhood tradition. Basil played it when he was Martin's age. And probably Michael and Sebastian too."

"You have four brothers?" said Brian.

"And one sister, Mary, but she got married and moved to Edmonton last year," I said. "Six kids in total and my Mom also had a couple of miscarriages."

"Wow," said Brian. "You like being part of a big family?"

"I don't know. Never really thought about it," I said. "Sometimes it's nice and sometimes it's a pain in the butt."

"Never lonely," said Brian.

"Hard to find any privacy," I said. "Slept with Basil until I was nine and now I share a bed with Martin. I can hardly wait till Basil goes to university."

"Don't know how you all live in this tiny house without killing each other," said Brian. "We have a two and half story, four bedroom house in Winnipeg and my Mom and Dad are always screaming at each other."

I'd never had a conversation like this before.

"Your parents fight?" said Brian.

"Sometimes," I said. "Last year when there was talk about the mill closing and my Mom said we should move to Alberta, they really went at it."

"I hate it when my parents fight," said Brian. "Can't talk to anybody, because you go to one the other thinks you're taking sides."

I didn't know what to say. I never talked to my parents about personal stuff.

"Maybe it's different if you have brothers and sisters," said Brian.

"Always someone to talk to, that's for sure," I said. "One thing about the Schmidt family is we like to gab. We eat dinner we argue. We play cards we debate. We drink cocoa we talk. Martin helps me deliver papers and it's non-stop questions."

"You're good to Martin," said Brian. "He looks up to you."

This personal stuff was getting uncomfortable.

"Basil looked after me and made sure I understood how the world works, so I pass it on to Martin," I said.

"I guess that's how family is supposed to be," said Brian, sounding sad.

"Hey, it isn't all good," I said, determined to make my new friend feel better. "Big families have a good side and a bad side."

"I'd give up some of my privacy to get what you have with Basil and Martin," said Brian. "You belong."

What was that supposed to mean? This personal stuff was weird. Time to change the subject.

"You know what the little bugger told me as we're walking to the game today?" I said. "You know that story I made up last week about a Mackie gang and how they were going to stop every kid from west of Ninth Avenue from playing in Elgin Park?"

"Very creative," said Brian. "And just in the nick of time to prevent the fight. Except of course the kick in the stomach I got."

"So creative, it came true," I said.

"What do you mean?"

"I guess the story was convincing enough that Steve and Doug started questioning kids at Queen Elizabeth about what was going on. Martin says they made a pack of eight and nine-year-olds confess to belonging to the Mackie gang. And not just that the gang exists, but that they are planning to take control of the park."

"They confessed to something that isn't true? That you made up?"

"Hey, we're playing Old Lady Witch," I said. "You heard of the trials where they made women confess to being witches? Basil says it happened to thousands of women all across Europe and New England and Mexico."

"In Spain they made people confess to being Jews," said Brian. "And killed them."

"Fear of Doug made those kids confess to belonging to a gang that never existed and to a plan I invented."

"That's pretty funny," Brian said, smiling. "Makes you wonder what's the point of torture if people just agree to whatever story you make up."

"Ya, but even more incredible, it looks like the Mackies heard about my story and liked it so much they decided to make it come true."

"What do you mean?" said Brian.

"Kids from west of Ninth Avenue told Sam Wong about their new gang and how he wasn't allowed in the park anymore," I said.

"No!" said Brian.

"What I figure must have happened is those kids that Steve and Doug tortured told Mike, or his evil brother, that kids from the west side of Ninth Avenue have gotten together in a gang to fight over who gets to play in Elgin Park."

"And, of course the Mackies' reaction is that kids from their side better do the same or else they won't be able to play in the park anymore," said Brian.

"Exactly," I said.

"Oh man, that's too much," said Brian. "You make up something and it happens."

He smiled as he raised his hands and wiggled his fingers at me.

"You got the power," he said. "You must be a god. Should I bow down?"

Maybe it was funny, but it was also serious.

"What are we going to do?" I said. "The Mackies are tough,

mean and crazy and now we got to fight them instead of Steve and Doug's stupid little gang."

"We?" said Brian. "I thought I heard you say we."

"We, family, brothers, team," I said. "Along with the good comes the bad."

"I heard about this Catholic guilt thing, but I never experienced it before today."

"Next month I'll take you to confession," I said, smiling.

"Hey Martin," said Brian, as my little brother ran by the steps.

"Ya?" he said while keeping an eye out for the old lady witch.

"Roy says I can join your family. What do you say? You want another brother?"

"Sure," said Martin shrugging. "You gonna sleep in Basil's bed?"

Brian laughed as Martin sped off to avoid being tagged with the broom.

"Okay," said Brian. "I guess I'm in."

Katherine, letter 6

October 16, 1962

Dear President Kennedy,

That Roy Schmidt is truly awful. He sides with that communist Fidel Castro over you every time. Sometimes I think he really believes that Cuba is a better and more important country than the United States.

Roy and I spend every social studies class arguing about you and Cuba and socialism and communism and Saskatchewan politics. He really is a know-it-all and I think some of the more impressionable children actually believe what he says. He is very popular with a certain sort of boy because he is a good athlete and most of the girls think he is cute. And, of course, since he usually gets the top marks it is easy to understand why some of the more feeble-minded would think he must know what he is talking about.

I must say Mr. Rebalski is the only teacher who understands the importance of questioning Roy's socialistic views. Twice now I have been awarded higher marks on tests than Roy. I believe that is so important because it sends the message that free enterprise can compete with and beat socialism. I know that is the same message you are trying to convey with your policies regarding Cuba, isn't that correct Mr. President? We must stand up for freedom and free enterprise and make sure Communism never gets a foothold in the Americas.

So, back to my story.

Instead of telling Cindy about her mother's meanness Katherine told her that the reason it was important to make as many friends as you could was because friends gave one influence and power. Only with influence and power could one really make a difference in the world.

It was funny but only after Katherine said it did she realize that it was true. What started out as sort of a white lie became truer than what she had thought was the reason for making so many friends. Her mother's meanness was no where near as important as the ability to influence people and shape events.

"What do you mean?" asked Cindy.

It was then that the plan came to Katherine.

"If you have friends you have a way of influencing what's going to happen," Katherine said. "Take for example the situation with the government and our doctors. The government says that on July 1 their socialist medicine plan will come into effect. The doctors say they can't do their jobs if the government goes ahead with their plan. What can we do to help the doctors? Well, if I have lots of friends and get each one of them involved, that's a lot better than if I am all alone, isn't it? We could all write letters and get people to sign petitions. Don't you see?"

"I guess so," said Cindy.

But the truth was Cindy really didn't care much about politics or doctors or anything like that, so Katherine had to find another way to explain the power of friends.

"Who is the person you'd like to get even with more than any other?" said Katherine.

"Roy Schmidt and his little brother Martin," said Cindy after thinking about it for only a moment. "The things they said to my cousin Mary. I was so embarrassed. All my cousins from Swift Current, Maple Creek and Medicine Hat laughed at me when we went to the wedding in Regina and they probably told everyone there. I can't stand Roy and Martin."

"And you'd like to get even?" said Katherine. "I bet all my friends could help."

Cindy smiled. Now Katherine was saying something she understood. They decided on a plan that was very simple. Katherine would talk to Roy and even pretend to like him again. Boys were stupid that way so it would be easy to fool him into thinking she liked him and besides he was a good kisser. If that happened again, Katherine really wouldn't mind. Sooner or later he'd tell her something that would be useful and then they'd use Katherine's friends to tell stories about Roy and Martin.

This conversation was near the middle of May and within a week Katherine had talked to Roy twice.

"Did you kiss him again?" asked Cindy, giggling.

Katherine nodded.

"Did he stick his tongue in your mouth?"

Katherine nodded.

"Did you feel anything? Like anywhere else in your body?"

Katherine nodded and turned red. The two girls laughed. After Katherine lost the colour in her face, she got serious again.

"I asked him about how he was feeling and was he all better after Doug hit him and he told me that his little brother is always trying to get him to fight older boys in order to impress Martin's friends. I asked him if he was scared of Doug and he said no but I think he really is. He said he's a pacifist like his older brother Basil."

Cindy smiled. "I bet I could get Doug mad real easy. He's very sensitive about his mother. I could tell him Roy said something. Doug likes me and he always wants to neck."

"No, not you. This is where my friends come in," said Katherine. "If we say the right thing to the right ones, then they will say something to someone who will say it to Doug. That way no one ever knows, but you and me, what's really going on. Get it?"

Cindy nodded and smiled. She got it.

Roy, letter 11

Oct. 22, 1962

Dear President Kennedy,

I can't sleep so I'm writing this at the kitchen table. I may have to finish it in the morning if my mom catches me. After 10 on a school night I'm supposed to be in bed. All that stuff you talked about missiles and nuclear weapons really scared me. Have you seen pictures of Hiroshima and Nagasaki? Paul says his Mom says those missiles in Cuba could hit here and Moose Jaw would be a target cause of the air force base. Is that true? I don't think it's fair to die before you become a teenager. I'm going to continue with the story. I'd rather think about that. So, here it is.

"Two more days of school," said Martin. "Two more days!"

"You don't like school?" said Brian, as he sat on the back steps waiting for me. I was in the porch getting my stuff together.

"He likes school," said Basil, stepping out of the house through the screen door. "But he likes summer holidays even more, right Martin?"

My little brother nodded as he took the newspaper from Basil.

"I'll be out in a few minutes," I shouted from inside the house.

"The papers were late today, so he just got back ten minutes ago," said Basil.

"No hurry," said Brian.

"Nice glove," said Basil.

"Ya, my new catcher's mitt," said Brian " You want to try it on? Just got it yesterday. My uncle from Minneapolis sent it to me after my Dad told him I was trying out for the all-star team. Professional quality. He played for the Winnipeg Goldeyes."

"Roy says you're pretty good," said Basil.

"Funny how no one noticed until I got a chance to play," said Brian.

"Ain't that always the way," said Basil.

"Roy says you're a great pitcher," said Brian.

"Not good enough to make the Regals," said Basil. "Doesn't matter. There's no team at the U. of S. anyway and that's where I'm headed in a couple of months."

"You finished all your exams?" said Brian.

"One more departmental that's it," said Basil. "Social studies, so I don't even need to study."

"I can hardly wait till I'm in high school," said Brian.

"I can hardly wait until I'm in university," said Basil.

"What are you going to take?"

"Everything probably. Political science and history, but I get my best marks in math and science," said Basil.

"I hear you won a scholarship," said Brian.

"Ya," said Basil. "The Robin Hood scholarship."

"One for all the 500 families of people working at Robin Hood," I shouted from the other side of the screen door. "And Basil won it."

"How much is it worth?" said Brian.

"Not enough," said Basil. "Covers tuition and a little more, but I've been saving up plus I got a job at the CPR this summer. Clerk."

"What does this mean?" said Martin, showing Basil a story on the front page of the paper. "'Algiers exo ...'"

"Exodus," said Basil. "It means leaving, usually a bunch of people at once."

"'Algiers exodus begins as explosives hit Oran,'" read Martin.

"Remember I told you about the French settlers leaving Algeria?" said Basil.

"Cause the people who were like the Indians were gonna get their country back from the French colorists?" said Martin.

"Colonists," said Basil.

"Colonists," said Martin. "They don't want to give the land back and there's been lots of people killed and stuff."

"He remembers everything," Basil said proudly to Brian. "Don't you?"

Martin shrugged.

"The Algerians have won their independence and now a lot of the colonists are leaving, but they're blowing up stuff cause they're mad about having to go," said Basil. "Algeria has been a French colony even longer than Saskatchewan has been a province and some of those settlers have lived there for generations, so they think the country belongs to them."

"Isn't that the part of the car that Dad got fixed last week?" said Martin.

"What?" said Basil.

"Generations," said Martin.

"Generator," said Basil, smiling. "The part of the car that makes electricity. A generation is the time it takes for someone to grow up and have their own kids."

"You're in one generation, then your Mom and Dad are in another and your grandparents in a third," said Brian.

Martin nodded and went back to looking at the newspaper.

"Is that a good book?" said Brian, looking at the volume in Basil's hands.

"Bertrand Russell 'On Happiness.' It's great," said Basil. "You ever read Russell?"

Brian shook his head.

"My favourite philosopher. He makes ideas simple instead of complicated."

"What's it about?" said Brian.

"On Happiness?" said Basil holding up the book. "Exactly what the title says. Happiness, what is it? How do you know if you have it? What parts are individual and what parts collective? All his stuff stimulates you to think for yourself, that's what's so great about it. Some philosophers, it's a struggle to understand what they mean, all your energy goes towards comprehension. But when I read Russell it's like he opens doors and you get to look inside. Usually something I never saw before."

"Same way I feel about Chopin," said Brian.

"Roy says you're a pianist," said Basil.

"People think he's hard to play and you do need good technique, but once you get inside his composition, he opens doors just like you describe Russell," said Brian.

"I've been told musicians think in sounds, instead of words."

"Music is a language that allows you to express things words can't," said Brian.

"Isn't that the goal of every great writer?" said Basil. "To find words to express what before was only felt? Or seen? Or only expressed as music?"

"Roy said you want to be a writer," said Brian.

"Some day, maybe," said Basil. "So does Roy."

"What does this mean?" said Martin, reading from the paper. "'Four counter rev…'"

"Counter-revolutionaries," said Basil, looking over Martin's shoulder.

"'Four counter-revolutionaries with $25,000 in cash'," said Martin. "'Four captured by Cubans.'"

"Counter-revolutionaries are people against the revolution," said Basil.

"Counter means against," said Brian.

"Roy said a counter was someone who is counting or the place in the store where you pay for the stuff you bought," said Martin.

"It means that when it's a noun," said Basil. "When it's an adjective it means against or the opposite."

Martin looked at his older brother like he was crazy. "How can a counter be a sister?" he said.

"What?" said Basil.

"You said when counter was a nun," I said, coming out of the house. I could always figure out Martin better than Basil.

"Ya," said Martin.

Brian smiled.

"Noun, not nun," said Basil to Martin. "A noun is a word that is an object or a person or a thing."

"Don't bother," I said, putting on my baseball glove. "I've tried explaining grammar, but it's no use. Give him another year."

"One word can have lots of different meanings," said Basil.

"I know that," Martin said sharply, reacting to his older brother's condescending tone. "I'm not a baby."

Our baby brother was angry. Basil raised his hands as if surrendering, then disappeared into the house.

"I didn't mean anything bad," said Basil from inside.

"You guys always talk like I'm stupid," said Martin.

"That's not true. We think you're very smart," I said.

"He told me that," said Brian. "Honest. He told me you're the smartest just-about-seven-year old in the whole city."

"Some things just don't make sense until you're nine and other things until you're twelve," I said.

"And some when you're seventeen?" said Martin.

"Ya, probably," I answered. "I can barely do calculus, but that doesn't make me stupid."

I remembered how frustrating it was to have an older brother who knew everything.

"I guess we better get going," I said to Brian. "Is that your new catcher's mitt?"

Martin was still sulking.

"You want to come with us to all-star practice or not?" I said to Martin. "Coach might let you be batboy when we start playing games. Maybe go to tournaments."

"Okay," said Martin, still sulking "Should I bring my glove?"

"Sure," I said. "And tell Mom you're going with me."

Martin disappeared inside the house. Brian handed me his new glove.

"It's stiff," I said, trying it on.

"Help me break it in," said Brian.

"We've got two weeks until the city playoffs," I said. "We can play catch everyday and then there's practice."

"If I make the team," said Brian.

"You've already made it," I said. "I told you."

Martin reappeared from the house.

"Let's go," I said. "Coach gets ticked if we're late."

We walked down Brown Street towards the park that was on Grafton across the street from Uncle Gregor's house. I didn't know how the coach would react to the idea of Martin as batboy, but Aunt Myrtle always welcomed us with cookies and lemonade.

"Basil didn't tell me what that story meant," said Martin. "Why did the counter-revolutionaries have $25,000?"

"They're working for the Americans," I said.

"The CIA," said Brian.

"You remember the CIA?" I said.

"Spies," said Martin.

"They give these counter-revolutionaries a whole bunch of money to bribe people," said Brian. "To cause trouble for the Cuban revolution."

"Remember what I told you about Fidel Castro?" I said.

"The Americans and the cannibalists hate him cause he's trying to help the poor people instead of the rich guys," said Martin.

Brian smiled at Martin's new word.

"The word is capitalist," I said.

"I know that," said Martin, smiling too. "But cannibalist sounds better."

I rubbed my little brother's head. The little guy could surprise you.

"Hey Martin, hey Roy, hey Brian," said Sam, who was sitting on the back steps of the Elgin Park Grocery and Confectionary.

"Hey Sam," said Martin.

"Where are you guys going?"

"Baseball practice," I said.

"Brian and Roy are trying out for the all-star team," said Martin.

"You going through the park?" said Sam.

"Ya," I said.

"The Mackies might be there," said Sam.

I shrugged.

"We're not scared of them," said Martin.

"Steve says we're gonna fight em next week," said Sam.

I looked at Martin.

"He says four of their toughest guys will be going away first week of summer holidays," said Martin. "So that's the best time to fight."

"Steve says if you can handle Kevin, we can wipe out the rest of them," said Sam.

"Steve's your fight manager?" said Brian. "You give him a cut of the purse?"

"See ya," I said to Sam as we headed across Ninth Avenue.

I didn't say anything to Martin until we got to the schoolyard.

"You knew about Steve's plan?" I said. "When were you going to tell me?"

"Steve talks a lot," said Martin.

"Has he talked to Mike or Kevin? Or to one of their little lieutenants?" I said.

"Maybe," said Martin.

"So maybe when's the fight?" I said.

"Maybe Monday," said Martin. "Maybe first day of summer holidays."

"Maybe what time?" I said.

"Maybe two o'clock, or maybe not if you have practice then," said Martin.

"Awfully considerate of him," said Brian.

I looked at my new best friend and then at my little brother.

"You still think big families are wonderful?" I said.

"You told me to let Steve be leader of the gang," said Martin.

"I told you to let him think he was the leader," I said. "But he was supposed to talk to you before making any decisions. And you were supposed to talk him out of doing anything stupid."

"I did," said Martin.

"What did you talk him out of?" I said.

"He wanted to fight on Friday night, last day of school," said Martin. "But I said that's a stupid plan."

"How is it any stupider than fighting Monday?" said Brian.

"Cause next week the doctors are going on strike," said Martin.

"And?" I said.

"Mark Collins said all the doctors and their families are going to Regina for a big valley," said Martin.

Brian looked at me.

"I think he means rally," I said. "A big rally."

"Mark and his big brother Frank and Dave Hendry, all of them are gone next week," said Martin.

"Hendry's Dad isn't a doctor," I said. "He's a trapper."

"But Paulie's Dad and his Dad are going up north for two weeks to fix up their cabin," said Martin. "Paulie's been talking about it for months. He's gonna get to sleep in a tent."

"Paulie for Dave Hendry, plus Mark and Frank Collins, that's a pretty good trade," I said.

Martin smiled,

"If we had to fight," I said. "Which we don't. We're better off ignoring them. Let them have the park for a week or two, then they'll start fighting among themselves. Everyone hates the Mackies."

"What about Sam?" said Martin.

"What about him?" I said.

"They beat him up once already."

"Who did?" I said.

"Called him chinky, chinky Chinaman and pushed him off the swings," said Martin.

"Who did?"

"He wouldn't tell me," said Martin. "They said he'd get it again if he told. And they scared his grandma."

"How do you know it was kids from Mackie's gang?" said Brian.

"They told Sam he couldn't play in the park anymore, cause it belonged to the Mackie gang and they don't allow no chinks or kids from the west side of Ninth Avenue," said Martin.

"Why didn't you tell me this before?" I said.

"Sam just told me after school and you were delivering papers," said Martin.

"Some kids are always picking on Sam," I said to Brian.

"Nazis," said Brian. "Like they did to the Jews. 'The Chinaman is the Jew of the West,' that's what my Grandpa says."

"We don't like Nazis, do we Roy?" said Martin. "They're mean."

"Very mean," said Brian.

"You and Basil said socialists have got to fight the Nazis, right Roy?" said Martin. "You said that."

I nodded. The little guy was annoying sometimes. The three of us said nothing for the next two blocks. I started throwing the ball up in the air as we walked down Hall Street. I was feeling guilty.

Truth was last winter I had joined in with a gang of kids from east of the park as they banged on the billboard outside the Elgin Park Grocery and Confectionary. I too had chanted 'chinky, chinky chinamen" and laughed. What had Sam and his grandma thought about that? Were they scared? It was mean. I was mean. Why had I done it? Because the other kids did? That's pretty stupid. Dad and Mr. and Mrs. Wong are friends. Dad's best friend back in Lancer when he was 12 was Chinese. Dad told that story a hundred times. About how Grandpa didn't like Chinese cause he fought in the Russian Japanese War. About how that made Grandpa prejudiced just like Americans were prejudiced against negroes. I should have known better.

"'If you let the Nazis get away with one thing they'll try to get away with everything,' that's what Basil said," said Martin, who had obviously been trying to remember the exact words. "Right Roy?"

"You're right," I said. "That's what Basil said."

Brian looked at me.

"So that's what we believe, right Roy?" said Martin.

I nodded.

"So we gotta fight em," said Martin. "We gotta."

I made eye contact with Brian. I felt embarrassed, as if some secret had escaped from a deep, dark place where the bogeyman lived and no one else was allowed to enter.

I threw the ball up in the air, as high as I could, then competed with Brian and his new mitt to catch it. We both missed and it fell to the ground, rolling down the hill towards the diamond at the bottom, where a crowd of kids were gathered, waiting for the first all-star tryout practice to begin.

As we ran down the hill, a kid picked up my ball. Brian stopped running as he was the first to get close enough to recognize him.

It was Mike Mackie.

"He's trying out?" said Brian.

I tried to look cool. I held up my glove and made eye contact with Mackie. After a few seconds he threw the ball to me.

"This ought to be interesting," said Brian to Martin as they made it to the bottom of the hill.

Katherine, letter 7

October 20, 1962

Dear President Kennedy,

I visited my father in Regina today and he says something very important is happening in the world and that it could mean war with Russia. He says it is about time and that the Reds should have been wiped off the face of the earth years ago.

I'd just like you to know that you have our support in whatever it is you must do.

Here is the next part of my story.

Within a few days Katherine had second thoughts about their plan. While Cindy was happy, having Roy beaten up by someone older and bigger than him just did not seem important or useful. Maybe it was even wrong. Perhaps if it was for a good cause it could be justified. But what was the point of Doug hitting Roy a few more times and maybe knocking him out again? Katherine had already seen that once.

"I've been having second thoughts," she said to Cindy as they sat in her mother's rumpus room drinking iced tea. "Maybe we should tell the girls that it isn't really true, that Roy never said anything about Doug's mother."

"No," said Cindy. "It's worked perfectly and it's too late anyway. Mary-Anne from William Grayson told her friend Elizabeth who is in the same choir as Doug and she is the biggest blabbermouth in the whole world so I'm sure she's already said something to him. They had choir practice today after school."

"I'm just not sure what the point of a fight is," said Katherine.

"To scare him," said Cindy. "To serve him right. To make him scared to walk around the neighborhood like I've been ashamed to because of what Martin said."

"It just seems like we could aim for something bigger, something more important," said Katherine.

Cindy got a look on her face as she stared at Katherine.

"Are you sweet on him again?" she finally said. "He kissed you again and made you feel all mushy and now you don't want to hurt his sweet angel face."

"No," said Katherine, but she had to admit it was a little bit true. She did like kissing him, even if he was a socialist. He was strong and smart and gentle and tasted good. When Doug had kissed her he was rough and pushed his teeth against hers and it was uncomfortable, not dreamy nice. And he'd just smoked a cigarette, which made the taste rather revolting. Of course Katherine never said anything to Cindy about that kiss.

"You've turned to Jello because he kissed you," said Cindy. "All wiggly, jiggly inside."

As Cindy was teasing her Katherine had another thought. Perhaps Cindy doesn't need to know everything that is happening either. Perhaps Cindy can think that having Roy beaten up is all that this plan is about, but something more can be happening. That could be useful. It's better if Cindy doesn't know what's really going on. A secret is always safest when only one person knows it. Her father had told her that. Katherine could use Cindy just like the other girls were being used.

So Katherine said nothing more to Cindy, not even the following week when everyone heard about the big fight on Tenth Avenue that never really happened. Of course Cindy was mad when she learned that Roy had only been pushed down and was even madder when Doug told her that he and Roy had joined forces to protect themselves against the kids from the other side of Elgin Park.

"That's terrible," Katherine said, trying to make Cindy feel better.

"All you care about is your boyfriend not getting a fat lip," replied Cindy. "You're worried that he won't be able to kiss you for a week."

"I just kiss him to get information," said Katherine.

"Sure," said Cindy. "And let him stick his tongue down your throat."

"That's gross," said Katherine.

"Gross and true," said Cindy.

Cindy is not very smart, thought Katherine. She can't see the bigger picture. But she will be useful. And that's good enough.

"He told me that he made up the story about kids from the other side of the park," said Katherine. "Roy told me exactly what he said about Mike Mackie. I think we can use it to get Mike and his big brother really mad at Roy."

That brought a smile to Cindy's face.

"They say Kevin Mackie is the meanest boy in all Moose Jaw," said Katherine.

"He's been sent to reform school twice," said Cindy. "They say he burned a cat to death."

"That's awful," said Katherine.

"Ya," said Cindy, but she had a smile on her face. "He's a lot more scary than Doug. Doug's big but he sings in a choir. He's got a beautiful voice. No one is scared of a beautiful voice."

What Katherine did not tell Cindy was that her new plan involved much more than the Mackie brothers. And while making Roy worry about the Mackie brothers might be useful as part of her bigger plan, it was really only a diversion, like when robbers in a cowboy movies did something to make sure the sheriff was out of town when they hit the bank.

What Katherine did not tell Cindy, and what she would not have understood anyway, was that the new Moose Jaw Keep Our Doctors committee had begun meeting. All the doctors in the province had vowed to shut their practices on July 1 if the CCF government went ahead with its plan for socialized medicine. Katherine had joined the committee and was the youngest person on it. She had volunteered to get at least one student from every school in the city to attend at least one meeting of the committee. With all her friends that would be easy. While most of the adults on the committee did not seem to think students were important, Katherine believed otherwise and her father agreed with her.

"Make someone an anti-communist when they are thirteen and you'll have an anti-communist for life," he said.

But there was much more to Katherine's plan than that. While adults never gave young people much credit, she knew teenagers could do a lot if they put their minds to it.

Roy, letter 12

Oct. 23, 1962

Dear President Kennedy,

I just put the letter I wrote last night into the mailbox on the way to school, so I know you might not have it before you get this, but could you please read them in order or they won't make much sense. I'm starting this at school, during English class. I want to finish the story before these Cuban missiles lead to World War III and the world ends. So here goes again.

By the third practice on Sunday it was clear who would make the North-West All Stars. I was the best pitcher in the league, undefeated all season with three no-hitters and also a good infielder, able to play every position. Brian was easily the best catcher and also the fastest player. Both of us would be starters. The guy who surprised me was Mike Mackie. He was third best pitcher, not fast, but could throw a good roundhouse curve that broke almost six inches, perfect to go the last inning or two in a close game. It would take opponents at least one at-bat to figure out the curve. Plus, with his good arm he was excellent in centre field and he hit with power, the only guy during batting practice who could regularly clear the fence. The team would be better if Mackie was on it, but pretty much everybody hated him or was scared of him. The question was: Should that matter? Wasn't fairness more important than liking someone or fear of bullies?

I spent hours thinking about it and once my mind was made up I had to follow through, no matter who got angry. So, when Sunday afternoon practice was over it was only a matter of waiting for the best time to say it.

"Who do you think made the team?" said Brian as we walked back to his place.

"We'll find out tomorrow," I said.

"I'll bet we can name them," said Brian. "It's not as if there's a lot of close calls."

"Some," I said.

"Something bugging you?" said Brian. "You've been somewhere else all day."

So I said it.

"Mackie is good enough to make the team," I said.

Brian shook his head.

"He's third best pitcher."

"We don't need a third pitcher," said Brian. "You and Frank are enough."

"In tournaments you need two starters plus a guy who can come in just in case."

"Johnny pitched for the Reds," said Brian.

"He's got control but he's too slow and has no junk," I said. "He got me out once in two games and that was on a line drive to shortstop."

"But he can pitch, if we need him, and he's a good third baseman."

"He should make the team, but we still need Mackie," I said. "We have no one else who can hit home runs."

"He's got power but he strikes out half the time," said Brian.

"Like Hank Aaron," I said.

"There's no way he makes the team. Coach hates him," said Brian.

"Coach hates Mike's brother. Basil says Kevin dumped sand in his gas tank two summers ago. Coach had to get the engine rebuilt."

"Mike's name won't be on the team list when it's posted," said Brian.

"But he deserves to be," I said. "The team will be better if he's on it."

"He's a Nazi," said Brian. "Calls me 'jewboy' right to my face. Plus we know it was him that threatened Sam and called him a 'chink'."

"Mike is an asshole and a bully," I said. "Kevin's been pounding on him his whole life. His old man is a drunk who stabbed a guy and got ten years in the P.A. jail."

"But you think he should be on our team?" said Brian.

"He's good enough and ..."

"You think Nazis ought to be treated fairly?" said Brian. "The way they treat us?"

"Us?" I said.

"Jews, socialists, Chinese, kids from the other side of Ninth Avenue," said Brian.

"If his name is not on the list, I'll talk to coach," I said. "I have to. It wouldn't be right. Basil agrees."

"I don't believe it," said Brian. "You're siding with a Nazi?"

"You think the coaches care if Mike calls you or Sam names? Our head coach talks about 'Jews this and Jews that' all the time and would never give Sam a chance cause he says 'chinks can't see straight through their crooked eyes'. Our assistant calls me 'square head' cause my ancestors back eight generations came from Germany and both coaches belong to the Orange Order, which makes damn sure Catholics don't get any of the good jobs at the CPR. Plus both of them come from families that helped break the Swift's strike. They hate Mackie cause his family is trash, not because he's a Nazi."

"So ten wrongs make a right?" said Brian. "We owe Mackie nothing. And I don't want him on my team."

"Your team?"

"Ya, when I make it," said Brian.

"Our team," I said. "And I say he deserves a chance."

"Is this just another scheme to avoid fighting his gang?" said Brian. "Suck up to Mike and become friends like you did with Doug?"

He could bait me all he wanted but I was not falling for it.

"There's better ways to avoid a fight," said Brian. "Who cares about the park?"

"I'm not scared of fighting and I'm not scared of getting beat up," I said. "I just don't like it when people are treated unfairly."

"Sometimes you have to take sides and Mike Mackie is not on ours."

"Because he called you and Sam a name? You don't think lots of kids have done that and maybe you just haven't heard them?"

"What are you getting at?" said Brian.

"Mackie should be given a chance," I said.

"A chance to play?"

"A chance to listen to what we have to say. My Dad has stories about lots of guys who were anti-union and then came around. You don't think it's possible?"

"With Mackie? He hates me."

"Hates?" I said.

"Ya," said Brian. "Hates. Not cause of anything I've done, but because of who he thinks I am. You've never experienced that because you're not …"

"Not Jewish?"

"Not Jewish, not Chinese, not Negro."

I stared at my friend. Maybe he was right. Mackie was a jerk. But, everyone I trust says people deserve a second chance and a third chance. Forgiveness is the best part of being Catholic. Just last week in religion class Sister Agnes said: "If a person is given a chance to do good, he'll do it." I believe that. I have to, because how could the world change if a person can't change?

But Brian didn't want to listen and I couldn't get into the whole forgiveness thing without sounding too Catholic. Maybe Brian and I could be friends, but not best friends.

So when he asked if I wanted to have supper with him and his Dad, I said no, I had to go home for Sunday dinner. My Mom had made chicken and rice, my favourite, which was true, and I wasn't allowed to eat at other people's houses on Sunday nights, which was not.

The next morning I walked to practice alone. Coach said the team list would be posted at 10:00 a.m. and the practice would begin at 10:30 so I made sure I arrived at 9:45. A few minutes later both coaches arrived in Mr. Roberts' car.

"Hi Roy," said Mr. Dixon.

"Hi Mr. Dixon," I said.

"You're here early," said Mr. Roberts. "You worried about making the team?"

I shrugged.

"We phoned everyone who was cut last night," said Mr. Roberts. "Wouldn't want them to come out today and learn they weren't on the team."

"Did you call Mike?" I said.

"Mackie?" said Mr. Roberts. "You don't have to worry about him."

He handed me a typed list. Mackie's name was not on it.

"You see I chose you for captain?" said Mr. Roberts.

"Thanks," I said.

"You're smart, you understand the game," said Mr. Roberts. "And the other boys respect you."

"Mr. Roberts?" I said.

"What is it?"

"I think Mike Mackie deserves to be on the team," I said. "He's third best pitcher and our best power hitter and it's not his fault about Kevin."

The coach looked at me like I was nuts. "He's a decent player but there are other factors we take into account. Team morale. Discipline. You know how disruptive the Mackies can be." Mr. Dixon was a referee during hockey season and had probably told Mr. Roberts about the fights I had with Mike. "In the bigger picture we're better off without him. Most of the players are scared of him, your friend Brian for example. We can't have our speedy little Jew catcher scared of his own teammate."

Why did coach have to call Brian Jewish every time he spoke about him? Wasn't that prejudice? "Is Brian Jewish?" I said.

"A Jew Communist is what I'm told," said Mr. Roberts, lowering his voice. "My brother-in-law works for Cohen's Furriers and he hears all the gossip. Even his own kind are uncomfortable about Brian's father."

"But you didn't hold that against his son, right?" I said. "You picked him for the team because he's the best catcher and we have a better chance of winning the city championship because of that, right? You're not prejudiced against Jews, are you Mr. Roberts?"

He looked trapped. "Prejudice is wrong," he answered, after a moment.

"And just because somebody called his Dad a communist, that wouldn't be a good reason to keep Brian off the team, would it Mr. Roberts?"

"Of course not," he answered. "The doctors went on strike yesterday and they're calling the premier of the province a communist."

"You believe in giving everyone a fair chance, right Mr. Roberts? So boys grow up into the kind of adults that future generations need?"

"You were listening at the end-of-season banquet last year," he said.

"Basil says you were the most fair coach he ever played for," I said.

"Basil has a great arm," said Mr. Roberts. "And he's smart, like all the Schmidt boys."

"I need a favour," I said.

"If I can," said Mr. Roberts.

"Give Mike Mackie a chance to play on the team."

"Roy ..."

"Please Mr. Roberts," I said. "I'll talk to him and explain the situation and I'll vouch for his good behavior and if he messes up, I'll tell him the kids voted him off the team so he doesn't blame you and tell his brother."

Coach stared at me as if I were completely crazy.

"Please Mr. Roberts," I said.

"Why? He hates your guts. Why are you sticking your neck out for him?"

I shrugged. "Do unto others as I would have them do unto me." It was my last talk with Sister Veronica. I promised to give religion another chance, to give God another chance. "And I think we have a better chance of winning the city championships if he's on the team."

"Will he listen to you? About team rules?"

"I don't know, but I can try," I said. "He doesn't live far away."

"You want to go over there now?"

I nodded.

"What would you say?"

I hadn't really thought about it, so I said the first thing that popped into my brain. "I'll tell him we had a team meeting and everybody wants him to play, but only if he follows the rules."

Coach gave me a look.

"It's better if he thinks everybody on the team wants him to play," I said.

"He'll slug you and then get Kevin to pound the crap out of you."

"Kevin is scared of Basil so he leaves me alone," I said.

"Maybe I should talk with Basil," said Mr. Roberts.

"I heard Kevin got caught breaking and entering and is probably going to juvenile detention again," I said. "Basil told me six months cause it's his third time."

Mr. Roberts shook his head. "What a family."

"His mother is nice," I said. "She works at the beach concession every summer and at the Civic Centre in the winter."

"I guess raising two kids with a husband in jail ..." Coach thought of something and made up his mind. "Okay, go try. Say what you said about the players meeting, but also say I want him on the team, if he follows all the rules. Say he'll be the starting centre fielder, bat fifth and pitch in later innings if we need him. Until he breaks one rule. He gets one chance, that's it."

I nodded.

"Go."

The rest of the team was crowded around the dugout looking at the list as Mr. Roberts walked towards them.

"Listen up, that list is not final," coach said loudly. "We're still considering our options, depending on certain discussions."

I stared at my new teammates. Brian stared back.

"So don't get too comfortable," said coach. "Every one of you is still competing for a spot."

Mr. Roberts looked at me and made a slight "get going" motion with his head. I broke eye contact with Brian and began walking quickly towards Mackie's house. They lived in a war-time house across the street from the "Ten Commandments" a row of identical buildings a few blocks from the diamond. As I stood facing the Mackie house, I was scared. Maybe this was stupid. Still, I was here. Better to try and fail, than to be scared of doing what you thought was right.

Mike appeared at the door almost the exact instant my knuckle struck the screen. "What do you want?" he said.

"It's about the all-star team," I said.

"Keep it down, my Mom is sleeping," said Mike. "She worked all night." He came out on to the front steps. "You're going to rub it in?"

I shook my head.

"I just think you should be on the team cause of your arm and your bat. You deserve it. Everyone on the team agrees."

Mike stared. "Is this some kind of trick?" he finally said.

I shook my head. "Coach agrees too, but only under certain conditions."

"I don't care about your stupid baseball team," said Mike.

"You deserve to be on the team, but some guys are scared of you. They think you're going to hurt them," I said. "They think you're tough and got a bad temper, but I played against you in hockey and baseball for a couple of years and I know you play fair. And you fight fair, at least against me, so I can't hold that against you either."

That look. What was Mike thinking?

"Point is we want you on the team so long as you follow rules, just like everyone else," I said.

"So why did I get a phone call last night saying I'm cut?"

"Cause coach is scared of Kevin and thinks, you know, he'll get sand in the tank again," I said.

"I never had anything to do with that," said Mike. "And no one ever proved Kevin did either. He gets blamed for lots of things."

It was good he stuck up for his brother, even if Kevin was the rottenest bully in Moose Jaw.

"Doesn't matter who did it," I said. "Coach is scared of Kevin."

"He got sentenced to six months and is leaving Wednesday."

He tried to look cold, but I could see Mike would miss his big brother.

"Must be tough on your Mom," I said.

"A lot of crying and screaming, if you know what I mean."

I nodded.

"Is that it?" said Mike, after an awkward silence.

"No," I said. "But go get your glove and I'll tell you the rest on the way to the diamond."

Mike was good at giving a blank look that hid whatever he felt.

"If you change your mind you can always swear at the coach or punch one of the guys and get kicked off the team," I said, my pulse twice normal.

Mike almost smiled.

"I'll be right back," he finally said and disappeared into the house.

My heart was still racing when Mike reappeared with his extremely worn, but once good quality glove.

"Coach is prejudiced against Jews and Catholics," I said, beginning the next tricky subject with the first words that popped into my head. "Which really pisses off Brian and me and some of the other guys who are Jews or Catholics," I said, fast so as to not let Mike say anything. "Which I'm sure you can understand cause I know the way some guys pick on you just cause your brother or your Dad … well, you know. It's not right that people judge you cause of some stupid idea they heard about 'people like that' or whatever. Makes me feel bad when somebody says all Catholics are going to hell, just like it makes Brian feel rotten if someone claims all Jews are greedy or you when some asshole says to you 'like father like son' or some other stupid ass comment."

I slowed down to catch my breath, but then started back up when Mike was about to speak.

"The point is who cares if somebody believes ignorant stuff like that. Keep it to themselves I say, at least when other people are around. I mean, like on a baseball team where you have all kinds of guys, Ukrainians, Germans, English, Irish, Scots, Catholics, Anglicans, Jews, Italians, Chinese, United Church, socialists, capitalists, French, Swedes, who knows how many, the best things to do is just stay away from that sort of stuff, right? That's the safest thing to do."

Was this sinking in? Mike was no dummy, but who knew?

"Be friends or at least be friendly, that's the way for a team to act towards each other, right? Everyone knows a team has a better chance of winning if players get along. I mean that's not exactly rocket science, is it? Even Grade Threes know that."

Mike's face was hard to read.

"So you'd think the coach would get it, wouldn't you?" I mean he's the guy who's supposed to think about stuff like that, right?"

"Supposed to," said Mike nodding.

"You think I should say something?" I said. "Coach made me captain so I guess if I said like a captain's speech, it wouldn't seem too weird. What do you think?"

Mike thought about it for a moment. "Sure, if you think it's a problem," he said. "Better you say something at the start. Like a team rule, for everybody, coaches too. Like a ref at a boxing match coming out and telling both guys no low blows."

"Exactly," I said.

"We don't have to be friends, but we should act like ones," said Mike.

The plan seemed to be working.

"At least while we're on the same team," continued Mike. "Anyone with half a brain understands that."

We were at the park. The players were running. Mr. Roberts was standing beside the dugout. I made eye contact. You know how you can say something without saying something? That's what I did. I let him know Mike had agreed.

Katherine, letter 8

October 24, 1962

Dear President Kennedy,

I am so glad that you are stopping all ships from going to Cuba. My father says this should have been done long ago and he only hopes that you have a good plan for invading the island as well. That Communist Castro needs to be crushed.

So many people are scared of a nuclear war, but I think all the so-called fear is really just a Communist plot. The Communists want us to be scared so that we back down. But real Americans do not back down from a fight. Better dead than Red, is what my father says and I agree with him. The Communists must be the ones who are scared of us. The enemies of freedom must understand that we are strong and fearless in defending our liberty. They must know we are powerful and are prepared to use our power.

This leads perfectly to the next part of my story.

Katherine was very busy during the end of May and all of June preparing for July 1 when all the physicians of Saskatchewan were to withdraw their services. She invited girls from every school to her house and her mother provided beverages, hors d'œuvre and wonderful sandwiches, which impressed everyone very much.

While some of the girls were reluctant to criticize the government, everyone agreed that it must have done something wrong to make the doctors so angry. Everyone agreed that doctors were nice, kind, important and necessary people. They talked about what should be done and Katherine was very confident that most of the girls would talk about the situation to their friends, classmates and parents. More than a dozen of the parents and two teachers joined the Keep our Doctors committee as a result and everyone was very impressed by Katherine's work.

But that was only a small part of what Katherine accomplished. She was even more proud of the work that nobody, not even her father knew about.

Despite how busy she was with school, her clubs and the KOD committee, Katherine made sure she spent time every week with Roy. Every few days she found a way to be alone with him. He never, not once, made any effort to be with her. At first she thought it was because he didn't really like her, but then she realized it was because he was immature, like all boys his age. She had to remember that even though he was in the same grade as her, he was almost a year younger. She was mature for her age and that made her more like a boy who was fifteen or sixteen, rather than one who had not even turned thirteen.

Still, she continued to pretend that she liked him. They kissed and she let him put his tongue in her mouth, but that was as far as she would let him go. Not that he ever tried to go any further.

But mostly they talked. Or he talked. He liked to go on and on about his ideas, which were just his older brother Basil's ideas. He was so foolish, but she never said anything. Katherine's mother had once told her that the surest way to a man's heart was by pretending to be interested in everything he had to say and that certainly seemed true with Roy. But Katherine was not after his heart but rather his information.

Roy talked on and on about his father's union and Basil's plans to help the government if the doctors went on strike. This was the information she wanted and the reason why she let him kiss her. Loose lips sink ships. Her father often said that and now she knew why, or at least had a pretty good idea. Her loose lips were going to sink the socialists' ship.

So far the information she obtained had been interesting, but not all that useful. Her father was pleased with some of it because he said it confirmed what the doctors of Saskatchewan already knew. The government was making plans to bring in socialist doctors from Great Britain. Some unions were talking about setting up community clinics to hire those socialist doctors, which, her father said, went to prove that the CCF's secret plan was to put all doctors on the government payroll, just like in Communist Russia. And some of Basil's friends were talking about getting even with doctors who closed their practices. Her father was most interested in the last part and asked her where she got the information. She told him the truth, but only a small piece of it. She said she heard it from a boy in her class. He told her to listen very carefully to what that boy had to say because it could prove important. Katherine was very happy that her father was pleased and knew her plan was working, even if she could not tell anyone exactly what it was.

To keep Cindy happy Katherine also used her network of friends to make sure the Mackie brothers were angry at Roy and Martin. She spread the rumour that the kids from the west side of Ninth Avenue were claiming Elgin Park for themselves and were prepared to fight for it. Soon enough Roy told her all about how strange it was that he had made up a story about the Mackies to stop a fight and now it seemed the made-up story was coming true. One thing Katherine learned from this was that mysteries were useful. Roy spent a lot of time trying to figure out why the Mackies wanted to fight and preparing for it. It kept him worried. And because of that and baseball he and his friends had no time to get involved with his brother Basil's plan, which was good because it meant there were fewer soldiers in the other side's army, but bad because maybe he would have better information to pass along if he were planning mischief along with his brother. On balance Katherine thought it was a good thing because, from how Roy talked, Basil told him everything anyway. There were no secrets among the Schmidt brothers.

All in all Katherine was very pleased with how well her plan was working. But it wasn't until July 1 came and almost every doctor in the province withdrew his services that she learned exactly how valuable all her hard work had been.

Roy, letter 13

Oct. 23, 1962

Dear President Kennedy,

I finished the last letter at school today and now I'm writing this in my room at home. I skipped hockey practice and told Mom I was feeling sick. The paper today is full of stories about the "Cuban missile crisis" and I read every one of them. I can't believe this is really happening. If the USA and Soviet Union go to war and shoot missiles at each other the world could end in a nuclear winter. The paper had a picture of the missiles' range. They can't quite make it all the way to Moose Jaw, but they could hit Winnipeg. Brian has moved back there and I'd like to visit him, if the city still exists. I better get this story finished, so here goes.

Basil and my Dad were angry as can be the day the doctors strike started. While they complained about the doctors who stopped work, the Times Herald was what made them the maddest. You'd have thought the government was sending the doctors to slave camps the way the newspaper described it. "The Day That Freedom Died in Saskatchewan" was the editorial headline.

"It's okay for workers to have bosses standing over their shoulders telling them what to do every minute of the day, but doctors? You can't have the elected government telling them what to do," said Basil throwing the page at me.

"I just deliver the paper," I said. "I don't write it."

"Exactly," said Basil. "You've got to deliver the newspaper whether you agree with it or not. But 800 damn doctors go on strike against a law passed by the elected government and this stupid newspaper says the bloody bandits are fighting for frigging freedom."

"Watch your language," yelled our Mom from the kitchen.

"The boy is right," said Dad, who was drinking tea at the kitchen table.

"He may be right but he doesn't need to swear," said Mom.

"These darn doctors have taken the province hostage," Dad said loudly. "Somebody is going to die."

"It still doesn't excuse his language."

"We'll fix them," said Basil in a whisper so our parents couldn't hear.

"What do you mean?" I said as Martin stared at us.

Basil put his index finger in front of his mouth before speaking in an even lower voice. "The air has a way of escaping from the tires of those doctors who close their offices. And from the fascists behind this Keep Our Doctors committee."

I smiled, but Martin didn't understand.

"Or maybe a dead gopher gets dropped off on their doorsteps," whispered Basil.

"The company fired everybody and then closed the plant when Swift's workers went on strike," shouted Dad from the kitchen. "The paper didn't complain about that. Maybe that's what the government should do with the doctors."

"All sorts of things can happen in the middle of the night," said Basil, as he stood up from the chesterfield and walked into the kitchen.

"What does he mean?" said Martin.

"The doctors are trying to scare the government by closing their offices," I said quietly. "Basil is saying the people who like Medicare can scare them back."

"Have you heard from the union about starting a community clinic?" Basil said in a voice loud enough to be heard from the kitchen.

"What's a commune titty clinic?" said Martin.

"Community clinic," I said. "It's like a doctor's office, only run by the community. We hire the doctors and pay them a salary."

I could see Martin didn't understand.

"Most doctors own their office and run it like a business, the same as Mr. Ray's son runs the Kentucky Fried Chicken place down in River Park, to make a profit. The doctors say Medicare takes away their freedom to do business the way they want, to charge what they want."

"Does it?" said Martin.

"Hope so," I said. "Medicine shouldn't be a business; it should be a right, a public service. People need doctors when they're sick, even if they're too poor to pay. But the government is trying to have it both ways. They know the doctors want to run their offices as businesses so it passed a law allowing that, but makes them take payment from the government instead of the patients."

"So everybody can see a doctor when they need to, even if they don't have any money?" said Martin.

"Exactly," I said. "But the doctors don't care if this is good for people or not. All they care about is what's good for them. They think the government is weak. That's why Basil says we should set up community clinics and pay doctors like nurses, teachers or university professors. Why should doctors be special? They're refusing to see anybody at their offices so the government should set up community clinics everywhere as soon as possible. Hire doctors from England or other places and pay them a salary just like other workers."

"The government is too chicken shit to do it," said Basil, walking back into the living room.

"Basil!" Mom's voice boomed from the kitchen.

"He's right," said our father.

"It's up to unions and ordinary people to start clinics on our own," said Basil.

"Put pressure on the doctors," our father said. "Scare the greedy so and so's."

"Community clinics are better than fee-for-service," said Basil. "It's crazy that surgeons are paid by piece work. They make more money the more parts of you they cut out."

There was a knock at the back door.

"Roy," shouted Mom.

I went through the kitchen, into the porch and saw Brian on the back steps.

"Hey," I said. Brian hadn't been around in a few days, but I tried to pretend it was normal to see him.

"Hey," said Brian through the screen. "You want to walk to practice?"

"Sure," I said.

"Take your little brother," said Mom.

"Martin," I shouted. "Time for practice."

As we walked up Brown Street I waited for Brian to say something. Instead Martin rattled on.

"My big brother Basil is gonna use dead gophers to scare those doctors," he said to Brian. "They're scaring the poor people and the government so Basil is gonna scare them right back."

Brian looked at me and I shrugged.

"You shouldn't talk about that stuff," I said to Martin. "It's a secret. It's okay to tell Brian cause he's a socialist like us but not some of your friends. They might say something to the wrong person and get Basil in trouble."

"What does he mean?" said Brian.

"Basil and some guys are thinking about what they might do to show the doctors and that KOD committee how most people support Medicare," I said.

"Show?" said Brian.

"These store owners and businessmen and doctors are trying to intimidate the government by scaring people that they'll die if they get sick," I said. "Basil thinks it's time to show two sides can play that game."

"Game?" said Martin. "What do you mean?"

"Sometimes Martin, you shouldn't say exactly what you mean," said Brian. "Sometimes it's better to say something people can understand in a few different ways."

"It's a way of avoiding lies," I said, nodding.

Martin still didn't get our point.

"Like the time you and me didn't want Mom to know we opened our presents," I said. "She asked us what we wanted for Christmas and we said exactly what we knew she already bought us. Maybe the absolute honest answer would have been to say we already knew what she bought us, but that wouldn't have been very smart, would it?"

Martin shook his head.

"But we didn't lie, did we?" I said.

Martin shook his head again.

"Sometimes to avoid telling lies you say something open to interpretation," said Brian.

Again Martin was stumped.

"You do it all the time Martin, without even thinking about it," I said. "If you're going out with Steve to scare old Tom when he comes home drunk you don't say that, do you? You say, 'Mom I'm going out to play' or something like that. Right?"

Martin nodded.

"Why?" I said.

"Cause she'd yell at me," said Martin.

"You'd get in trouble for saying it and then if you still did it you'd get in even bigger trouble," I said.

"And if you said it, but didn't do it, but someone else did, you'd still get blamed, because the fact you said it would be proof you did it, even if you didn't," said Brian.

Martin's eyes revealed a new, more sophisticated level of understanding about truth and consequences.

"And just like you're protecting yourself from getting in trouble with Mom when you say 'I'm going out to play' instead of 'Steve and I are going to scare the crap out of old Tom when he comes home drunk' we're protecting Basil and ourselves by saying 'two sides can play that game' instead of 'Basil is planning to drop a stink bomb onto Dr. Wilson's back porch.'"

Martin stared. "What's a stink bomb?" he said.

"It's a bomb that makes a stink instead of an explosion," said Brian.

"How do you make it?" said Martin.

Brian shrugged. I shrugged. Martin stared for a moment.

"Are you lying or protecting yourselves?" said Martin.

Brian shrugged. I shrugged. Both of us smiled. What was the word Basil told me about this sort of thing? "Ambiguity." That was it. Ambiguity made me feel more powerful than simply telling the truth.

As I was contemplating the power of ambiguity, we could see a circle of kids at the corner of Hall and Connaught, just four houses away from where Mike Mackie lived.

"Are they waiting for us?" said Brian.

I shrugged.

"Maybe they're going to jump us," said Martin. "The Mackies never play fair."

"Act normal," I said. "Pretend like nothing is happening."

We walked silently towards the six of them, all probably under the age of 10. If this was an ambush, it was either very clever or really bad.

"Hey Roy," said one of them. "Hey Martin."

I nodded but couldn't remember the kid's name.

"Hey Fred," said Martin. "Hey Pete. Hey Johnny. Hey Allan. Hey George. Hey Brent. Are you waiting to fight us?"

How did Martin do it?

"No," said Allan. "We don't have a gang anymore."

"You heard what happened to the Mackies?" said George, oldest of the group.

"What?" said Martin.

"The cops came last night and took away Kevin a day early cause he threw a brick through the detective's car window and then this morning they show up again with an ambulance and a fire truck," said George.

"His Mom got drunk and swallowed a whole bunch of pills just like Marilyn Munro," said Fred.

"She's dead," said George.

"Mike found her," said Fred.

"I was standing right here this morning watching all the cops and Mike walks up and says: 'She wouldn't wake up and I touched her and she was cold like a piece of meat,'" said George. "A piece of meat, honest to God that's what he said."

"That's what he said," said Fred. "Honest to God."

"Just like Marilyn Munro," said Allan. "That's what my Mom said too."

"Booze and pills can kill you," said Fred. "Honest to God."

"The cops were here until just about an hour ago," said George.

"All day long they were sneaking around Mike's house," said Allan. "Even poking in the yard. No respect, that's what my Mom said."

"No respect," said Fred.

"Where's Mike?" I said.

"Took him away," said George.

"My Mom says a foster home cause his Dad's in jail and his Mom was an orphan so she didn't have no family," said Allan.

All nine of us shared a moment of silence as we thought about this grim fate.

"Took him away and he's never coming back," said Fred, after a few seconds.

"Told me he'd run away and come back here," said George, a

revelation to the other boys. "Told me he could live on his own, did it anyway most of his life."

That had a ring of truth.

"He'll come back," said Fred and the other boys from the block nodded. "He won't stay in a foster home."

"No foster home can hold Mike," said Allan. "He'll come back."

"He'll come back," said Pete. "That's for sure."

"You guys thought Mike was a bully, but he always protected us," said George.

"Always," said Fred. "Even from Kevin."

"No one picked on us when Mike was around," said George. "Not even the Fishers and his east-end guys."

"No one," said Fred. "Not even the Fishers."

"You guys can join us and Roy will protect you," said Martin. "Now we're all part of the same gang, right Roy? We'll call ourselves the Elgin Park gang or maybe the northwesters."

Brian gave me a look. What was it?

"No one will pick on you when they know Roy is your friend," said Martin, who then lowered his voice. "Everyone knows he beat up Mike twice in hockey season and even Kevin was scared of our big brother Basil."

It was kind of nice to hear Martin talking about his big brothers like that. But it was also like a rancher talking about his prize bulls.

"We're going to be late for practice," said Brian.

"We better get going," I said. "Martin."

"I'll come in awhile," he said.

"You're okay?" I said. Mom would get mad if she found out he wasn't with me, but Martin would do what he wanted anyway.

"This is our terry tory now," said Martin.

"Territory," I said.

"Our territory," said Martin. "Just like in the cowboy movies. Right George? You'll make sure I'm safe?"

"Sure Roy, Martin is safe on our block," said George. "You don't have to worry."

I never worried about Martin. Not about his safety anyway.

"We're going over to the coulee to catch garter snakes," said Fred. "Some of the teenagers will give you fifty cents for one."

"Martin can come with us," said George. "You want to?"

"Ya," said Martin.

I knew the spot in the coulee. It was not far from the diamond.

"Okay," I said to Martin. "But make sure you meet us at the diamond before practice is over."

Brian started walking and I followed. The worst that could happen was we'd have to go to the coulee to get him and that wouldn't be bad. The snakes were kind of neat. And I had heard right before dark was the best time to catch them. Maybe a bag of snakes would be just what Basil had in mind for the doctors.

"Geez, that's pretty crappy about Mike's mother," I said, catching up to Brian.

"Ya," said Brian, still acting weird.

We walked quickly and quietly.

I could tell Brian was mad. "You're not going to say anything?" he finally said. "After I come to your house, even though I was the one in the right. You hurt my feelings and you're just going to pretend everything is okay?"

I never before had a friend like this. Only girls talked about feelings.

"What are you saying?" I said.

"I shouldn't feel bad you chose Mike, a Nazi, over me?"

"I never chose Mike over you," I said. "I just wanted to be fair to everybody, including Mike, that's all. And he isn't a Nazi."

"Just a Jew hater?"

I sighed.

"But that's okay?" asked Brian.

"I'm sorry about what he said," I said. "You made him mad, which is pretty easy to do, and he said a bunch of things he shouldn't have. Terrible things. He slugged you in the shoulder and then got kicked off the team. He had his chance and he blew it. That was fair. That's the important thing."

"More important than being loyal to your friend?" said Brian.

"I have to choose between fairness and being friends with you?" I said.

"You had to choose between hurting Mike's feelings or hurting mine," said Brian. "You knew he'd do what he did, everybody knew."

"That's not true," I said. "No one was surprised he did it, but that doesn't mean we knew he would. I mean there was a good chance sure, but that isn't the point."

"What is the point?" said Brian as we came to the corner near the diamond.

"Mike has never been treated fairly in his whole life, except maybe by his Mom," I said. "Somebody has to try. Doesn't everyone deserve that chance? Doesn't him blowing up at you yesterday make a whole lot more sense now we know what was going on at his house? Don't you feel a little sympathy?"

Brian shook his head.

"I'm sorry he called you those names," I said. "I am."

"You're a bloody missionary, Saint Roy among the heathens trying to save their souls," said Brian.

"What do you expect after seven grades in a Catholic school?"

"Atheist Jews don't share the missionary burden," said Brian.

I shrugged.

"Do you still want to be my friend?" said Brian.

"Sure," I said. "You're fun to talk to, the best guy I know. As good as Basil."

"You want to come over to my place after practice?"

"Sure," I said. "If you make me one of those milkshakes in the machine you guys have."

"Blender," said Brian.

"Ya," I said. "Banana and butterscotch."

"And chocolate for Martin," said Brian.

"Sure," I said, smiling. Brian was okay.

"I'm still mad at you," said Brian.

"I'm always mad at my brothers," I said. "One thing or another. It passes."

We walked down the hill to the diamond, friends again. Maybe this talking about emotions and stuff was not so bad.

Katherine, letter 9

October 25, 1962

Dear President Kennedy,

My father says it is war for sure. There is no backing down now. I haven't told you this before but my father supported Richard Nixon in 1960. He always said you were a liberal, maybe even a socialist sympathizer and he especially didn't like your brother Bobby. Said he is a hypocrite. Said your father was a gangster so how could Bobby claim to go after gangsters now? He also said you deliberately messed up the Bay of Pigs invasion, because you secretly support Castro. But he's not saying anything bad about you anymore. Now he's behind you one hundred percent and so am I.

My father is planning to move to California. He says he is tired of the socialists in Saskatchewan. He has been offered a very prestigious job as chief of surgery at a hospital in Los Angeles. Neither my mother nor my father has said anything about what will happen to me. But, I can tell you this, one way or another I will go to California with my father. I will not stay in Moose Jaw. I told you that my father was the youngest chief of surgery ever in Saskatchewan? I think the only reason he ever came here was because he knew he could gain experience that would help him later in his career. He wants to be head of the American Medical Association one day. And he will be too. He worked very closely with top officials of the AMA during the physicians' withdrawal of services last summer. Very closely indeed and I'm sure they were impressed, even though the result wasn't very encouraging.

Which brings me to the next part of my story.

Despite all of Katherine and Cindy's efforts, the fight between the Mackie brothers gang and the west of Ninth Avenue gang never happened. Roy was once again very lucky. The Mackies' mother committed suicide and the older brother was sent to juvenile detention just before the fight was supposed to happen. As a result the east of Ninth Avenue gang disappeared. In fact, most of them joined with Roy's crowd. He never called it a gang, even though his younger brother Martin did.

Cindy was furious. Katherine had a lot of trouble keeping her in line. Cindy went so far as to break up with Doug and was talking about going to a necking party with Mike Fisher, an east-side boy who hated Roy and whose father was a prominent businessman. Cindy said she was going to let Mike touch her wherever he wanted, if he promised to beat up Roy.

Katherine was disgusted with Cindy. Not that she was a prude or anything, but Cindy never thought things through. She just reacted with emotion. Katherine would have dropped her as a friend immediately, but when she mentioned Mike Fisher and how much he hated Roy, Katherine knew Cindy and Mike would be useful to her plan of keeping an eye on Basil Schmidt and his gang of socialist hooligans.

The day Mrs. Mackie died was July 1, the day that the physicians of Saskatchewan withdrew their services. Roy told Katherine on the last day of school that Basil and his friends were planning to do something to any doctor that shut his practice. Exactly what was not made clear and Katherine knew that her father would need more details if the information were to be of any use. But, before she could get any details out of Roy, they had a fight. He asked Katherine what her father was going to do during what he called the strike and she told him the truth. Or at least too much of the truth. She told him that as chief of surgery he was legally obligated to perform emergency surgery, but that he supported the withdrawal of services one hundred percent. Roy started yelling at her. Who knows what he would have done if she had told him that her father was the main contact with the American Medical Association and had come up with the idea of the Keep Our Doctor committees. The committees were very useful as a way to show how ordinary people supported the doctors. They put a lot of pressure on the government.

After their fight Katherine knew it would be hard to get any more information directly out of Roy so Cindy would be essential. She had to make up with Doug because he was now friendly with Roy. Cindy had to use Doug to either get Roy to tell him what was happening or, even better, through Doug joining Basil's gang.

Katherine absolutely needed to know what Basil was up to. She had to know the hooligans' plans so they could be caught. She needed to show their links with the unions and the CCF and the government. And she needed to get all that into the newspapers. If she could just prove that the government had ties to gangs of teenaged vandals, the physicians of Saskatchewan would enjoy a great victory. So, Katherine didn't care what Cindy had to do to convince Doug. And Katherine would do anything to make Cindy help her.

Roy, letter 14

Oct. 24, 1962

Dear President Kennedy,

The paper tonight says you're sending ships to blockade Cuba. The story says a blockade is an act of war and I'm scared. Sister Veronica says you must realize how serious this is and know what you're doing. I hope so because I'd really like to make it to my thirteenth birthday. I also hope you're reading my story and getting the point. Basil says a good story is not too obvious. He says writers should make a reader think. I hope this is making you think. It is getting close to the end. Here goes again.

Paul and I began arguing right after he knocked on my door. I was in a good mood because Mom had made waffles. (Basil won a waffle iron in the Manitoba Hardware Easter raffle a few months earlier.) Covered in chokecherry jelly I like them almost as much as the fried bread dough we call smoochkeekla (I don't know how to spell that because it's German, or maybe Ukrainian.)

"The paper says 63 doctors have already left the province," said Paul, who never read a newspaper, so he must have heard the story from his mother.

"The paper says lots of things," I said. "You think it's all true?"

"Sixty-three in four days — what's going to happen if the strike keeps on?"

"We'll get community clinics and doctors who care about helping people," I said. "Instead of businessmen who use sick and injured people to make money."

"Even that priest from Wilcox, that Father Athol Murray, is against the government," said Paul. "He says they're communists."

Father Murray ran this school called Notre Dame in a small town near Moose Jaw. Most of the kids who went there were bullies and tough guys and their hockey teams were the dirtiest we ever played.

"Basil says the Church supported fascists in Spain and Italy and Quebec too," I answered. "And Sister Veronica says he's just one priest with his own opinion."

"My Mom says the government is ruining the province," said Paul, fiddling with something in his pocket as we sat on the porch. "Communists taking away our freedom."

The previous night's newspaper had called the doctors strike a "fight for freedom" and the words made me so angry I almost emptied my paper bag in the gully that ran in the vacant lot between two houses on Montgomery Street. Instead I had dreamed up examples of "freedom" the doctors were fighting for and now I used them on Paul.

"Freedom for a doctor to tell a worried mother: Pay me what I want or your son will die," I said. "You think that's a freedom worth going on strike for? Or freedom to refuse an operation if people can't afford it? Freedom for doctors to make as much money as they want, even if it means poor people have to go without proper care? Freedom to blackmail an elected government? Freedom to call doctors heroes when they go on strike but never have a good word for ordinary people making a quarter the money when they walk off the job? Are you going to the pro-doctor rally to fight for that?"

Paul didn't respond. He was crushed into silence by my superior arguments, or more likely, because he always agreed with whatever was the last thing he heard.

"Me, I'm going to help Basil and some of his friends take down the names of every business that shuts its doors to support the doctors," I said. "We're going to make up a list. Why should we shop at a store that tries to stop Medicare?"

"Everyone has his opinion," said Paul, words he used when he had nothing to say.

"Sure," I said. "But some are smart and others stupid."

"My mother isn't stupid," said Paul.

"I didn't say that," I said. "She spends too much time with the doctors at the training school, that's all. She'd probably get fired if she stuck up for Medicare."

It was no fun winning an argument when your opponent was so easily beaten.

"I'm not stupid and neither is my mother," said Paul, mostly to himself as he sulked. "And the doctors at the training school are smarter than you."

This was why we didn't hang out anymore. At least with Brian I could have an intelligent disagreement.

"What's in your pocket?" I said to change the subject.

He produced a box of .22 shells then opened it to show me it was almost full.

"Holy!" I said.

"I found it in a big box Jiggs brought back from the farm," said Paul. "Junk my Mom told me to go through to see if there was anything I wanted."

His smile almost covered up the worry that Jiggs would find out and get mad. His stepfather was mean when angry.

"How many bullets?" I asked.

"Ninety-one," said Paul. "I counted."

"Holy!" I repeated.

"You want to go shooting down on the flats?" said Paul.

"Sure," I said. "This afternoon, after all-star practice? You'll bring the .22 and the pellet gun?"

"Okay," said Paul.

"Is it okay if Brian comes?" I said.

"Brian?" said Paul. "What for?"

"He's never fired a gun," I said. "I told him about your .22."

"I heard he plays piano," said Paul.

"So?"

"Kind of sissy," said Paul.

"He took a punch from Doug and I didn't see you there," I said.

"Nobody told me," said Paul. "I would have been there if Martin asked."

"Brian stood up to Mike Mackie," I said. "Pushed his shoulder when the guy called him 'jewboy'." Every time you see a Mackie, you cross the street."

"That's not true," said Paul.

"It's not true Brian's a sissy," I said.

"He's a Jew," said Paul.

"So?" I said. "Jews, Catholics, we're all going to hell anyway, according to you."

I was mad and he was mad. We sat for a while then Paul stood up to walk away. "Got to wash the breakfast dishes before my Mom gets up or she'll be mad."

I said nothing. Paul was ignorant and stupid and mean. How could anyone on Brown Street side with the right wing doctors?

So, after practice I went over to Brian's place for lunch and instead of shooting a .22 at frogs or tin cans, I got a tour of the accounting classrooms at the STI and listened to some Chopin, played for an audience of two in a 500-seat auditorium. While exploding frogs might have been more exciting, music was more refined, more mature and I didn't have to pretend Paul was my friend.

Still, later that day when he showed up at the back door after my parents left to play whist at a cousin's house, I forgot about politics and we were soon in my yard experimenting with a hammer, .22-calibre bullets and a new sidewalk that had been poured between our house and driveway the previous month.

"Did you go down to the flats with the rifle?" I said, lining up a bullet on the grey-brown concrete slab.

"No," said Paul. "I had to go downtown for my Mom to pick up a stupid dress. She's on night shift, so she wanted to sleep but needed it for some party at a doctor's house tonight and Jiggs and Billy are at the farm, so I got stuck doing it. And then it wasn't ready so I had to go bowling for an hour."

"What did you shoot?" I said, swinging the hammer, but stopping an inch above the bullet.

"Two-forty and 210 in five pin and 164 in ten pin," said Paul as he lined up a half dozen bullets on the sidewalk.

"I don't like ten pin," I said. "The ball is too heavy. Stupid American game."

Paul nodded and then looked towards the back fence. "Think you could put a hole through the fence by firing one of these with a hammer?"

Without even thinking I swung the hammer again, only this time landed it on the brass bullet casing. Pow. Sounded like a really loud firecracker.

"Holy," said Paul, his eyes wide.

It was fun to see Paul impressed. "Look where it hit," I said.

Paul shook his head as he looked at the fence. He stood up and ran towards the back of the yard, then checked out the boards between the corner and the gate. He turned and hollered.

"It's here, stuck in the post," he shouted, waving his hands.

Paul turned back to look more closely at the bullet. After a few seconds, he ran towards me.

"It's gone right in," he said. "You got pliers?"

As Paul sat down on the sidewalk a few feet away, I swung the hammer again. Pecow! This time I heard an echo off Old Ray's house across the street.

Paul was grinning in amazement.

I lifted the hammer up and then slammed it down a third time. Pecow!

"Holy!" repeated Paul, his eyes and mouth wide open.

"Can you see where they hit?" I said.

"You got to look close up," said Paul shaking his head.

"I'll fire off a few more then you go check them out," I said. "I'll get pliers."

Paul laughed, like he was having fun, but he didn't reach for the hammer, so I put the fourth bullet into the same spot as the previous three and swung the ball peen once more. Pecow!

It felt good even though a part of me knew this was stupid. We giggled some more as I set up one more .22 shell. And again I swung the hammer. But this time there was no sound. We looked around and then down at the sidewalk. The intact bullet was still there. I must have missed. Then I noticed something crazy: The bullet on the sidewalk was pointed straight at me!

Paul had noticed the same thing at the exact same moment and when our eyes met we burst out laughing.

"Holy, I could have shot myself," I said, giggling.

"Ya," said Paul. "It's aimed right at you."

We continued to laugh as I turned the bullet around and re-aimed it towards the back fence. I swung the hammer once more and pecow!

Where did it hit this time? I looked at the back fence and then over to Paul. "Can you see ..."

Paul was staring at me, dead serious. He was white and his eyes wide like the negro kid on Little Rascals.

"You're shot," said Paul, nothing more. Then he continued to stare at me.

What was he talking about?

"You're shot," repeated Paul.

Something wet traveled down my cheek and dropped off my chin. I looked down at the sidewalk. Brownish red. I looked back at Paul and then rubbed my right index finger across my left temple. Sticky. Blood.

"Geez," I said.

"Did it go in?" said Paul. "Is there a hole?"

Finger back up to the source of the liquid. Raw flesh, but no hole.

"Holy geez," I said. "It must have grazed the side of my head."

Paul leaned towards me to feel the wound. It didn't hurt. Least not yet.

"You okay?" said Paul as he rubbed the blood between his fingers.

"Does it look okay?" I said.

"Lots of blood," said Paul. "Sticky."

"Coagulated," I said. "It gets sticky so the wound closes and bleeding stops. If blood doesn't coagulate, it doesn't clot and you'd bleed to death."

"I know that," said Paul.

"Like Ralph, who lives across the street from St. Mike's," I said. "He's a hemophiliac. If you cut him, he could die."

"I know that," said Paul.

All the kids in the neighborhood knew that, so why was I saying it? Because I was lucky, that's the point. Compared to Ralph.

"Roy," said Paul.

I looked up.

"You're still bleeding," said Paul. "And you're talking crazy."

I looked down at the small pool of blood on the sidewalk then put my finger back up to the wound. The hair on that side was matted and gooey. A couple more minutes and it would be like when Martha Banks squirted white glue at me in art class. By the time I made it to the washroom ten minutes had passed and a big clump of hair had to be cut off. Blood was just like glue, I knew because of the time Paul had cut me with a rock and when the Bowie knife we had been throwing at the barn door bounced back and landed right in my shoulder, pointy side sticking in almost an inch.

"Maybe we should go to the hospital or something," said Paul.

"I'm okay and besides the doctors are on strike," I said and then realized the humor of the situation. I grinned.

"What?" said Paul, reacting to my look.

"Dad will be pissed," I said. "But not at me, at the doctors."

Maybe some good will come out of the doctors strike. That was funny.

"You okay?" said Paul.

Once more I reached up to touch my wound. The clotting was almost complete. I was no hemophiliac, that's for sure.

"Just got to let it stop completely and then I can clean up," I said.

I looked down at the three bullets still on the sidewalk.

"You better take them," I said.

Paul nodded, picked up the bullets and put them in the box.

"You're not going to tell your parents where the bullets came from?" said Paul.

Jiggs would be mad as hell if he found out.

I shook my head. "Don't worry."

I stood up and suddenly my head cleared. What had I done? How could I have been so stupid? Bullets are dangerous. This was almost as dumb as the time Paul and me fired the rifle in Matt Hawkins' basement and the shot ricocheted about a dozen times off the cement walls. We laughed about how close we had come to being shot.

Dumb.

"Maybe we should go to the hospital, just in case," said Paul. "There's supposed to be one doctor for emergencies. Just to look at you, to be safe."

"And tell him what?"

"You could say we were down in the flats and heard a shot and next thing we knew you were bleeding," said Paul.

Not a bad story. For Paul.

"Walk there?" I said. "It takes half an hour."

"We could ask Mr. Bowler for a ride," said Paul.

"Except he probably heard the shots, so why would he believe the story?"

Paul often came up with good stories and then undermined

them because he didn't think the details through. Good lying depends on paying attention to details.

"He'd tell my Mom," said Paul.

I nodded.

"I don't mind walking," I said. "It's a couple of hours till it gets dark."

Might be fun. The wound wasn't serious, but maybe I should go to the hospital. And if the doctors refused to see me, even better. Mom and Dad would be mad at them, not me.

"I better get Martin," I said. "I'm looking after him."

Paul smiled at this. "The babysitter got shot," he said.

It was kind of funny.

Katherine, letter 10

October 25, 1962

Dear President Kennedy,

I haven't been able to fall asleep, so I decided to write you again. This talk of war is so exciting and maybe a little frightening, because we don't know what will happen next. The only real comfort we have is the knowledge that you are in charge. We know you will do what is right and best for freedom and free enterprise.

I wonder if it is true that the missiles in Cuba cannot reach Moose Jaw. That is what the newspaper here says. We have a big air force base, but probably the Russians do not care so much about Canada. My mother says we should go to my grandfather's cabin north of Prince Albert. It is very beautiful up there and certainly not a target for any nuclear missiles. But my father says that would be an act of cowardice. He says we must show courage and defiance in the face of our enemies. I do not know who is right. Hiding in the bush with my mother could be very difficult but being vaporized in a nuclear explosion would not be any fun either.

I need to stop thinking about such things. That is why I decided to write you again tonight. It makes me focus on my story rather than about nuclear war and dying.

At first Cindy refused to help Katherine.

"I don't want to see Doug ever again," she said. "He promised to help me, but he didn't. Besides, he's a terrible kisser."

Katherine had to keep herself from smiling.

"He refused to help because you were asking him to beat up Roy and he could have been hurt," said Katherine. "Doug's not a fighter. He's a singer. Roy is pretty strong and he's had lots of experience fighting."

"Just come out and say it," said Cindy. "Doug is scared of Roy. He's a chicken."

"But he'll spy for us," said Katherine. "He wouldn't be scared to do that. Especially if he gets something out of it."

"I hate him," said Cindy. "I won't do it."

"Please."

"He called me a slut," said Cindy. "Someone told him that they saw me necking with Johnny Baxter."

"Were you?" asked Katherine.

"What difference does that make?" said Cindy. "I know Doug is kissing lots of other girls. So why can't I do the same?"

She had a point, but it was not the point Katherine was concerned about.

"It's terrible when people start talking about you," Katherine said. "Saying bad things."

Cindy looked at her as if she understood what was coming.

"People say the cruelest things when they get mad at you," continued Katherine. "It's never a good idea to make girls all over the city dislike you. Like if you used them for what you wanted but then didn't help them when they asked for a favour. They might get mad and say bad things about you."

Katherine could see from the look on Cindy's face that she understood.

"What do you want me to do?" Cindy wasn't smart, but she wasn't stupid either.

"Let Doug kiss you a few more times or at least make him think you will let him," said Katherine. "Do whatever it takes to make him spy on Roy and Basil for us."

"My Mom and Dad say the doctors are wrong and the government is right," said Cindy.

"When do you ever listen to them?" said Katherine.

"This is not fair," said Cindy. "I have to do what you want, but I don't get anything I want."

"I'll get Mike Fisher to beat up Roy," said Katherine. "His father is on the KOD committee and he hates Roy already anyway. As soon as you get Doug to agree to spy for us, I'll get Mike's promise to beat up Roy. And he'd probably also beat up Martin, just for fun."

"What choice do I have?" said Cindy.

"It's free country," said Katherine.

"I'll do it," said Cindy, still pouting.

"Right away," said Katherine. "We need the information

now. Last night someone let the air out of Dr. Ballard's tires. I bet that was Basil and his gang. We need to know what they're up to."

"Okay," said Cindy.

"We'll go see Doug now," said Katherine.

"Together?" said Cindy.

"You can see him yourself at first, if you want," said Katherine. "And then I'll just happen to be walking past his house and you see me and we talk so I can make sure Doug understands exactly what he needs to do."

"You don't trust me?" said Cindy.

"I trust you," said Katherine. "But I trust me more."

"What if he won't do it?" said Cindy.

"He'll do it," said Katherine. "One way or the other. For pleasure or pain."

As soon as Katherine heard herself say those words she felt guilty. But only a little. Sometimes, to accomplish great things, one must make sacrifices, do things that make you uncomfortable. Her father told her that. And now she learned it was true.

Roy, letter 15

Oct. 25, 1962

Dear President Kennedy,

The radio says today that you ordered the army, navy and air force to the highest alert ever. Please don't go to war. Please let me finish this story. I'm writing this at home. I told Mom I was sick. Nothing important at school on a Thursday afternoon. I'll tell her I'm still sick tomorrow morning so I can keep writing until I'm done. Here goes.

We found Martin and five of his friends in Barry's back yard. Even though I had cleaned off most of the blood from my cheek, my little brother stared like I was the ghost of Pope Pius XII come back to life.

"What happened to you?" said Barry.

"He got shot," said Paul.

I put my hand on Paul's shoulder. I had to calm him down. He was the world's worst liar when he was excited.

"We were down in the flats and heard a shot from somewhere and I looked at Roy and he was bleeding," said Paul.

"Holy," said Barry.

"Holy," repeated the other three boys.

"Did it go in?" said Martin.

"No," I said, shaking my head. "Just grazed me."

"We're going to the hospital to get him checked out," said Paul.

"Stupid doctors are on strike," said Barry, whose father worked for the CPR and was a union man. "My Dad says someone is going to die."

"Ya," said the twins whose names I didn't know. "Stupid doctors."

"Supposed to be someone available at the emergency," said Paul.

"We're going to walk," I said to Martin. "You have to come."

For once my little brother didn't complain about leaving his friends. Instead, he had a look that said questions would follow. And as soon as the three of us began the journey downtown, the grilling began.

"Is that true what Paul said about being in the flats and hearing a shot?" said Martin. "I thought you and him were playing in our yard. You never said anything about going to the flats. If Mom found out you left me she'd be mad."

I put my index finger over my mouth to signal silence. Paul shrugged as we exchanged a glance. Should I tell Martin the truth? As we walked down Ninth Avenue, I debated what to do.

While Martin could keep a secret, perhaps this was information my little brother should not possess. It was about the stupidest thing I'd ever done and maybe wasn't what a little brother should hear. Or maybe it was the stupidest thing I'd ever done and that was exactly what a little brother should hear.

"I shot myself," I said, as we crossed Caribou Street.

"You better not tell anyone," said Paul.

"He doesn't have to be told that," I said. "Do you Martin?"

"With a gun?" said Martin, shaking his head to answer my question. "With Paul's .22?"

"With a hammer," I said.

That stumped him. He looked at me, then at Paul, then back at his big brother.

"With a hammer," repeated Paul, enjoying himself. "A .22 calibre hammer. Pow."

Martin looked at Paul then back at me once more.

"I was smashing bullets on the sidewalk beside the house," I said.

"Pow, pow, pow!" said Paul, miming the motion of a hammer.

"Shot them through the fence," I said.

"And one doesn't fire, even though Roy hit it pretty good. We look down and the bullet is pointing straight at him and we laugh, thinking that's pretty funny, then he straightens it out and smashes it again," said Paul. "Pow."

"And I'm staring at the fence trying to see where the bullet went when I see Paul is looking at me and his eyes are getting bigger and bigger," I said. "Finally he says 'Roy, you're shot'."

"'Roy, you're shot,'" repeats Paul. "Blood is pouring down the side of his face. Looks like the bullet has gone straight into his brain."

"Straight in?" said Martin.

"I'm thinking maybe he's dead, you know like in the cowboy shows where the guy is shot but he stands there for a little bit before falling over," said Paul.

"Like that chicken Mom chopped the head off at the Five-Mile Dam who ran around and around and then I had to crawl under the car to get it," said Martin.

"Only Roy wasn't running around," said Paul. "Just kneeling there."

"Like a chicken with his head shot off," I said, enjoying the telling of this story.

"Finally he talks to me so I know that stuff oozing down his cheek isn't brains squirting out of his head," said Paul.

Martin made a face as if he were disgusted by the thought of it.

"Maybe a bit of my brain did ooze out," I said. "That's why I have to go to the hospital. 'Hey doc. I think you guys are jerks for going on strike to stop Medicare, but I need to ask you something: Are all my brains still in my head?'"

Paul and I enjoyed a good laugh, but Martin looked scared. As we cut across the last few yards of the William Grayson schoolyard, I noticed the concern on my little brother's face.

"Hey Martin, you don't think that's funny?" said Paul.

Martin shook his head. When the little guy was quiet, it was a bad sign.

"What's the matter?" I said.

Martin shook his head again.

"Tell me," I said, taking Martin's hand.

At first Martin avoided my eyes, but then he gave me a look I'll never forget.

"You coulda been killed," he said.

"The bullet just grazed my forehead," I said, sighing.

"But it coulda gone right in," said Martin. "It coulda hit you just a little bit over."

It was true.

"Or it coulda hit your eye and made you blind like that girl in the movie that's coming to the Capitol," said Martin.

Patty Duke in the Miracle Worker. Martin had seen the preview with me last Saturday.

"It coulda gone right in your head and made you dead," said Martin.

I realized I was still holding my little brother's hand. I squeezed it. Martin looked like he was about to start crying.

"It could have," he said.

"But it didn't," I said. "I was lucky."

Stupid and lucky. Martin's reaction made me embarrassed. Hitting bullets with a hammer, that was a very dumb thing. Why did I do it?

"You told me playing with guns is bad," said Martin.

One problem with being a responsible big brother is taking responsibility for what you said.

"Were you lying?" said Martin. "Or just saying it cause you think I'm too little?"

"He wasn't playing with guns," said Paul, who was about the worst excuse maker I ever knew. "Just bullets."

Both Martin and I gave him 'are-you-stupid-or-what looks'. He shrugged and slowed down to follow a few yards behind us.

What I did was stupid. I was stupid. Why hadn't I thought about it before I did it? Was I showing off to Paul? Or to myself? I couldn't remember why I did it. I just did it. And now my head hurt, both the wound and inside.

We walked in silence and were almost downtown before I spoke. "Sometimes big brothers do stupid things," I said. "Me, even Basil."

"Ya?" said Martin, more as a question than a statement of agreement.

"Everybody does stupid things," I said. "All of us. You know that, right?"

"Ya," he answered. "That's why they make you go to confession."

"Exactly," I said.

"Protestants don't go to confession," said Paul, "so I guess we don't do stupid things."

I glared and Paul retreated again.

"Is a sin a stupid thing?" said Martin.

"Mostly, I guess," I said. "Committing a sin is stupid, but I don't think all stupid things are sins."

"Is hammering a bullet a sin?" said Martin.

Good question.

"Maybe, maybe not," I said. "If I killed myself that would be a sin, cause it would be suicide. Or if I killed Paul, that would be the sin of murder. Or if Mom told me not to do it but I did it anyways that would be disobeying thy father or mother."

"Do you have to break a commandment for it to be a sin?" said Paul.

I shook my head.

"Swearing is a sin," said Martin. "Sister Elizabeth said so when she heard Cindy call Bernadette Laberge a bitch. Cindy said that's just the name of a female dog, but Sister Elizabeth said it was a swear word and a sin if you said it in anger at another person."

"And there's no commandment against swearing except for the one about taking the Lord's name in vain, which only applies if you cuss with His name in it," I said, pointing to the sky.

"What's 'cuss'?" said Martin.

"Another word for swear," I said.

Martin thought about it for a moment and then said: "Can you cuss on a bible?"

Paul laughed.

"You said you have to swear on a bible if you're gonna talk in front of a judge," said Martin.

"That's a different kind of swear. It's like a promise," I said. "Cuss only means the kind of swearing that's a bad word."

"If you cuss in front of a judge he'll throw you in jail," said Paul, smirking.

"Point is," I said, getting back to what I wanted to say, "smashing bullets with a hammer on the sidewalk is stupid. I was stupid to do it. Anyone who does that is stupid."

Didn't feel bad. Maybe it even felt good. This being honest stuff that Brian talked about was okay.

"I don't know why I did it," I continued. "Didn't think, that's what is most stupid. I didn't think about what I was doing. You should always think about whether it's good or bad or dangerous or could hurt somebody. You know that, right Martin?"

Paul rolled his eyes, but I didn't care if I sounded like a goodie-two-shoes. Martin looked up to me and I had to be responsible just like Basil almost always was with me.

As we crossed into Crescent Park, Martin was the first to spot Mike Fisher and a half dozen of his east-end friends.

"Oh, oh," said Martin, as he grabbed my hand and pulled me behind the gate to the park.

"What's wrong?" I said.

"Mike Fisher," said Paul, waving. "Mike!"

"Don't let him see us," said Martin.

As Martin and I concealed ourselves behind the fence, Paul walked towards Mike and his friends.

"What's going on?" I said to Martin.

"It's not safe," answered Martin. "These east-end kids want to fight us."

"Who said?"

"Barry and all the kids from the other side of Elgin Park," said Martin.

"Mackie's gang?"

"Ya, Barry was with them at the beach yesterday and Mike Fisher was there and they started talking about who was the toughest 12-year-old in Moose Jaw."

I knew where this was headed. "And Barry challenged Mike to fight me?"

"Allen did, but Barry said he told Mike you could beat him up with one hand tied behind your back."

Great.

"Mike was really mad and said next time he saw you, he'd make you eat Lick-a-maid off his smelly feet."

That was something to look forward to.

"Maybe he won't fight you today when he sees you're shot in the head," said Martin.

Something good might come out of hammering bullets after all.

Paul had reached Mike and his friends and the scene looked peaceful so I stood up and pulled my little brother onto the path and began walking towards them.

"Don't act scared," I said.

"I'm not scared," said Martin, who looked like he was headed to his own funeral.

As we neared the crowd of eight kids, we could see Paul talking about a hammer, bullets and a wound to the head. Everyone stared at my forehead.

"Hey Mike," I said.

"Schmidt," said Mike, only he pronounced it "Shit."

As Martin reeled off every kid's name, I made eye contact with Fisher, who was the best pitcher and hitter on the East Side All-stars. We would be facing each other on the diamond in a few days, in the three-team tournament for the right to represent the city on the road to the Little League World Series.

"Hey I hear you were almost shot to shit, Shit," said Mike. "Too bad you weren't using shotgun shells and blew up your mouthy little brother too."

The east end kids laughed, while Martin glared and Paul looked embarrassed. I kept my eyes on Fisher, but said nothing. We stared at each other for a few seconds. Martin remained behind me.

"Well, we better get going," said Paul. "Have a doctor look at the wound."

"Doctors are on strike," said Fisher. "Shit here knows that, because his commie brother Basil is going around town causing trouble for anybody who thinks the doctors are right and the government is wrong."

Fisher's father was a businessman prominent in the Keep Our Doctors committee.

"But the doctors promised to keep the hospital emergency room open," said Paul. "That's what my Mom says and she's a nurse."

"He can see a doctor on his own side of town," said Fisher. "Find a hospital there."

Both city hospitals were east of Main Street.

"He doesn't look any worse than normal," said Fisher. "Unless Shit wants to fight me and get the shit beat out of him, then maybe I'll allow him one free passage."

"You're pretty tough when it's six against three and one of the three is seven years-old," I said.

"Actually, it's six against two," said Fisher, "because your buddy Paul here is such a chicken I keep on expecting to find him in a bucket of Kentucky Fried."

As Fisher's gang laughed and formed a semi-circle facing Martin and I, Paul backed away.

"We're not scared of you," said Martin. "But Roy was just shot in the head. You can't make him fight now. It's not fair."

"Fair like kicking my brother in the balls when he's not ready," said Fisher. "Fair like jumping me and grabbing my head before I even have a chance to get ready."

"Hey, you were the one who wanted to fight and same with your brother," I said. "I never started anything."

"Course you never started anything, because you're a chicken shit," said Fisher.

I took a step towards him. We glared at each other.

"I'll fight, if that's what you want," I said. "But you leave Martin out of it. Any of you guys touch him and you'll answer to me and Basil."

"They're scared," said Fisher.

"They are, unless they're stupid," I said.

"I'll fight em Roy," said Martin. "I'm not afraid."

"You go with Paul," I said. "You'll get your chance when we get all the west side kids together. We'll show these east end bullies."

Martin stayed close.

"Don't worry about me," I said, making sure everyone could hear what I was saying. "I pounded the crap out of this guy once before and I'll do it again. If he thinks I'm scared just cause a bullet grazed my forehead, he'll learn. I tasted blood and it made me hungry for more. And if all these wimps are planning to jump me six against one, that's okay too because I'll make sure to hurt each one of them before they get me down."

I was bigger and stronger than Fisher. I was not scared. He'd regret taking me on. He'd pay the price.

I took another step towards Fisher and pushed Martin away at the same time. My little brother took a few steps toward Paul.

"Hey Fish, you going to do your own fighting? Or do you need these five stooges to help you?" I said, moving another few steps away from Martin and Paul.

The six boys formed into a circle surrounding me.

"I'll take you on Mister Big Shit and I'll make sure to leave Little Shit for the other guys."

"Very funny," I said. At least Fisher was the right enemy. The guy wasn't stupid and he was a good baseball player. Plus his family had money and supported the doctors strike.

The circle around me grew a little tighter as I moved on to an open spot of lawn. I tried to focus. Get myself pumped. Get ready to grab him.

Just as Fisher took a step towards me, something caught the corner of my eye. Someone surprising. A few of the guys in the circle turned their heads. It was Mike Mackie! Had he run away or found a foster home nearby?

"What's going on?" said Mackie as he marched into the middle of the circle.

"What are you doing here?" said Fisher.

"It's a public park, ain't it?" said Mackie.

"It's none of your business," said Fisher. "Me and Big Shit are going to fight."

"Looks like he's already been in a fight," said Mackie, staring at my head.

"He shot himself with a .22 shell, smashing bullets on the sidewalk with a hammer," said Paul, who had followed Mackie close to the circle. "Just grazed his forehead."

Mackie looked at me and shook his head.

"We were going to the hospital, but these guys won't let us," said Paul. "They want Roy to fight them."

"Six against one?" said Mackie.

"Stay out of it," said Fisher.

Mackie swung around to face him. He smiled.

"No, I think I'll stay here and help the Big Shit," said Mackie.

"It's none of your business," said Fisher.

"Maybe, but I feel like fighting and beating up six East Enders would be a hell of a lot more fun than smacking an injured guy across the forehead," said Mackie.

Fisher's nostrils flared.

"What do you think Big Shit," said Mackie. "Can we take them all?"

"Easy," I said, smiling.

A couple of Fisher's friends backed away, then the others followed.

"What's the matter, you changed your mind?" said Mackie, taking a step towards Fisher. "Not so tough when you have to do your own fighting?"

"It just occurred to him it makes a lot more sense to do battle with me on the mound and at the plate in the tournament next week," I said. "Right Fisher?"

His gang scattered, Fisher stared at me for only a few seconds before turning and walking towards the Natatorium. Mackie shook his head, first at Fisher and then at me.

"Is it true you were smashing bullets on a sidewalk?"

I nodded.

"That's pretty stupid," said Mackie.

"Ya," I said. "Didn't think. I guess everybody does stupid things sometimes."

"I guess," said Mackie.

I made eye contact. Mackie was not as bad as everyone thought.

"Thanks," I said.

"Just making sure everyone is treated fairly," said Mackie. "Doesn't mean I like you."

Katherine, letter 11

October 26, 1962

Dear President Kennedy,

I hope the Russians back down and take their missiles out of Cuba. The more I think about war, the more scared I get. I had nightmares last night. I don't know if it's true that both Russia and the United States would be destroyed in an all out nuclear war, but what if it is? I really want to move to Los Angeles with my father. Disneyland is supposed to be lots of fun, although maybe I'm too old for it. Still, I'd rather it be there, not blown up.

Anyway, I'm getting close to the end of my story and want to finish mine before Roy finishes his.

Of course Doug agreed to help just as Katherine knew he would. He didn't really have any choice after she explained to him that her friends could get him kicked out of the choir by telling stories and it wouldn't really matter whether or not they were true. Besides, Doug really liked kissing Cindy. And she may have agreed to something else as well. Katherine didn't really want to know about it. She honestly didn't know why Cindy liked kissing and that other stuff so much. Sure Katherine thought it was okay and she knew that books and stories talked about how wonderful it was, but to her it wasn't anywhere near the best thing in the world, which Cindy seemed to believe it was.

The very next day Doug reported that he had talked to Roy and learned that Basil was planning something.

"It's got something to do with snakes," Doug said. "Roy's little brother is getting all his friends to collect garter snakes. Roy says they have almost 50 of them."

"Garter snakes?" said Katherine. "What do they plan to do with them?"

"I don't know," said Doug. "I don't think Roy knows. All he said was that Basil really liked his idea of collecting garter snakes."

"Did you ask?"

"Ya," said Doug, who sounded a little reluctant. "I asked and Roy said he didn't know, but something good he was sure."

"Garter snakes," repeated Katherine.

"Ya," repeated Doug.

"What do you think they're planning to do with them?" asked Katherine.

"I don't know," said Doug.

"What would you do with 50 garter snakes?"

Doug thought about it for a few seconds as he sipped the chocolate milk shake Katherine had bought him at the Exchange Café.

"Frighten somebody who was scared of snakes?" said Doug. "Most boys use snakes to scare girls."

He was right, thought Katherine. "Why do boys do that?" she asked.

"Why are girls scared of them?" asked Doug. "Garter snakes are yicky, but they don't hurt you. Sort of like grasshoppers. Lots of girls are scared of grasshoppers too, but I don't see why."

"Doctors aren't scared of garter snakes," said Katherine. "It doesn't make any sense."

"Aren't any woman doctors," said Doug.

"There are a few," said Katherine. "My Dad says there will be more and more."

"Never heard of any in Moose Jaw," said Doug.

"There are none in Moose Jaw," said Katherine. "I think there's only a couple in all of Saskatchewan."

"Maybe Basil is planning to scare them?" said Doug.

Katherine considered this possibility. It didn't seem likely, but perhaps she had better call her father.

"Did Roy say anything else?"

"He said something big was going to happen across the province," said Doug.

"Something big?"

"Something big and it had to do with snakes," said Doug.

"Across the province?" said Katherine.

Doug nodded.

"Not just in Moose Jaw?"

"He said across the province."

Now Katherine was really confused. She needed to speak to her father. Maybe he could make sense of this. Snakes and something big across the province. What were they planning?

"I've got to phone my father," she said. "I'll pay the bill on my way out."

"Thanks for the milkshake," said Doug.

"You're welcome," said Katherine, as she headed for the cashier.

It was important that her network of friends understood that she offered both the carrot and the stick, thought Katherine. Her father had talked about the carrot and the stick for as long as she could remember. But it wasn't until the past few days that Katherine really understood what he meant.

Roy, letter 16

Oct. 25, 1962

Dear President Kennedy,

You should get the letter I wrote this afternoon on Saturday if it is sent by airmail. I hope that's not too late. You know what I mean. I will try finishing one more letter tonight. I sure hope you read my story before you decide to go to war. I'm pretty sure it will help. Here goes again.

While it wasn't the Seattle World's Fair, the 1962 Moose Jaw Exhibition was something I'll remember forever. The time from my pitching at the all-star tournament to the rumble at Kids Day was only a few hours but the ride was wilder than the roller coaster plus the Tilt-O-Whirl and the Rotor put together.

I didn't mean to bean Sam Kalinski, but I did, hard on the cheek, as the South Hill's best batter turned away from an out-of-control screwball. If he had just stood still it would have bounced off his helmet, but instead it smashed the bone below his left eye. Maybe not smash, but it made a sound like stepping on an egg carton. I felt bad and not just cause Sam was hurt. It was the day of the Keep Our Doctors rally in Regina and there'd be no one to see him at the hospital. I knew he'd have to wait hours before the doctors got back from the capital. They had more important things to do than fix a 12-year-old South Hill garlic-eater. They had to bully the government.

Of course, with South Hill's top player out of the line-up my job was easy and by the end of the game I had another no-hitter. I only gave up one hit-batter and two walks in a 6-0 victory in which I also hit two loaded-bases doubles that knocked in all our team's runs. We were only one win away from a trip to Grand Forks, Montana, and the Little League World Series regional playdowns.

I was still feeling pretty good the next day when Brian and I took Martin to the Moose Jaw fair. Every year since I could remember we stuffed ourselves with greasy burgers and cotton candy, stood outside the freak shows and tested exactly how much food, midway rides and summer sun you could take before getting sick. The fair was fun. For months afterward kids told stories about the best rides and how they puked their guts out. And 1962 was the best one of all.

Even the walk to the fair grounds, just east of Main Street on the north side of town, was great. As we were walking along Main Street, Sally McCutcheon, a 14-year old who may have been the most beautiful girl in Moose Jaw, said: "Hey Roy, where are you going?"

"Hey Sally," I said. It was the first time she had ever talked to me. "We're going to the fair. Have you been?"

"Not yet," she answered. "See you."

"See you," I said.

Brian smiled too, but Sally walked past him without saying a word. He turned to me. "You're famous."

"Her Dad coaches midget hockey. He wants me to move up and play for him this season."

"She likes you," said Brian.

I didn't know if was true, but the idea sure made me feel good.

Once we got to the fair it was my little brother's big mouth that started it all. The three of us were waiting in line for the Tilt-O-Whirl. Martin was too young to get on the ride, but he liked to be seen with older boys and the midway was crowded with kids from every corner of town.

I was still smiling because of Sally. My world was perfect. My picture was almost for sure going to be in the paper because of the game last night. My teammates treated me like a hero. Basil and his friends had liked my idea of using garter snakes to get even with doctors who were trying to make the government back down from Medicare. Yesterday, during the Keep Our Doctors rally in Regina, they put four or five snakes through the mail slots or in the mailboxes of each striking doctor's house. And also in a few mailboxes of the best known KOD committee members. Basil had friends who did the same thing in Regina and Saskatoon. Guys even did it in some smaller towns. But in some places they used rats instead of snakes. Rats and snakes, that's what Basil said we should call the doctors who were on strike, and their supporters. Every one of the dozen or so kids I had already told about the rats and snakes that morning laughed when they heard about it. Probably every single kid in Moose Jaw had already heard. Especially since a lot of them were at the Fair.

We were having lots of fun as Brian and I climbed up to the ride and Martin joined a crowd of kids his age in front of a nearby candy floss stand. The spinning helped my good feeling and as I climbed down from the ride five minutes later I was imagining my first home run of the season as Sally watched from the stands. I'd be a hero, carrying my teammates to glory at the Little League World Series. They'd run my picture on the front page of the Times Herald.

These thoughts spun in my head as I looked where I last saw Martin. The gang of little kids had grown larger and moved behind the candy floss stand. A crowd of about 30 six-to-nine year olds surrounded two boys, one of whom had the other in a headlock. Even though I couldn't make out either fighter, I knew my little brother was somehow involved.

"Come on," I said to Brian, bouncing down the stairs towards the action.

"What's going on?" he said.

"Martin," I answered.

We pushed through the crowd of little kids a lot faster than an adult making his way from the other side.

"Hey, what's going on?" the adult was shouting. "What are you kids doing?"

It wasn't until I was almost on top of the fighters that I saw Martin held in a hammerlock by a much bigger boy who looked familiar but I couldn't immediately place.

"Give? Give?" the older boy repeated.

Martin was squirming and trying to gain position for a move I recognized. Just as I was about to grab the bigger boy by the shoulder, my little brother brought up his knee hard into the guy's private parts. The bigger boy groaned. I grabbed Martin's arm as he was about to lunge at his weakened opponent.

"Are you boys fighting?" said the adult as he broke into the open space in the middle of the crowd. "I'll call the police."

"They're not fighting," I said, holding Martin back. "My little brother was just showing his friend a move we saw last month at All-Star Wrestling."

The man wasn't buying the story.

"Right Martin?" I said, putting pressure on my brother's arm. "It's a way of getting out of the hammerlock, right Martin? You were showing your friend."

Martin calmed himself and nodded. The adult looked at the bigger boy, who shook off his pain and nodded as well.

"They were just playing," I said. "You know what happens when you get this many little kids in one spot."

The adult was unconvinced. "Go on, get out of here," he said to no one in particular, but everyone in general.

As the crowd began to disperse, Martin continued to glare at the bigger boy.

"Who is that?" I whispered.

"Don't know his name," said Martin. "He's from South Hill."

"I'm going to keep my eyes on you," said the adult as he walked away.

"He called you a baseball ass in," said Martin.

"Ass in?" said Brian. "Ass in?"

He thought about it for a few seconds. "You mean assassin? Baseball assassin?"

"Ya," said Martin "And a rich North Hiller who loves the stinking doctors who keep poor people from having good medicare."

I remembered where I had seen the kid: At the all-star game the day before. He'd been in the stands cheering for South Hill.

"We hate the doctors and we're poor people," Martin shouted at the South Hill kid who stood about ten feet away, half ready to fight again. "Socialists too!"

I pulled my little brother back.

"What's a ass ass in?" Martin said to Brian.

"An assassin is someone who kills, like John Wilkes Booth was the assassin of President Lincoln," said Brian.

"My brother never killed anyone," shouted Martin at the South Hill kid.

"Ya, but he threw a baseball right at my cousin's face and he is still waiting for a doctor to see him," said the South Hill kid.

Sam Kalinski's cousin. That explained the assassin comment. Lots of South Hill Ukrainians were communists, Basil had told me, so that would explain why the kid called us rich.

"When I tell my brother the guy who hit Sam is here at the fair, he's going to come after you," said the South Hill kid.

"Like we're scared," said Martin.

"You better be," said the South Hill kid. "My brother Frank is fourteen."

"Roy beats up fourteen-year-olds all the time," said Martin.

"My brother will clobber him," said the South Hill kid.

"If he wants to fight Roy, you'll have to fight all of us," said Martin. "We got kids from all over the north west."

"There's a hundred kids from South Hill."

"We got double that," said Martin.

"I'm so scared," said the South Hill kid.

"You better be," said Martin.

"Oh ya!"

"Ya!"

As I pulled my little brother away from the South Hill kid I noticed that a crowd was once again forming around us. If this kept up the cops would soon be here.

"Look," I said, stepping in front of Martin. "I'm sorry for hitting Sam. I never meant to. The pitch got away from me and he turned right into it."

"You hit him cause he's the best batter, to get him out of the game, everyone knows that," said the South Hill kid. "Rich kids from the north side never play fair, everyone knows that."

Many of the kids in the crowd shouted agreement. "Just like the doctors," yelled one.

"We aren't rich," said Martin. "Tell em Brian, you said our house is tiny, even for poor people and you're a communist."

Brian nodded, embarrassed.

"Our Dad works at Robin Hood. We aren't rich, right Brian?" Another nod.

"Lots of our dads got laid off from the CPR," said the South Hill kid. "All the fancy houses are on the north side, everyone knows that."

A half dozen kids voiced their agreement.

"What's your name?" I said to the South Hill kid.

"Sam, same as my cousin," he answered. "They call me Little Sam."

"How old are you?" I said.

"Eight," said Little Sam.

"Your cousin is still at the hospital?" I said.

"Stupid doctors wouldn't see him yesterday," said another older kid who Roy also remembered from the crowd at the game. "They said it wasn't an emergency."

"Doctors were partying all night in Regina," said Brian. "My Dad says the businessmen and lawyers and them were having a good time after the rally."

"Sam came home last night," said Little Sam. "His face is all swelled up so this morning they took him back to Providence. He missed the game after the first inning and now he's missing the fair. He saved up since Christmas."

"I'm sorry," I said. "Ask Sam, him and I have always got along. We played hockey against each other last three seasons. Never had a fight. We were in the same oratorical contest this year."

"He won," said Little Sam.

True, but he gave a sucky speech about the importance of the Blessed Virgin while my title was: 'Why I am a Socialist'.

"Can you tell him I'm sorry?" I said.

Little Sam looked down at the ground.

"And also say that our coach told me if we win the tournament and he is okay, we're going to ask him to play for us in Grand Forks," I said. "We're allowed to pick up two players. Coach said he's the best power hitter in Moose Jaw."

As I spoke I noticed Brian turn to look at something. As I was about to follow, I felt a sharp pain from the back of my head. Someone or something had hit me.

"Watch out Roy," shouted Brian. "Fisher!"

Off balance and hurt I turned to see Mike Fisher about to sucker punch me again. I followed the momentum of the first blow to roll away from my attacker and hit the ground. As a result Fisher's fist missed its target, but the fall onto the rough pavement probably hurt worse than any punch.

"Get up you chicken," said Fisher. "You're not getting away this time."

"Leave my brother alone," shouted Martin, as he tried to tackle the much bigger guy.

"Graduated to sucker punches now," said Brian as he moved between Fisher and me.

"Get out of my way," said Fisher to both Martin and Brian.

As Fisher pushed Martin away, I got up.

"Touch my little brother or my friend and you'll regret it," I said.

"Get the little monkey away from me then," said Fisher, as some kids laughed at Martin pushing a kid twice his size.

"Martin," I said, motioning for him to get behind me.

Brian and Martin both stepped away to allow Fisher and I to face each other.

"No one is coming to your rescue this time," said Fisher, who moved from side to side as if he were about to lunge at me.

"Six against one or a sucker punch," I said, remaining perfectly still. "You ever hear of fighting fair?"

The crowd of kids grew larger and shrunk the space available to do battle.

"Here, now, you, me," said Fisher. "Is that fair enough?"

"He was looking forward to crushing one of your weak-ass pitches over the centerfield fence tomorrow," said Brian.

"Keep out of this, commie Jew boy," said Fisher.

"Afraid to meet him on a baseball diamond?" said Brian. "So you have to sucker punch him in a crowd of kids?"

"Hey pansy, you want a piece of me too?" said Fisher.

"There isn't enough to go around," I said, taking a step towards him. "There won't be anything left after I finish you off."

"Come on then," said Fisher.

"What are you waiting for?" I said. "Expect me to turn around so you can sucker punch me again?"

As I glared and Fisher circled, there was a commotion in the crowd of kids that surrounded us for a radius of at least twenty feet. It was the same adult who broke up Martin's fight making his way from the edge of the crowd.

"This guy has already threatened once to call the cops," I said, motioning with my head towards the oncoming adult.

"So?" said Fisher.

"So you want to fight, meet me somewhere a little more private," I said.

"Ya!" said one of the kids in the crowd.

"Where?" said Fisher.

I shrugged.

"Over by the stables," said another kid in the crowd.

"Ya!"

"Over by the stables!" came another voice. "There's no adults there, just some old piles of dried up horse manure."

"We'll fight 'em in the horse shit," came a very young sounding voice.

"North Hillers are horse shit," came another.

"South Hillers eat shit!"

"That shit belongs to the East Siders!"

"Cause they all got diarrhea."

"You've got shit for brains."

"Least we got brains."

"Fight!"

"Okay," I said. "Over by the stable."

"Half an hour?" said Fisher.

"Okay," I said. "Half an hour."

"Half an hour," said Little Sam. "We'll be there too."

Some of the South Hill kids cheered.

Fisher and I glared at each other for another few seconds and then, just as the adult entered the circle, we turned away and headed in opposite directions.

"Hey," said the adult. "I told you I was going to call the police if there was anymore rough stuff."

But no one listened. Within a minute the crowd of a few hundred kids had evaporated back into the midway.

Katherine, letter 12

October 27, 1962

Dear President Kennedy,

On Saturdays I usually sleep in until 9 o'clock, but I was up before six this morning. I sure hope you are getting some sleep because I don't think many people around the world are. My father says a good sleep is very important to good decision making, although I know he, as a surgeon, often must work all night long. My father is very happy that you are holding firm on Cuba, but he says you should have sent troops by now. He says the only way to deal with the Russians is by force and that they must learn we mean business when we make a threat. He says that those missiles in Cuba offer an extraordinary opportunity to demonstrate our resolve and armed might to the Reds. He says you better not compromise, just to save some lives.

Sometimes I'm not sure if I agree with everything my father says. I know he is a very smart man and if he says something there must be a good reason for it, but sometimes I just don't understand.

I asked my father if he knew how many people would be killed in a nuclear war and he didn't know. Maybe millions. Maybe tens of millions. Maybe hundreds of millions. But he said the number really doesn't matter. It's the principle. You have to do what's right regardless of how many people die. What I don't understand is that it seems like my father doesn't believe saving millions of lives by avoiding war is doing right. Yet he works very hard to save every single patient who comes to him on the operating table. He doesn't ask who is at fault for their injury or disease. Saving a person's life is the only principle that counts at that moment.

I know I'm not quite 14 and there's lots for me to learn, but sometimes I think my father doesn't get enough sleep and then says things that are more about being grumpy than about being right. I sure hope you and your generals are getting enough sleep.

I just have two short parts left to my story.

Katherine called her father that morning and told him about the snakes.

"Have you heard about the socialists' plan to use garter snakes against the doctors?" she said.

"Snakes!" he said. "Garter snakes?"

"Little socialist boys have been collecting them and giving them to teenage socialist gangsters who are going to do something with them very soon," said Katherine. "I couldn't find out what they're going to do, but it definitely involves snakes."

"You didn't hear anything about rats?" said her father.

"Rats?" said Katherine.

"There's been a few police reports about kids with bags of rats," said her father. "The attorney-general phoned the head of the College and said some kids were planning to do something that involved rats and doctors."

"Rats and doctors?" asked Katherine.

"And now snakes," said her father.

"What are they planning to do?" said Katherine.

"We don't know," said her father.

"Can't the police arrest them?" said Katherine

"For collecting rats and snakes?"

"But we know they're planning to do something," said Katherine.

"Perhaps we could go to the police if we knew their actual plan," said her father. "Can you find out what it is?"

"I can try," said Katherine.

And so she did. She spent the next two days calling and visiting every one of her friends across the city. Some of the girls had heard about the collecting of snakes, but no one knew what for. Katherine begged and pleaded and threatened, but she had no new information by the day of the big Keep Our Doctors rally in Regina, when she next saw her father.

"I didn't find out anything more about the snakes or the rats," said Katherine standing next to her father near the front of a crowd of thousands. "But I do have an idea."

Her father wasn't interested. Instead he talked with the important businessmen and politicians and physicians who stood at the front of the crowd. Katherine was disappointed, even though she understood that her father was an important person who other important people wanted to talk to. She had worked so hard to get the information and now he wasn't even interested.

The next morning when Katherine and her mother returned to Moose Jaw, Cindy was waiting on the steps to their house.

"Did you hear?" said Cindy, as soon as Katherine got out of the car.

"About what?" said Katherine.

"They put snakes and rats in every doctor's house yesterday," said Cindy. "Snakes and rats. And now all the little kids are calling the doctors snakes and rats. They think it's funny."

"Snakes and rats," repeated Katherine.

"The little kids are running around giggling about snakes and rats. They just keep saying the doctors are snakes and rats."

Was that their plan? To make the little kids call doctors snakes and rats? That was it? Why would anyone care what little kids thought?

"By the end of the day everyone will know," said Cindy. "Including the adults."

That's right, thought Katherine.

"I hate snakes and rats," said Cindy. "They're creepy."

Katherine felt defeated, but she was also smiling. A good trick. There was a lesson to be learned.

"And there's something else," said Cindy. "I got a phone call from Sally McCutcheon about twenty minutes ago. Roy and his stupid piano playing friend Brian are at the Exhibition. She saw them on the way there. And guess who I called to tell about that? Mike Fisher. He's going to pound the crap out of Roy and anyone else who tries to stop him.

Roy, letter 17

Oct. 25-26, 1962

Dear President Kennedy,

I'm starting this pretty late Thursday night and I'm tired after writing two letters already today, so I think this will get finished tomorrow morning. Since I was in my room all afternoon and Mom thought I was sleeping she let me watch the late news. Things seem pretty bad. The guys on TV are talking like war is a sure thing. I hope that's not true. There was a story about some people in Regina stocking up their bomb shelters, preparing for at least a year underground, they said. We don't have a bomb shelter. I don't want the world to end in a nuclear explosion. I better stop thinking about that and get back to the story.

The area on the other side of the barns was only used during the annual rodeo, so when almost two hundred boys from all corners of town showed up on a hot summer afternoon there was not a single adult in sight. They were either working or enjoying themselves on the midway.

Martin had spent the half hour rounding up every kid from the northwest side of town, and boys from the eastside and South Hill did the same. I spent my time talking with Brian about what we should do. With only a few minutes to go before the fight was to begin we were still on the midway arguing.

"Fisher will be there in a couple of minutes and if we don't show we might as well move out of town," I said.

"You're welcome to the spare bedroom at my Mom's place in Winnipeg," he said.

"You'd really do that?" I said. "Run away?"

"Think of it as living to fight another day. It's better than a shootout at the Moose Jaw Corral," said Brian. "I saw that movie and we all end up dead."

At least he hadn't lost his sense of humor.

"Who says we lose?" I said.

"You got kids from the eastend and South Hill all trying to clobber you," said Brian. "It's going to be two-against-one."

"I can manage this," I said. "Just follow my lead."

"Somebody is going to start throwing punches before you get the opportunity to manage anything," said Brian. "There's too many kids. All it takes is one hothead to say a bad word or throw a rock or touch somebody the wrong way."

"I know what to do," I said, even though I hadn't a clue.

Think on my feet. That was the key. Be prepared for anything. A good idea would spring up, something that would allow me to gain control. Something always came up.

I began walking towards the stables. Brian reluctantly followed.

"This is crazy," said Brian. "There's no point."

"The point is to prove we won't back down," I said.

"Let's have a fight to prove we're not scared to have a fight?"

"What was the point of the First World War?" I said. "The war to end all wars."

"Exactly," said Brian. "And something like twenty million soldiers died."

Life was full of things you had to do and not think about it: boring stupid homework, cleaning your room, table manners, being nice to adults who were jerks, and fights. Brian didn't have any status, that's why he failed to see the importance of standing up for himself. He had nothing to lose.

"I thought you were a pacifist?" said Brian.

"I am," I said.

"A fighting pacifist?"

"Even pacifists fight for what they believe."

Brian gave me a look.

"We all fight for something or against other things," I said. "Pacifists fight for peace, doctors against medicare, bosses against unions, students against principals, Jews against Nazis, Ku Klux Klan against negroes, socialists for medicare, unions for higher pay, capitalists against communists, negroes for equal rights. Life is all about fighting or fighting back."

"There's fighting and then there's fighting," said Brian, pretending to box. "I prefer to do mine non-violently."

"Me too, but sometimes there's no choice," I said.

"You always have a choice," said Brian.

"You don't have an infinite range of choices," I said. "Sometimes you have to choose the best of a bad bunch."

Brian stared.

"I don't want to fight and I'll do everything I can to get out of it, but if it's the best alternative, I take it," I said. "If you don't make the same choice, I won't hold it against you. I understand. You don't have anything to lose."

"Everyone thinks I'm a sissy Jew anyway?" said Brian.

"It's just the way things are."

I stood next to the grandstand, around the corner of which was a short walk to the passageway between two stables. "I gotta go," I said. "Don't want to be late for my funeral."

I smiled. Brian smiled back. I turned and headed for the other side of the stables. As I entered the passageway I glanced behind.

"I'm covering your back," said Brian. "I'll scream and then run like hell if anyone tries to jump you."

I couldn't help smiling despite my nerves about what was ahead of me.

As we entered the open area between the stables and the grandstand, kids hung out in three groups. The eastside was on my left, South Hill in the middle near the side of the grandstand and northwest on my right. It was mostly nine-, ten- and eleven-year olds, with a smattering of younger and older kids scattered throughout. There were only a few guys as big as me.

As we walked towards the northwest gang, a loud voice came from the eastsiders. "Hey Shit, glad you could make it," said Fisher. "Thought you were going to chicken out."

Some of the younger kids around him "clucked" like hens and one imitated a rooster.

As I glared at Fisher, Little Sam, who stood at the front of the South Hill gang flapped his arms then pulled a much taller, older kid forward.

"My brother Frank gets to fight you first," said Little Sam. "To pay you back for hitting our cousin in the face."

Frank looked uncomfortable as he sort of smiled and sort of scowled. I sort of knew the guy. He hung around Moose Jaw beach and was kind of weird, shy, not a fighter and definitely not a bully. Mostly he was interested in girls. No worry about fighting him.

"I get you first Big Shit. I'm gonna rub your face in that pile of horse manure," said Fisher, pointing to the dried remains of the rodeo a month earlier. "Come on, you want to start right now?"

As Fisher moved towards the pile of seasoned manure I looked back at Frank from South Hill.

"I don't know, Frank has a pretty good reason to fight me first don't you think Mike?" I said, loud enough for most kids to hear. "I did bust his cousin's face. What did I ever do to you?"

"The real reason Fisher wants to fight Roy is to hurt him and knock him out of the all-star final tomorrow," Brian said to Martin as they stood near the border between South Hill and northwest kids. "He's afraid because Roy is the best pitcher in the city. Just watch, he'll go after his right arm."

The few South Hill kids near enough to overhear the conversation quickly relayed the information back into the crowd.

"You looked at me with your ugly face," said Fisher, with that same smug grin he had when bragging about how great a baseball player his Dad had been or how much money the family's new Cadillac cost. "And your northwest gang of little monkeys has been trying to stop us from stepping foot on the west side of town."

"That's a lie," shouted Martin. "It's the eastenders who are stopping us from going to Crescent Park or the Natatorium or the Y."

An assenting chorus rumbled through the northwest crowd.

"Little Shit lies just like Big Shit," said Fisher, to the approval of the eastenders. "All the Shits are lily-livered-lying losers."

As he said this Fisher shoved my right shoulder, then slugged me, not hard, on the arm. Some of the kids in the South Hill crowd noticed this and passed along confirmation of Brian's analysis.

I ignored him and took a few steps towards Frank and the South Hill gang. Fisher began clucking like a chicken and was joined by many of the eastenders.

"Hey Frank, Fisher is trying to make me fight him first," I said. "What have you got to say about that?"

Little Sam nudged his cousin towards me.

"I'm thinking I should fight the easiest guy first," I continued. "So I got something left for the second. What do you think? Which one of you guys will be the easiest to beat? Fisher thinks it's him."

Most of the northwest kids laughed and were joined by a few South Hillers.

"Hey, I agree with that," said Frank, smiling. "His mouth is tough, so I'd worry if you were a ham sandwich. But since you're not, maybe you should fight him first."

This time the taunts and laughter came from the South Hill gang. Fisher took a few angry steps towards Frank.

"Make up your mind Fisher, you want to fight me or Frank?" I said.

The toughest 12-year old on the east side stopped and turned back to me.

"Eastenders are all alike," I said to Frank. "Yap yap yap, like a little Terrier puppy, but when it comes time to put up or shut up, they always got an excuse. 'Oh you didn't fight fair' or 'my mommy told me to come home.'"

Frank laughed, as did the kids around him. One started to "yap" like a puppy. Fisher turned towards the culprit, glaring, but the crowd emboldened him to change the mimicked noise to a puppy's whimper. The South Side and northwest kids roared with laughter, further taunts and more canine impersonations.

It was at that moment, surrounded by almost two hundred kids prepared to fight each other for nothing more important than the part of town on which their house happened to be located, that the idea came to me. I had to act fast. The words that had been tumbling out of my mouth could be made, retroactively, part of my plan.

"These eastenders think they're something special cause they have all the good stuff on their side of town," I said to Frank. "Crescent Park, the Y, the Natatorium, the Exhibition grounds. It's not fair they have it all, but just to make it worse they want to hog it all for themselves."

There were cries of "it's not fair" and "they can't stop us" from the South Hill crowd.

"That's a lie," shouted Fisher above the rest of the denials from his eastenders. "We said Big Shit and Little Shit and their gang aren't allowed, that's all."

"If they get away with stopping us who do you think will be next?" I said to Frank and the other kids nearby.

"Stop talking and let's fight," shouted Fisher.

"The whole city pays for Crescent Park and the Natatorium and the Y and the exhibition grounds. Why should the eastsiders say who can and can't use them?"

The nods of agreement and the buzz of kids talking confirmed that I was getting through to the South Hill gang.

"Stop talking and let's fight," repeated Fisher.

I could hear conversation fragments from the South Hillers over top of the eastsiders who had begun to chant: "Fight. Fight. Fight."

"He's right. ... If they can stop ... we'll be next. ... Ain't right. Let them try ... we'll stop 'em going to the beach."

I took a few menacing steps towards Fisher. Hands down at my side I stared into the bully's eyes.

"Okay you want to fight now, let's do it," I said.

"About time," said Fisher, who put his fists up like a boxer.

"Everyone," I shouted as loud as I could. "Everyone who thinks the eastsiders should be able to say who can use the Natatorium and Crescent Park and the Y and the exhibition grounds against everyone who thinks those things belong to all of Moose Jaw."

I noticed a smile appear on Brian's face.

"Everyone who supports the eastsiders over there and everyone else over here," I shouted, as I pointed behind Fisher and myself.

"Come on," shouted Brian. "Everyone who supports the eastsiders over there and everyone else over here. Hurry it up so we can start the fight. Hurry it up."

A few of the South Hill kids walked to the marshalling area that Brian was directing them to, then the rest quickly followed. Within a few minutes there was a crowd of 135 kids facing an eastside group half that size. Cries of "not fair" and "what's going on" swept through the smaller gang like the mumps through a Grade 1 class.

As Fisher glared, I focused on my opponent and maintained my centre of gravity by keeping my knees bent and equal weight on both feet, just like Basil had shown me. A sudden attack would not catch me off guard.

As the larger group of kids felt their power a few voices could be heard inciting a charge. "The city belongs to all of us," said one. "They can't stop us from going anywhere," said another. "Let's teach 'em a lesson. Let's fight."

As the combined force of the northwest and South Hill surged forward and began surrounding the outnumbered eastenders, I could see Fisher panic.

"You still want to fight?" I said quietly.

Fisher said nothing, but backed up a few paces, as did the rest of his east-of-Main crowd. I maintained the distance between us, by pressing forward as I spoke.

"Come on, let's pound the crap out of them," came one particularly loud and clear voice from the middle of the bigger gang.

"There's not enough of them for us each to have someone," said another boy.

"You grab the top half of one and I'll take the bottom," answered another voice, resulting in a wave of laughter.

"Let's beat up each one of them twice," said another.

"I've got no reason to fight, unless you force me to," I said, my body almost pressed against Fisher's as the combined forces of northwest and south pushed me forward.

"Last chance," I said, watching Fisher's eyes.

He knew that I knew his situation was hopeless.

"You want to give now or after we fight?" I asked him quietly so no one else could hear.

His reaction was predictable because I'd gone up against Fisher since we were eight or nine in hockey and baseball. He never wanted to fight if he thought there was any chance of losing.

"What do you want?" he mumbled.

But just as he was about to back down, I saved him.

"What did you call me? A Catholic bastard? I can't believe you said that," I screamed as loud as I could. My voice was powerful enough to grab the attention of every kid in the crowd.

Fisher looked confused.

"You're telling me I'll go to hell cause I'm Catholic?" I yelled. "You go to hell!"

Fisher took a step back from me and turned to the kids around him as if to ask: "What's going on?"

"I'm not putting up with your Protestant bullshit anymore," I continued as loud as I could. "The hell with you. You're all bastards.

Anglicans, United, Baptists, all of you. You're rich bastards who think you can run the world. Keep all the good jobs at the CPR for the Orange Order. Discriminate against the Irish and French and Ukrainian and Polish just cause we're Catholic. I say you're the ones who are going straight to hell."

Well, you would have thought I was a farting cow the way kids reacted. They all backed away from me.

Brian looked more stunned than anyone. I ignored him. I knew what I was doing.

"You're always picking on Catholics," I shouted. "Protestants think they're so tough, but I'm not afraid. Come on, I'll fight you all."

A rumble of mumbled conversations rolled through the assembled crowd. I could hear kids agreeing with me on both the eastside and northwest-South Hill gangs.

"All of us Catholics are going to fight back when you attack us," I screamed. "Not like back in the 1930s when the Protestants started the Ku Klux Klan here in Moose Jaw to pick on the Catholics in Saskatchewan just like they did to the negroes in the United States. This time we won't let you get away with it. This time we'll beat the crap out of you."

I knew most of the Catholic kids had heard the story about the KKK and how almost every important Protestant family in Moose Jaw had joined. The Klan tried to stop nuns from teaching and lit crosses on the lawns of French Canadians and even paid prostitutes to dress up as nuns, then sent them into bars, just to make Catholics look bad.

Basil said the important Moose Jaw families now pretended it never happened.

"What about it Fisher? You got pictures of your grandpa wearing a white sheet like all the Klan members did?" I shouted.

"That's a lie," said Fisher.

I could hear the arguments develop inside both the massed gangs. "I hate Catholics. Protestants go to hell!" The united forces of northwest and South Hill had begun to disintegrate because the garlic eaters from the south were mostly Catholic, while the white bread, with the crusts cut off, north side kids were mostly Protestant.

"We got just as much right to be in Canada as any Limey Protestant," I shouted. "Catholics have always been the majority, even if you damn Protestants run the country."

The arguments over religion had spread to every corner of the massed crowd of kids. Even Martin was losing control of his immediate circle of seven and eight year olds from our neighborhood who were almost all Protestant.

"Okay Fisher, if you want to fight me let's do it properly," I shouted. "Let's fight over something more important than what side of town we live on. Let's fight for our religion. Protestants against Catholics."

My voice was loud enough to drown out the other kids. There was silence for a moment.

"Come on, Catholics over here and Protestants over there," I shouted as loudly as I could. "Come on."

Some of the kids moved quickly, others reluctantly, but all, except for Brian, Sam and two other Chinese kids I didn't recognize, were soon formed into two almost equal gangs.

"I'm not a Protestant or a Catholic," said Sam and the other two Chinese kids both said, "Me neither."

Brian stared at me like I was crazy.

Katherine, letter 13

October 28, 1962

Dear President Kennedy,

Everybody I talk to thinks the world is going to end soon. War was much simpler before the atom bomb. You could think about just destroying one country, but now it could be the whole planet. It's hard to imagine why everyone should die just because of some stupid little Communist island.

My father says it's not really true that the atom bomb changes everything. He says chemical weapons could destroy the world too and they haven't been used at all since the First World War. He says we will continue to have wars, just not ones where countries use atom bombs. I hope he is right.

I'd much rather think about my story.

Katherine was very unhappy that day, after she came back from the Keep Our Doctors rally in Regina. First was the news about the snakes and rats. Katherine couldn't get over how stupid she had been not to figure out the plan and warn her father.

"They made everybody laugh at the doctors," said Cindy.

And she was right. People were laughing at the doctors. Kids at first, but soon enough it would be adults too.

Then Sally phoned Cindy, who went to Katherine's place.

"He did it again," said Cindy as soon as Katherine opened the door.

"Who?"

"Roy," she said.

"Did what?" said Katherine.

"Got out of the fight with his big mouth," said Cindy.

"Who told you?"

"Sally called. Her little brother Wayne and his friend Sam were there and saw everything. They said Roy got punched once and went flying, but then he talked his way out of it and every kid there was cheering him."

Katherine didn't really care about Roy being beat up, so that wasn't too bad, but all the kids cheering him bothered her. And that he could talk his way out of another fight, that bothered her too. Why did the other kids always seem to follow him? The fact Roy was socialist and the other kids listened to him bothered Katherine a lot.

The rest of that day and the next Katherine was miserable. All she could think about was Roy's success and her failure. She moped around the house, reading her father's old National Geographic magazines and her mother's Chatelaines, then two Nancy Drew books that she had read before.

The next afternoon her father made a surprise visit to take her to the Exhibition.

"I'm withdrawing my services for the night to take my daughter out for a good time," he said.

And so they went to the Fair and Katherine held her father's hand as they walked down the midway.

"What's wrong?" he said. "Why so glum?"

"The snakes and the rats," she said. "The socialists won."

"How do you figure?" he said.

"All the kids were laughing at the doctors yesterday, calling them rats and snakes," Katherine said. "And lots of the adults too."

Her father stopped walking and looked right into his daughter's eyes.

"Good," he said. "That's exactly what we need right now."

Katherine did not understand.

"Don't you see?" said her father. "We want physicians to leave Saskatchewan. If people are laughing at them and calling them names, why would any of them stay?"

Katherine stared at her father.

"This is war, my darling, and in a war you must do whatever it takes to win," said her father. "If you must lose a few battles, sacrifice a few soldiers for ultimate victory, that's the price you pay."

"It's okay that they made people laugh at the doctors? And that we did nothing to stop it?"

"I knew something like this was going to happen the day before you called me," said her father. "Why else would they be collecting rats and snakes?"

"But you didn't tell me," Katherine said.

"Of course not," said her father. "Your friends and their stories, they go both ways. I didn't want anyone to stop this."

"So that more doctors would leave Saskatchewan?" said Katherine.

Her father nodded. "You have to understand the bigger picture. Saskatchewan is a just a small piece of the problem. Even all of Canada. What's important is preventing socialist medicine from coming to America. That's what this is really all about."

Katherine was amazed again at how smart her father was.

"Do you understand?" he said.

She nodded. She did understand. She understood about the doctors and about the bigger picture and that her father used her the way she used Cindy and the other girls. She understood that the smarter people used stupider people and that's the way life worked. It was a lesson she would never forget.

Roy, letter 18

Oct. 26, 1962

Dear President Kennedy,

Basil came home for the weekend and he's been pretty nice to everyone. I think it's because he knows the whole world is just about over. Is there anything you can do?

I know you're smarter than me, but I don't understand the point of blowing up everything and everybody with atom bombs. This might be my last letter because the story is just about over. Here comes the ending.

There we were lined up Catholics against Protestants. The kids were all jumbled, guys who lived on the same block their whole lives faced off against each other. Martin was about to fight Billy from across the back alley.

While Fisher still had not figured out my plan and didn't like to see his best friend (who was also the best fighter on the east side) lined up beside me, he was more confident standing at the head of a gang of Protestants that was pretty evenly matched against Catholics than he had been when outnumbered two-to-one. His look had changed back to one of meanness.

Religion made a lot of kids mean. Guys were saying things against the Catholic kid from down the block or the Protestant boy from the next street over. The words were no different than I heard before, but something about so much of it in one place made it seem scarier. Guys were feeding off each other, competing to say the meanest things, so it got worse and worse really quickly.

A few shoving matches broke out and I got scared that I had lost control. Then Brian said something. I don't know if he figured out my plan, but whatever the reason, it worked.

"Hold on there," he shouted at two eight year olds who had exchanged a few quick punches. "We're going to do this right or not at all."

The two kids looked at him like he was crazy.

"Did anyone say the fight had started?" screamed Brian, in his whiny tone of voice. "Well, did they?"

The two offending fighters shook their heads.

"Who the hell made you referee?" shouted Fisher.

"Fate," said Brian. "I am neither Catholic nor Protestant. I am a Jewish atheist."

There were oohs and ahs from throughout the crowd.

"As far as I'm concerned all of your religions are ridiculous," he continued. "I am above it all, which is why I make the perfect referee."

"Or maybe we change the rules to Christians against Jews," shouted one of the boys from Mackie's block.

A few kids laughed.

"Ya, let's make it Christians against Jews and Chinks," shouted another.

A pack of about ten kids began to make a circle around Brian, Sam and the other two Chinese kids.

"Christians against Jews and Chinks," repeated another.

We were losing control and I had to do something fast.

"Christians against Jews and Chinks," the same kid shouted again.

Another half dozen guys broke off from the main group to surround the four non-Christian boys, who looked frightened.

"Christians against Jews and Chinks," a few of the kids were now chanting.

While most guys stayed in their Catholics versus Protestant pairings, some broke away and began pushing the smallest Chinese kid, who was no more than seven or eight.

"Chinky, chinky Chinaman," chanted one boy, ten or eleven, as his buddy pushed the Chinese kid, who was now whimpering.

"Chinamen and Jewboy," said another, with three other kids around Brian.

"Catholics will burn in hell for all eternity," said a kid a few feet away.

Shoving matches had broken out between Catholics and Protestants, the non-Christians were surrounded and it looked like the whole crowd was about to blow up when the words came out of my mouth almost before I had the thought.

"Slug me hard on my nose," I said to Fisher, who had been distracted by the fights breaking out around us.

"What?" he answered.

"Slug me hard as you can on my nose," I repeated. "Now."

He looked at me like I was planning some sort of trick.

"Just do it," I said. "I won't hit back. I promise."

Fisher stared.

"Do it," I said.

And he did. He pulled his right hand back a few inches and then swung it at me as hard as he could.

It seemed like slow motion as I watched the clenched fingers get closer and closer to my face. I held myself still as long as I could and then right at the last moment, just before the punch was about to land on my nose, I threw myself back as hard as I could. The combination of Fisher's fist landing and my take off gave me so much momentum that I flew through the air like in one of those saloon fights in a cowboy movie. Throwing my arms wide I plowed down three of the six guys who had surrounded Sam.

While I had avoided some of the blow, Fisher still caught me hard enough to burst a vein in my nose and as I sat up, on top of three kids, blood spurted everywhere.

My flight, the bowling ball effect, the blood and the resulting screams gained everyone's attention. Kids scrambled to get a good look and in a few seconds almost two hundred boys were spread out in a circle around me.

While I hadn't planned on the blood, it proved useful.

"Oh my god, he knocked off his nose," shouted one little guy.

"Did you see him fly through the air?" said another.

"Holy cow!" screamed another. "Look at that red stuff!"

"Roy," I heard Martin shout.

I was kind of woozy as the kids I flattened crawled out from under me.

"Roy!" shouted Martin again. "Are you alright?"

"He knocked him out," said one voice.

"What a punch!" said another.

"Did you see that?"

"That was the hardest punch I ever saw!"

I could hear lots of oohs and ahs as I opened my eyes to see Brian and Martin staring down at me.

"Did he kill him?" came one little kid's voice.

"He's alive, but I bet his nose is broken," said another older boy.
Martin turned to Fisher.

"That was a dirty trick," he said. "A sucker's punch."

"Sucker punch," said Brian.

"You hit Roy when he wasn't looking," said Martin.

"And broke his nose," said Brian.

"He better go to the hospital," said the loudmouth kid from
Mackie's block. "He could bleed to death."

"Ya, he could bleed to death," said another.

I had suffered a real gusher. Probably the worst ever, although
there was one time in Grade 3 when I got a tetherball straight
on the noggin during recess and was still bleeding when I got
home from school.

"He better go to hospital," repeated the loudmouth.

"What's the point?" said a kid beside him. "The doctors are still
on strike."

That was my cue. I stood up, a little wobbly on my legs, but not
too bad. It wasn't the first punch to the face I'd ever taken and it
certainly wasn't the hardest, even though it had looked good.

"Roy's getting up," came a voice.

"Now Fisher is going to get it," said another.

"Fisher's in big trouble."

Absolutely everyone stared. As the blood pumped out of my
nose on every heartbeat, I glared at Fisher. He was scared. I
looked like the guy who climbs out of the coffin in Premature
Burial. I took a step towards Fisher and he backed away, but
then I stopped. Instead of threatening the guy who slugged me I
looked around at the crowd and said: "It's not right that the doctors are on strike."

While the blood covering my clothes probably gained me some
extra sympathy, I knew most of the kids came from families like
mine. Most people in Moose Jaw believed in Medicare. While
some didn't want to go against their own doctor, most people,
other than rich business families, were behind the government.

"They won't see me, just like they wouldn't see your cousin,"
I said to Little Sam and his brother Frank, who were about a
dozen feet away. "But if I was rich like Fisher they'd see me right
away. Or if I was the son of doctor."

Little Sam and his brother nodded.

"They'd see you then," said an older South Hill kid whose name I didn't know.

"Rich kids always get special treatment," I said, to the nods of many.

"That's for sure," said Brian.

"Rich kids are assholes," said the loudmouth from Mackie's block.

"I hate doctors," came a voice from the edge of the crowd.

"Me too," rang out from multiple locations.

"Rich kids against the rest of us, that's the fight we should be having," I said, loud enough for everyone to hear.

"Ya!" shouted Brian.

Nods of agreement everywhere.

"Rich kids against everyone else," I shouted. "That's the real fight. The important fight. Teach them a lesson."

"All the rich kids over here," said Brian.

"Rich kids over there," shouted the loudmouth.

"Rich kids over there," said Little Sam.

Cries of "rich kids over there" traveled through the crowd like the wind through a field of wheat. But no one moved. No one would admit to being rich.

"What's the matter?" said Brian. "No one wants to be rich? Usually the rich kids are showing off."

"Hey Fisher," I said. "You're always bragging about how rich your Dad is."

The kids who knew Fisher nodded or voiced their agreement.

Other guys shouted out the names of kids in their neighborhood who they knew to be rich. Cries of " rich kid" and "he's a rich kid" came from ahead, behind, left and right. A half dozen guys were pushed out and deposited in the middle of the crowd.

A bunch of kids started chanting, "rich kids, rich kids, rich kids" and the boys who had been identified looked scared. "Doctor lovers," screamed the loudmouth. "I hate rich kids," said another.

The crowd was worked up. Boys pushed forward to get a swipe at the rich kids in the middle, but before things could get out of hand again I shouted, as loud as I could, which made a spurt of blood gush from my nose onto three or four kids near me.

"Hold on, wait a minute, I want to say something before you beat up the rich kids."

"Hold on, Roy wants to say something," shouted Brian.

"Hold on, Roy wants to say something," echoed the loudmouth.

The spurting blood and my being a sucker punch victim gave me everyone's attention, at least for a few seconds.

"What do you want to say, Roy?" shouted the loudmouth. "Before we pound the dollars and sense out of them."

Kids laughed.

"Get it? Dollars and sense?" said the loudmouth.

More kids laughed.

"I guess I must look kind of funny with my nose gushing blood."

"Like Rudolph after Santa slugged him," said one smart aleck.

As the laughter died down I made sure everyone could hear me. "But not as funny as everyone who was willing to fight the kid from the other side of town, the kid with a different religion or the kid who has more money."

The crowd fell silent for a few seconds as my words sunk in.

"I look ridiculous because my nose is probably broken and my blood is everywhere, but you guys look even more stupid because you're like sheep being led by a dog."

I saw Brian smiling.

"Woof woof and you want to fight the South Hillers or the East-enders or the northwest kids. Woof woof and you want to fight Catholics or Protestants. Woof woof and you want to fight Jews and Chinese. Woof woof and you want to fight rich kids."

Many of the kids looked down at their feet.

"That's what I call ridiculous," I said, loud and clear. "I'd rather have blood all over my face than be a sheep that gets fooled into fighting."

I walked a few steps, as if to leave, but turned around.

"Why are you fighting? To prove what? How stupid you are?"

I let that sink in for a few seconds and then spoke again.

"Go ahead, fight all you want," I said, looking at Martin. "Just don't ask me to be as stupid as you are."

Then I turned and walked away. I didn't look back until I had passed by the grandstand.

Brian was behind me, followed by a long line of kids.

Katherine, letter 14

October 30, 1962

Dear President Kennedy,

My father is mad at you for promising never to invade Cuba, but also says you made the Russians back down. I think he's pretty happy, but he won't say it because he really doesn't like Democrats. My father says it's too early to tell how this all will work out and everything could still change because the Communists can't be trusted, but I think you must know what you're doing. I also think that getting the missiles out of Cuba is important so making promises is okay. Promises are easy. I mean the Russians never keep their promises so why should we keep ours?

You want to hear some really good news? I am moving to Los Angeles with my father at the beginning of December. A California Christmas! I am so happy.

My father got my mother to agree by doubling the amount of alimony he will pay. He really didn't want to, but I'm getting better at figuring out ways of getting him to do what I want. Smart people can always come up with a way.

This is the ending to my story. I had planned to tell you what my story meant but after talking with Mr. Rebalski I'm not going to. Mr. Rebalski says a good story speaks for itself and that each reader is supposed to figure out what it means to him. He says that if you must tell the reader what the story means then it is a failure.

I've thought a lot about how to end this. I thought maybe I should leave it the way it ended last letter, but I really want to tell you about what happened to the socialist Roy. He thought he was so smart, but in the end Katherine got even. It's important to understand that you can lose over and over, before you finally win, so never give up.

All through the summer Cindy complained to Katherine about how their plan to have Roy beaten up had failed. Actually Cindy said it was Katherine's plan that failed, despite the fact she would have taken credit if the plan had been successful. Then, in the last week of summer holidays, after about the tenth complaint, Katherine thought of a new plan, even better than the rest.

"I know how to make the principal give Roy the strap," said Katherine, as the two girls lay on their towels at the beach in River Park.

Cindy always attracted boys, who she paid more attention to than Katherine, but these words made her listen.

"Mr. Kalinsky? Give Roy the strap? No way," said Cindy. "Roy and his big brother Basil are Mr. Kalinsky's two favourite students ever."

Cindy was right about that. Katherine's father said Mr. Kalinsky was a socialist and had once tried to run for the provincial legislature for the CCF. Of course he liked Roy. But it wouldn't matter. Mr. Kalinsky would not have a choice. He'd have to strap Roy if he wanted to keep his job.

"The plan will work because Roy will do something that makes the principal strap him," said Katherine.

"What?" asked Cindy.

Just then two 15-year-old boys stopped to talk to Cindy so Katherine didn't have to tell her anything more about her plan, which was just as well because the fewer the people who know about something the easier it is to keep a secret. Katherine certainly had learned that over the past few months.

By the second week of school Katherine knew exactly what she had to do. It was really very easy. Duncan White Junior was a new kid in Grade 8 at St. Michael's. He looked like he should be in Grade 6, but he was a year older than Roy. His father, Duncan White Senior, was the owner of White Construction, one of Saskatchewan's largest builders, whose new house, a few blocks from the school, was the biggest in the new subdivision being built on the northwest outskirts of Moose Jaw.

By the afternoon of the first day of school, all the kids were calling him Junior, partly because of his name and partly because at the first recess he told everybody who would listen that his father was the richest man in the city. Duncan was a little spoiled and most of the kids in Grade 8 took a quick dislike to him.

Unlike most of the kids, who avoided Junior, Katherine made friends with him. It wasn't easy. He was a real little twerp. Every time he opened his mouth it was about all the toys he had in his very own rumpus room or the horse on his father's really big farm. Plus he was always trying to touch some girl's chest or look down their blouse, even though he didn't look much past eleven. But that made him all the better for Katherine's plan.

It was really very simple. Every so often, when Katherine learned about something bad one of the boys in class had done, she'd tell Junior.

"You know what Mario Fillipi did?" she said during morning recess. "He pulled the fire alarm yesterday."

"Mario did it?" said Junior.

Katherine nodded.

"Mary dared him," she said.

Just after lunch Mario was called to the principal's office and Katherine knew her plan was working. That day, after school, everyone was talking about who told on Mario. No one knew, but a few of the boys said they would find out.

Three days later Katherine again found out something interesting that she passed on to Junior.

"You know who wrote those swear words on the school door?" she said, walking home with Junior after school "Everyone says it was Maurice Lafleche. You know he lives just across the street? I was told he got up in the middle of the night and did it. Maurice told a bunch of the boys that he did it because Mario got the strap."

"Really?" said Junior.

Katherine nodded.

The next day Maurice was called into the principal's office. At lunch time all anyone could talk about was who could be the tattletale.

"When they find him, the boys will beat him up," said Cindy to a group of a half dozen girls.

"Ya," said Diane. "I wouldn't want to be him."

"Then they'll get the strap too," said Katherine.

"If the principal finds out," said Marie-Anne.

"He seems to find out everything," said Cindy. "There's a little squealer in this school."

"The boys will beat him up real good," said Diane. "But they'll do it on the weekend or something. They always get squealers."

"Yes," said Katherine. "That makes sense. You know what the boys used to do at my old school in Regina? They'd pick one of the boys to do something like that. They'd pick the one who would get into the least trouble."

"Least trouble?" asked Diane.

"The boy who the principal liked the most or who had a rich father or something like that," said Katherine. "The boys would pick someone like that to beat up the squealer. Then he'd do it away from school. That way even if the principal somehow found out, nothing too bad would happen to him."

"That's pretty smart," said Diane, as the other girls nodded in agreement.

After that Katherine was even more confident that her plan would work.

The following week Katherine was walking home with Junior and again she revealed a secret.

"Did you hear about the stolen cigarettes?" she said.

Junior shook his head.

"Maurice stole a whole carton from the 11th Avenue grocery and half the boys in the class go out to smoke them at lunch time," she said.

"Where?" said Junior.

"Behind the shack in the vacant lot," said Katherine, who thought everyone knew where that was, but could tell from Junior's look that he didn't. "Half a block down the alley behind the store."

Sure enough, two days later six boys were called into the principal's office. That evening Katherine received a phone call from Cindy.

"Did you hear? The boys had a meeting after school today and they decided Roy should beat up Duncan Junior," said

Cindy. "He's the tattletale. Diane saw him go into Mr. Kalinsky's office and she put her ear to the door and she heard him tell about the cigarettes."

Katherine smiled, but did not say anything.

"Was this your plan?" said Cindy.

"I don't know what you're talking about," said Katherine.

"Your plan?" said Cindy. "The one you started to tell me about on the beach?"

"I really don't know what you are talking about," said Katherine. "And I must get off the phone. My mother is expecting a call."

So far everything had worked perfectly. The hardest part of the plan was keeping it secret. Everything else had been easy.

The following Monday before school Diane told Katherine that Roy had beaten up Junior outside the Natatorium after Saturday public swimming. The next day Roy was called into the principal's office. At lunchtime he told everyone that he had gotten the strap. Five hits across his hands.

Katherine smiled at Cindy, but never said a word.

Roy, letter 19

Oct. 31, 1962

Dear President Kennedy,

One more letter. It's Halloween and I'm not going out trick or treating. I kind of miss it, but I'm twelve and five-foot-nine and people gave me funny looks last year when I was four inches shorter. Martin will give me some of his candy. First time he's gone out with friends and not a big brother, but no need to worry about him. He'll come home with the biggest bag of candy in the whole city.

It's hard to tell from the newspaper how things are going with you and Khrushchev. The Times Herald last night said you cancelled the spy planes over Cuba. That's good, I think. Anyhow, the story is over and I don't have anything more to say, except about what's gone on since that day at the fair. No more fights, except for a bit of pushing and shoving at the game on Saturday. And that didn't have anything to do with Martin or gangs or Fisher, just hockey. Martin's smarter now, about fighting and stuff like that. He didn't mean to be stupid and start all that bad stuff. He was just little. He learned. That's what we all have to do, right? The doctors and the government both sort of backed down and we got Medicare. Basil says it's too bad the government didn't open more community clinics and put more doctors on salary, but Mom and Dad say it was a good compromise. I don't know. I do know that at least sometimes it's a good thing to compromise instead of fight. Only bullies think they can win all the time. But you probably already know that cause you're president of the most powerful country in the world.

Anyway, I hope you know that.

Roy, letter 20

Dec. 26, 1962

Dear President Kennedy,

I still haven't heard from you, but I guess you get lots of letters and have more important things to do than answer a 12-year old from Moose Jaw. Sister Veronica says maybe you did read my letters because of the way everything turned out between you and Khrushchev. Or maybe someone close to you, like one of your brothers, read them and told you about it. Basil doesn't think you read the letters at all. He's joined a Trotskyist club at the university and Mom is really mad at him. He told her that women should have the choice to have an abortion and she kicked him out of the house. He had to go stay with his friend John Larkin. I hope you had a merry Christmas. Ours was okay, but a little tense because it was the first time Basil was back after the big fight. I got a new pair of hockey gloves because my old ones were awfully ratty. Martin got a road race set, which he bugged Mom and Dad about for months. I never seen him follow all the rules and be so polite as he was all this month. But it ended with a splash yesterday. Christmas dinner is one of the only times Mom lets us eat as much as we want so Martin pigged out on turkey, stuffing, mashed potatoes, gravy, cabbage rolls and mincemeat pie. He really likes mincemeat pie. I swear he ate twice as much as me and I'm twice as big. Anyway, he threw up on Aunt Myrtle when she tried to give him a hug before leaving. You should have seen the look on her face.

Maybe I'll write again and maybe I won't. Basil says you're still doing some rotten stuff against Castro and sending troops to a place called Vietnam. I know you have a good conscience and you should follow it. I'm pretty sure you'll get elected again in 1964 so there will be lots of times for me to think of another story to tell you.

Yours sincerely,
Roy

DIARY ENTRY, DEC. 9, 2000

She took her time reading the last dozen pages as he stared at her. She smiled after putting down the last page of his story, to indicate that it was okay to speak.

"You set me up four times?" he said.

"Three times I believe. Once was Cindy, if my story is to be believed," she said.

"You pretended to be my friend to get what you wanted," he said. "You've lived your whole life lying, twisting, cheating and manipulating. You really are the wicked witch of the west."

"How kind of you to say so," she said, then cackled. "And your story reveals an equal talent for manipulation."

He was offended. "To prevent war," he said.

"Different goal, same method," she said.

"You're twisting reality once again," he said. "I never tried to gain power over other people. I tried to help them gain power by understanding how they could overcome divisions and barriers."

"Cut the crap," she said. "You manipulated those kids for political ends. You and I were sharing the same political lesson with President Kennedy: Politics is all about manipulation."

Her words angered him, at least in part because the point she made had some validity. Or at least it was one plausible interpretation of his story.

"You used people," he said.

"So did you," she said.

"You pretended to like me," he said. "To set me up."

She shrugged. "I liked kissing you and you appeared to like kissing me. Both of us got what we wanted."

She oozed smugness, but he could still turn the table. "The irony is none of your set-ups worked, not once," he said.

"The principal strapped you," she said.

"Sorry, not true," he said. "Mr. Kalinski took me into his office and asked what happened and I told him the truth. I told him about Junior being a tattletale and bothering all the girls and how the boys decided I should beat him up because I would get into the least trouble. I told him about my fight with Junior and how I lifted him up in the air but didn't do anything except pull his pants down and make him walk home in his underwear. He laughed and told me how Duncan White Senior had called the superintendent and insisted that the culprit who assaulted his son be punished severely. He told me that, under the circumstance, the least he could do was give me the strap. Five whacks. I held out my hands and he pulled a tube of lipstick from his file cabinet and said, 'rub some of this on your hands and if anyone asks, you got five.'"

"You talked yourself out of that one too?" she said.

"Right wingers always think it takes courage to engage in violence, but the truth is, it takes a whole lot more not to," he said.

"More of your left, liberal, loser mumbo jumbo," she said. "Like your story, what's the ultimate point? That compromise is the greatest good?"

"Living with other people in a democratic society where everyone is respected inevitably means compromise and cooperation," he said.

"I thought you Marxists believed in revolution?" she said. "Are you going to compromise your way to revolution?"

"Yes," he said. "Compromise is the only way to real, lasting change."

"I'm afraid you've lost me there," she answered.

"Short of killing your enemies what is the choice?" he said. "Compromise is just a word meaning opposing sides learning to live together."

"I can live with my opponents just fine after defeating them," she said.

"Can you really?" he said. "If you aren't willing to compromise your only other choice is repression."

"If that's what it takes," she said, smiling. "I thought you Marxists found this liberal urge to compromise as distasteful as us."

"You're confusing Marxism with Stalinism," he said.

"You're claiming to be a better Marxist than Stalin?"

"I find it interesting that you approve of Stalin's views regarding compromise, but I guess I shouldn't be surprised. After all the pantheon of American right-wing heroes includes Pinochet, the Shah, Duvalier, Trujillo, Somoza and scores of other lesser known tyrants and bullies from every corner of the world."

"Do you really want to argue about whether the Left or the Right has produced more repression?" she asked.

He shook his head as he thought about this. "The historical answer is obvious, but I do not want to discuss it with you."

"I'm surprised at your lack of fighting spirit," she said. "You're as mushy as the liberals I crush every day."

There was no point in talking to her.

"You don't even know what you want," she said. "Our side is the only one with any new ideas."

"Neither side has any new ideas," he said. "The fight is between building a real democracy or defending oligarchy. The fight has been the same for a long time."

"If one side plays to win and the other side is always willing to compromise, who do you think is going to win?" she said, triumphantly.

"In a democracy the side with the most people on it," he said. "Slowly, but inevitably, we'll compromise the ruling class out of existence."

"Right," she said sarcastically.

"Compromise has always been the way of those who believe in democracy," he said. "Winning through whatever means necessary has always been the way of the minority who seeks to rule the majority."

"And that's why the smart minority always rules the majority," she said. "We always win."

"Yes, we always lose," he said. "And we always will, until we win."

"What's that supposed to mean?" she said.

"You figure it out," he said. "I've got a plane to catch."

"You're leaving?" she said.

He nodded.

"Will I see you again?"

"You want to see me again?" he asked.

She nodded. "I enjoyed myself."

"Maybe it was your hypomania," he said.

"Probably," she said. "Did you enjoy yourself?"

He looked at her before picking up his pile of papers from the bed. What was the truth?

"Yes," he said, after deciding that was the honest answer. "It was an adventure."

"It was," she said.

She smiled, but it was slightly rueful.

"We generate sparks," she said.

"We certainly do," he answered. Where was she going with this?

"Sparks often lead to fire," she added. "Passion is good."

"Fire can be the key to human survival," he said. "But it can also destroy everything in its path."

They looked at each other.

"Give me a kiss?" she said.

He stared again. Love thy enemy. The words from one of his St. Michael's catechism classes stuck in his brain. Love thy enemy. It was just another way of describing compromise. Love thy enemy. She was definitely his enemy.

"Why not?" he said.

"Why not," she said.

They kissed.

"Come visit me in Washington after we finally win this election. I'll invite you to the Inauguration Ball."

He laughed, but then saw she was serious.

"I'll be one of the most powerful people in the world," she said.

"Oh boy," he said.

She smiled.

What did she want?

"Come and live with me. Learn what happens in the real world."

It was his turn to smile.

"I'm serious," she said.

He shook his head in disbelief.

"I like talking to you, even if we never agree," she said. "You can be my sounding board. I'll come home from Cabinet meetings and ask your opinion about the stuff I can talk about."

"I'm waiting for the punch line," he said.

"You're one of the smartest people I know, even if you can be an idiot," she said. "It would be good for you to face real world problems, instead of living in the world of airy-fairy socialism. And it would be useful for me to know how someone with your airy-fairy opinions would respond to whatever we might be planning."

"You're actually asking me to help you destroy the world?" he said.

"I'm asking you to come visit with me in Washington and see how it goes," she said. "Maybe we'll have fun. Maybe we won't. You'd be free to leave at any time. Think about the material you'd gather for a novel or screenplay."

That was interesting and tempting.

"You can take a leave from your job and I'd put you on salary as a aide. You could indirectly influence the most powerful government in the world," she said. "Maybe you'll change the course of history. Isn't that what you always wanted? It may be your only opportunity."

"You are certifiably crazy," he said.

She looked hurt and he immediately felt guilty.

"I didn't mean ..." he said fumbling for words.

"Come for six months and try to convince me that your politics are better than mine," she said, smiling again. "Give it your best shot."

She was serious.

"I promise to listen carefully, but you have to promise the same," she added. "And if my arguments are better than yours, you have to admit it."

She was serious.

"I've got a plane to catch," he said. "I've got your number."

She said nothing as he picked up his bag and opened the hotel door.

"I'll think about it," he said. And the really weird thing, he already was.

The Class

Emma had spent the whole week once more going through her father's diary, which was written in the form of short stories, novels and film screenplays, and fragments of all three, covering his life from age 11 to the day before his death. But there were no more clues about why he had decided to move in with Katherine. Emma told her mother, but her word wasn't good enough. Her mother demanded the opportunity to look through the material as well, even though the will had been explicit. Her father's instruction was that she, Sylvia and Louise could read it, but their mother was not to have any access at all.

Of course this led to another fight, the latest chapter of which her mother wrote that morning, so Emma was once again distracted and not as prepared for class as she would have liked. And once again Louise had taken their mother's side.

"He's dead and Mom's need for closure is more important than any of his requests," she said.

And, as always, Sylvia tried to play the mediator. "I'm not saying do it, but just think about it, consider it," she said.

Emma understood why her mother wanted to read the diary, especially any parts that might shed light on why their father left her for that awful, rightwing bitch. But an executor's job is to follow the instructions of the person who made out the will. And there was nothing that she could find in the diary that directly dealt with the question her mother wanted answered. There were hints of possible affairs her mother had and a sort of leftwing missionary zeal to convert the Queen of Rightwing Talk Radio. Louise could read all this and tell their mother, if she wanted. There was no way of preventing that. So, why were they demanding something they could achieve by other means? It was a tempest in a samovar, as her father would have said. Why then do I even think about it? Why do I let my mother get under my skin? Why can't I grow up? Focus on my class.

"I'd like to start with something written as an introduction to your reading assignment," Emma said to the five seminar students. Her father had written this in 2010 when he was trying, once again, to turn the letters into a novel.

"'What follows is not entirely history, but also not simply fiction. It is fiction and history making out in the backseat of a 1959 Chevy. Those of us who have been there know that in the heat of the moment emotions are exaggerated and lies may be told. Passion is not entirely rational. The same can be said of history, historians, authors, politicians, scientists and ordinary people.

"'History is not a mere recitation of facts. It is also not simply memory. But it does require both memory and facts. History is the transformation of memory and facts into a narrative whole — in simplest terms a story. History is always an interpretation of the past — it cannot be anything else because it requires selectivity — written to make some point, usually about the present.

"'But history does not necessarily make sense. Sometimes it is simply what happened and offers no lessons beyond some simple facts. It is certainly not a teacher with a lesson plan guiding us into a better future. On the other hand a good education must include knowledge of what happened in the past because history often warns us that one path is preferable to another.

"'Sometimes the point of history is simply to relive the past, enabling people who weren't there to understand and to offer validation to those who were there. Some stories must be told in order to escape the past. These can be personal — acknowledge what you did — or social — the Truth and Reconciliation commissions that looked into South African Apartheid and Canadian residential schools.

"'Good history is literature and good literature is history. Only a few great works of either have ever been recognized as both.'"

Emma put the paper down and glanced at the graduate students around the table.

"Who would like to begin the discussion?"

"I understand what you're trying to make us think about — the difference, if any, between history and literature — but I really think that blurring the line between the two is not good for either," said Marc, who almost always started these discussions. "History must base itself on documents that are more verifiable than mere stories someone has made up about the past or even the present."

"So you wouldn't consider the diaries of Bernal Diaz about the conquest of Mexico as a primary source?" said Raj.

"Or the journals of explorers?" said Katie.

"Or letters written by monarchs or prime ministers?" said Dorothy. "How do we know they are any less fictional than a story some ordinary Joe or Jane recorded at the time of an event?"

"We should be skeptical about any document that may have been written with a purpose other than simply recording events or communicating policy," said Marc.

"We should be skeptical about everything," said Michael.

"We should consider any source that offers insight about events or periods or people," said Dorothy. "But of course we should be skeptical."

"So you guys are saying there's no difference between studying a novel that's set in the French Revolution or studying police records of the time? Made up stories and speeches in the National Assembly, they're both the same," said Marc. "If you're right, what are we doing in the History Department? Why not combine English and History into one big, let's read books department?"

"Who is saying there's no difference?" said Raj. "I never heard anyone say that. I heard them say we should look at both."

"Police records can tell you a lot about who was being arrested and for what, but a novel written by someone who lived through the revolution might give you a better insight about why certain types of people were arrested and not others," said Dorothy. "Or help you understand what people were thinking. A novel might do that better than a speech in the national assembly by a politician."

"I don't know if I'd go as far as to say that all novels are historical documents," said Katie. "Some novels may be, but other clearly aren't. The emergence of the genre of vampire romance novels over the past decade may be of some historical interest, but I doubt very much if any historian will someday study the texts of the Twilight series to gain insight about what people thought in the first decade of the 21st century."

"I don't know about that," said Michael. "'The Twilight Series and the Emergence of Doomsday Cults in the 21st Century' sounds to me like a good title for a PhD thesis."

Everyone around the table laughed, but the conversation quickly continued. These graduate seminars were fun because everyone contributed. Unlike undergraduate courses, everyone here loved history. Emma was the only one who wasn't engaged today. She couldn't stop thinking about her mother's outrageous and illegal request to go against the instructions of the will. Her mother wanted to read her ex-husband's diary to search for a phantom answer rather than face the simple truth that when two people fight all the time and an opportunity arises for one of them to leave, it sometimes happens. The simplest explanation is almost always the best explanation. Still, when you care passionately and personally about something a simple answer is often not satisfactory. In fact, the closer one gets to a topic, the more nuanced answers often become. If I know a little about some event and am asked a question about it, my answer is usually simple. The more I know about someone or something the more complicated explanations are.

"Look, if you guys want to step into the realm of Psychology and English Literature and Women's Studies, go ahead," said Marc. "I'm sticking with shipping manifests and the longue durée."

As Emma tuned back into the conversation she looked down at her seminar plan.

"You're welcome to spend your entire life in dusty archives calculating yearly variations in wheat trade," said Dorothy. "Just don't disparage those of us who wish to get a wider picture of the past through other methods."

"Including Women's Studies," said Katie.

"I think we've got a fairly wide range of opinions on the appropriateness and utility of fiction as an historical tool — at least for now," said Emma, interrupting. "But I'd like you now to narrow in on the particular material at hand, as a case study, before we return to the general question. How does the material you read inform us about the 1962 Saskatchewan doctors strike? Or does it? Who would like to start? Dorothy?"

She was quiet, but always thoughtful and well prepared. If I have a favourite, it's her, thought Emma.

"I found the stories very useful," said Dorothy. "Especially to illustrate how ideological the opponents of Medicare were. I never realized that they saw taxpayer-funded, government-run health insurance as a blow to capitalism. We take it for granted now as just another government program like pensions or unemployment insurance. I mean we've had Medicare in Canada for half a century and it's not like capitalism has disappeared. In fact, most people would say it's stronger than ever. Isn't that the point of the Occupy movement, for example?"

Nods came from around the table.

"To me this raises the question of why the doctors were so ideological," continued Dorothy. "Did they believe their rhetoric or did it simply serve their purpose?"

"They were attempting to manipulate public opinion," said Michael, "just like Katherine and Roy were attempting to manipulate the people around them. That's what the stories are about, politics."

"What I liked about the material was it gave us insight into the context of the times, how different people saw things," said Raj. "Events like the doctors strike and the Cuban Missile Crisis expose the broad divisions that are always there, but which in normal times get glossed over because things just move along slowly and so damn normally. I liked how the analogy is drawn between the Cuban Missile Crisis and the doctors strike, the brinksmanship of both events."

"And the boys fighting," said Katie. "That could be seen as a feminist understanding of the roots of politics and war."

"I don't think 'Betty Bitch' would agree with that one," said Marc.

Katie looked horrified. She looked to Emma for support.

"What?" said Marc. "I can't quote the text?"

"Can we leave that discussion for another day," said Emma.

Katie glared at Marc, who struggled to maintain the faux innocent smile that was so incredibly irritating.

"I think the text illustrates what fiction can do better than other more studied types of historical documents," said Dorothy, rescuing the seminar from another bout of Katie versus Marc. "It's like Raj said, it offers a sense of why people did what they did, how they saw things in the context of the times."

"I think it shows that the supporters of Medicare were right and supporters of the doctors were wrong," said Michael. "Both in the context of the times and today, looking back on it. I mean, it's like one of the quotes about history being written to make a comment about today. How do you avoid sounding like a fool if you say the doctors thought they were right in the context of the times? Of course they did. That's trite. Why would they do something if they thought they were wrong? But they were wrong. I mean isn't that the point of the author? The doctors, the rightwing 13-year old and the neoconservatives all think they are right, but they're not, they're wrong. That's the point you're left with. The doctors put their own narrow economic interests ahead of the community. They were judging Medicare strictly from their own business point of view. But medicine isn't just another business."

Raj nodded in agreement. "Ya, it's like the doctors and their supporters were talking about something entirely different from what most people think Medicare is about. For most of us, socialized medicine is about achieving more or less equal access to healthcare. But all the doctors of Saskatchewan and their supporters in 1962 seemed to be talking about was the freedom to do business the way doctors as businessmen saw fit."

"Exactly," said Michael. "That's the central point of the story — the two solitudes of right and left talking at each other about completely different things, never really having a conversation at all."

"No," said Katie. "That's not the point I was left with."

Katie stopped as she saw Marc roll his eyes.

"What's the point you were left with Katie?" said Emma.

"That extremists on all side must learn to compromise," said Katie. "That you never get all you want. People take extreme positions for political purposes, not necessarily because they believe what they say. But, in the end, real progress is made by compromise, by moving forward, then retreating and then moving forward again. We need to learn to love our enemies. That's the point."

"What's the point you're left with Dorothy?" said Emma.

"That 1962 was the pivotal year in these people's lives," said Dorothy. "That was the year they became who they were. Certain events shaped their lives permanently. That 1962 was the year we became us, Canada certainly, but probably also the United States."

"That's the point I got out of it too," said Raj. "1962 was the year Canada became Canada. It took the fight over Medicare to create one of the key things that makes us different from the United States. And the Cuban Missile Crisis revealed the limitations of U.S. power. It was the beginning of the end of their empire, even though it was a tiny, tiny crack in their armour."

"Marc?" said Emma.

"The real point of the material you had us read is that 'all history is bunk' to quote Henry Ford," said Marc. "It's just a story made up by one person. Human beings are suckers for a story and they'll choose one every time over the truth. You ever see the movie Braveheart? Mel Gibson's version of Scottish history. How many people do you think believe that compared to the truth? That's the trap you fall into if you buy into the notion that history must have a narrative. The best story becomes accepted truth regardless of reality. That's the point Katherine makes and she's right."

"No," said Katie. "You're missing the point once again. The male authority figure — whoever plays that role, whether or not it's a she or a he — is fooled into thinking he won, but the passive female figure — whoever plays that role, whether or not it's a she or a he — never gives up. She does not go away, just like your enemy never goes away. The only real victory, the only permanent change comes through compromise, which is the ultimate female trait."

Perhaps that's my mother's problem, thought Emma, as the students continued their heated debate. Mom thought marriage was nothing more than a series of compromises, but my father wanted a challenge, not another compromise. The Queen of Rightwing Talk Radio was the ultimate challenge. Going back to my mother would have been just another in a long line of compromises. Katherine never got to him by calling him a failure. He didn't fall prey to her definition of success, he fell prey to her challenge.

"Maybe the point of the book is that rightwing types and leftwing types are exactly the same," said Marc. "Politicians of both persuasions manipulate us and in the end they go off and live together."

"Or that the rightwing and the leftwing will always be with us and so they had better learn to live together," said Dorothy. "In Canada we took a leftwing path in 1962. This eventually led to a rightwing reaction — the Reform Party and Harper's Conservatives— which will eventually lead to a leftwing reaction. Which goes back to the reason for learning to compromise because both sides will always be with us."

Emma's thoughts drifted further away. All us girls were grown up, on our own, when Dad left. He had a right to do what made him feel best at that point in his life. If that was the challenge of trying make 'Betty Bitch' into a decent human being, who are we to criticize? Maybe he was even successful at some level. We'll never know, because when the two started living together they agreed to never write or talk publically about the other or about their relationship. Her father's diary made that clear.

"Maybe the real point is that Roy is a social democrat and that path leads to the sort of compromise where you go off and live with the fascists in Washington," said Raj. "Maybe the book isn't defending compromise, it's demonstrating where it leads. The Saskatchewan government should have crushed the doctors by replacing them with community clinics and Medicare would have taken an entirely different path. We'd have doctors on salary and everyone would be better off. Instead we have social democratic governments all over the world cooperating with the U.S. Empire and happily going off to war to keep the brown people in line."

"You guys are all wrong about this compromise stuff," said Marc. "This Roy character believes in compromise about as much as the Queen of Rightwing Talk Radio. He only argues in favour of it because he is trying to stop President Kennedy from nuking Cuba. The leftwing is always in favour of compromise when it has no power. When the left comes to power all of a sudden it's the right that's talking compromise."

The last time she spoke to her father Katherine and him were having fun together, he told her. Katherine had been diagnosed with breast cancer and the two of them had decided to have some adventures before she started therapy.

"No, the real question here is: Does this material have a place in historiography?" said Michael. "And you have to answer yes after listening to the discussion we've had. I mean look at the questions and different points of view that have come up. Isn't provoking discussion one of the jobs of historians?"

Emma had to stop herself from crying as she thought about the plane accident that killed her father, a pilot and Katherine six months earlier. They were going up to skydive for the first time in their lives. That was a good way to go. Their fire was still burning. They died while passionate for life.

"Anyone can ask questions," said Marc. "The job of historians is to provide answers to those questions."

"You're wrong," said Dorothy. "A critical part of the job of a historian is to provoke questions. All good research provokes questions. That's what keeps the academy relevant."

"If we don't provoke intelligent questions with the material we study, where will they come from?" said Katie.

Emma realized she had let the seminar get away from her again, but the students seemed to be enjoying themselves despite her lack of control. They cared about history. They cared about the question of sources. They had strong opinions on the idea of fiction as a fit subject to study. They were engaged and animated. They were arguing about the doctors strike, President Kennedy and 1962. They had learned from the material she assigned them and they were learning from the seminar. That was the point, wasn't it?

"Looking at events from different points of view raises different questions," said Michael. "That's the utility of material like this. It enables thinking outside the current historiographical box."

The seminar had even helped her understand something important. Or at least it shone some light on a possible explanation for what her father did. Isn't that the job history is supposed to do? Shine light on the past. Help us understand.

The seminar was not over, but already Emma felt content. It was a good class. She was a good teacher. Something was learned today.

The End